Call Me
When You Land

Call Me
When You Land

MICHAEL SCHIAVONE

THE PERMANENT PRESS
Sag Harbor, NY 11963

For information, address:
    The Permanent Press
    4170 Noyac Road
    Sag Harbor, NY 11963
    www.thepermanentpress.com

Library of Congress Cataloging-in-Publication Data

Schiavone, Michael–
    Call me when you land / Michael Schiavone.
        p. cm.
    ISBN 978-1-57962-221-3 (hardcover : alk. paper)
        1. Self-realization in women—Fiction. 2. Mothers and sons—
    Fiction. 3. Domestic fiction. I. Title.

PS3619.C354C35 2011
813'.6—dc23   2011023957

Printed in the United States of America.

For Abbie, who endures the madness of
my writing process.

And for my two-year-old son, Colton,
who shows me what it's like to live with someone
as impatient and temperamental as me.

ACKNOWLEDGEMENTS

I thank my many parents for their continued support: Mom, Dad, Joyce, Jim, and June.

I thank my no-nonsense literary agent, Barbara Braun, who championed this novel. I thank everyone at Permanent Press—Martin and Judith Shepard, in particular—for bringing this book to life. I thank Lon Kirschner for creating a perfect book cover. I thank Susan Ahlquist for her precision. I thank Joslyn Pine for her thoughtful insight and eagle eye.

Thank you Jenna Blum, Jennifer Haigh, Michelle Hoover, and Pamela Painter for reading and recommending this book.

I thank those who helped shape this novel in its various stages: Stace Budzko, Dave Demerjian, Cathy Elcik, Steve MacKinnon, Marc Simon, and Sue Williams. I'd also like to recognize all members—past and present—of the Hanover Street Writers Group for their generous input and honesty.

WINTER 2007

CHAPTER 1

He's found dead in Nevada.

"Your information was in his Camelbak," the deputy says.

Katie holds the line. Last she heard Craig was in Montana. A few months ago he'd sent them a sunny postcard from Bridger Bowl. He usually sends one or two a year. She's repeatedly sorry as she pushes those cards under C.J.'s door, but she doesn't want to be one of those mothers who hides the father from the child.

The deputy clears his throat.

"Where?" she finally asks, removing her smock. She stands up and rinses her dirty paintbrushes, the water a grey, gloomy color.

"Mr. Hunter was discovered in a motel room here in Carson City," the deputy says. "An apparent heart attack. They're still investigating."

"At forty-six?"

Katie hears a toilet flush in the background. While she's imagined this phone call many times before, *heart attack* hadn't played through her mind. Buried by an avalanche, squashed by a tree trunk, frozen on the wrong side of a ski boundary. Always on a mountain. Always fierce.

"There's a storage bin here," the deputy continues. "A pod. He left you the key." He tells her instructions were written on the back of a restaurant placemat they found folded up in fours inside his Camelbak.

"What's inside?" she asks, picturing broken skis, bent poles and snowshoes, a container full of donations.

"We'll send it out tomorrow," he says.

"Here?"

"There," he confirms. "Newquay, Massachusetts. For you and Calvin."

"For you and Calvin," she mumbles away from the phone.

Katie pours herself a glass of Grand Marnier from the bottle she keeps behind the gallery mats. When Craig left for good fifteen years ago, C.J. wasn't even C.J. then; he was nine-month-old Calvin James. Her son claims to remember his father's hands. "Like sandpaper," C.J. said; but he was less than a year old the afternoon Craig drove away, her mint green Rossignols still strapped to the roof rack of his truck.

"So where's Craig going?" she asks. "Is he inside too?"

"His mother's handling the body."

She hangs up the phone. When it rings again, she leaves it to her voicemail. The ice cubes crackle and snap as the sweet orange liqueur settles into the tumbler. Circling her callused index finger around the rim of the glass, she pauses before taking her first drink of the day. As always, Katie waits—an instant of consideration before the plunge, one last chance to dump the contents down the drain. Later on she'll reflect upon this moment and wonder why she didn't just drive to the gym or clean the inside of the microwave. She could have stuffed her face with brownies instead, but once the drink is poured, all other options seem absurd. As Katie's lips now touch the glass, she reminds herself she can make a different choice next time.

"His mother's handling the body," she says to the cat. Of course she isn't acquainted with Craig's mother. Katie never met anyone who really knew him. No brothers and sisters, no friends. The poor woman probably has no idea she has a grandson. Leaning back in her late father's brown leather chair, Katie considers leaving C.J. a note on his pillow. She could even ask Walter to deliver the news while she stays in the studio. In fact, she doesn't have to tell her son anything at all, but when he finds out it will give him yet another reason to resent her.

Outside the window, Katie watches the workers finish removing debris from last night's ice storm. The street's strewn with trash, sea vines, dirt and sand. The sky's cold silver. When the New England wind chill goes below zero, she gets headaches, the kind aspirin can't resolve. Apparently, wind took out Mr. Kashgarian's cherry tree across the street, Katie's view now altered. One man in an orange suit reattaches a sagging telephone line to Mrs. Seton's house, his thick body dangling by a belt strap. Most of the crew huddles together, a swarm of cigarettes and Styrofoam coffee cups, their shift ending with the February light. Her dad would call these guys "working stiffs," but Katie admires these men and their guts.

The mail startles her as she hears it shoot through the slot in the front door. Ten years in this house and she still can't get used to the postman's invasion. In the kitchen it's another world—sunlight douses the room, the floorboards warm and dusty against her feet. Their outdated refrigerator buzzes as if it's on the brink of an explosion. Scattered across the counter are C.J.'s flax seeds, which look like mice droppings. Katie swears her blood pressure rises in this room. She sorts through the mail stack, separating three piles onto the butcher block. Art gallery flyers, three credit card offers, and an electricity bill for her, *Maxim* for C.J., *Poets and Writers* and a letter from his prison pen pal in Illinois for Walter. No postcards from Craig. She hears the annoying bells from Saint Joachim's ring four times, the church less than a mile from their three-story house. Her son will be home soon.

Katie scurries back to the studio and shuts the door. As she collects her dirty clothes from the floor, she wonders what possibly could've happened to Craig in Carson City. Like many people, he drank and smoked pot, but he exercised religiously, his body durable and strong. Layered in muscle, Craig was a specimen, a man who felt crowded in dress clothes. His Popeye forearms were too ample for long sleeves, his legs so thick they rubbed together when he walked, turning his thighs red and rashy. Yet his waist was narrow, almost dainty, which gave his barbaric shape a sense of grace. She just can't imagine how that body could surrender, but he was only thirty years old then— Katie's image of him forever frozen. When she considers their son's jarring fifteen-year metamorphosis, Katie can imagine how Craig *must* have changed. After all this time, she may not have even recognized him in Nevada.

She hears the front door bang open. Against an earlier promise, Katie adds another finger's worth of Grand Marnier to her glass, careful to tread quietly across the studio floor. Her glass is streaked black from the paint still on her fingertips. From the kitchen, the blender churns and she envisions the lip-stick red potion of creatine powder and fruit punch, one of three daily doses her son guzzles down. With an ear to the door, Katie listens as C.J. rummages through the refrigerator. She pictures him wolfing down cold cuts and hard-boiled eggs, cottage cheese and pickles. He eats like a pregnant woman, chronically hungry. Cabinets frantically open and close, drawers are slammed shut. He can't seem to do anything quietly. And not until Katie hears his heavy footsteps on the stairwell does she spit the ice cubes from her mouth.

Above her head, she can hear the Ramones blaring from the stereo in his room, an upgrade from the German industrial music he played for three months straight. Katie can remember the way music struck a nerve when she was his age, how vital it was to her existence. Now it's just a distraction while she drives. She'd like to tell him that a portion of her own teenage years were consumed by the Ramones' punk anthems, but a remark like that would most likely aggravate him. Whenever she tries to reach out, C.J. just rolls his eyes and waits for her to leave.

Katie grabs a hockey stick and taps the ceiling—his floor— with the butt end of the shaft. A collection of little divots from previous strikes decorate the white plaster above her head. The volume eventually drops. Then silence. Some nights this is the only exchange between mother and son, one she's come to depend on. She used to ask him what he learned in school, how the biology test went, what girls he liked, but routine questions are now invasive. And so she's stopped. When he wants to speak, she'll listen. "Just please tell me if anything bad is ever happening," she said recently. "Promise me that."

Katie forces down her drink as sea gulls cry outside the window. As she leaves the studio behind, her courage shrinks. Walking up the staircase, she hears C.J. counting out reps: *Forty-two! Forty-three! Forty-four!* He makes it to forty-seven push-ups before his body drops. Next he'll work through sit-ups. Then more push-ups. The routine can last over an hour. Usually Katie's in the studio painting while he's exercising, his regimen the soundtrack to her artistic process.

She pauses in front of his door and brushes the grey cat hair from her sweater. Her throat is dry. As if freshly introduced on a daily basis, Katie is nervous in front of her son. She and Craig certainly hadn't imagined puberty when they mingled beneath the sheets. They hadn't considered any harm.

She knocks.

Five! Six! Seven! He grunts in between reps.

She knocks again.

C.J. finally opens up, six feet and muscular in the door frame. Vein trails map his forearms. He hasn't cut his hair all winter, the stringy black bangs almost long enough to shield his eyes. His chin is dried out from too much acne cream, his face a blend of the two of them: his father's blue eyes, her nose and ears, Craig's cocky smile when C.J. allows it to appear. A faint shadow of hair shows beneath his white undershirt. Not very long ago, his chest was bare. How suddenly C.J. had transformed, how severe he'd become.

Katie remembers the morning he turned twelve, how his feet had grown a size overnight, instantly clownish on his gawky frame. Soon after, the hairs on his legs had darkened—sweet blonde giving way to that awful, primitive black. As his jaw widened, the eyes narrowed. Top to bottom, he had shed his skin. Top to bottom, C.J. had hardened. Like a gallery exhibit, Katie had stared curiously at her son, amazed and alarmed she'd borne such a creature. Before puberty, he used her shower on the first floor, only a towel wrapped around his waist as he passed through her bedroom to the bath. Now he was suddenly pissed off he only had a toilet and sink on the second floor. Katie told him she'd be happy to add a shower stall to his "water closet," but he'd have to give up hockey, cable, and steak tips for a year to cover construction costs. So he became accustomed to using the third floor bathroom where the tiles are moldy and Walter hangs his plants, C.J. likely as upset as Katie over her son's bodily invasion.

"What?" he says.

"How are you?" she asks.

"I'm busy." He squints when he speaks, a tic she hopes will fade in time.

Pushed deep into the dormer, Lewis nibbles on a catnip toy. She notices a new poster of the Dropkick Murphys taped to the wall near other bands she's never heard of like Wolfmother, Godsmack, and Disturbed. Magazine photographs of NHL hockey players are tacked behind his bed, a small shot of Megan Fox in a bikini above his desk. No pictures of her, of them. The few photos she has of Craig are in storage, C.J. showing no interest in seeing his father's face since he was a little boy.

"What do you want?"

"I'm doing a load of whites," she says. "Do you have any whites?"

"No whites."

Katie breathes in and smells traces of pot. She'll ignore this for now. After all, it could be coming from Walter's room above them. The truth is she'd love to share a joint with her son, to be there when his guard unravels. Some way in. On the rare occasions she does smoke in the bathtub, Katie wonders if all three of them might be getting high at the same time, each from their own floor.

C.J. snaps his fingers. "Anything else besides laundry?"

"I need to talk to you," she says.

"You are talking to me."

"Maybe I'll come back after you're done exercising."

"Spit it out, Mom."

"Craig's dead," she blurts out.

He thumbs down the volume on his iPod, then frowns.

"So what?" he says, removing his headphones.

"Are you upset?" she asks.

"No."

"Do you want to ask me anything?" Hands shoved in her pockets, Katie pinches the skin on her thighs and digs her nails in deeply.

"I'm busy."

She wants to hug him to save herself from saying anything more, but Katie doesn't want to embarrass him. Touch between them no longer exists. Some nights she'll sneak into his room while he sleeps. There she'll sit by his bed and watch him, sometimes brushing her hand lightly across his hair, his forehead and cheeks, careful not to wake him. C.J. sleeps soundly throughout, the covers moving up and down with his breath. It's then Katie feels most like a mother.

"I'm here if you want to talk about anything," she says.

"I'm not going to any funeral."

"We don't have to," she says. "I doubt there'll be one anyway."

He focuses on the hardwood floor. All she can see is his hair. If only he had a brother, someone to share all this confusion. When he was a small child C.J. had begged for a sibling, like other kids do for a pet or a video game. But that was one request Katie could not honor, telling him "you're it." She feels guilty for this now.

"Was it a motorcycle crash?" he asks.

"No," she says. "Heart attack."

She'd all but forgotten about Craig's postcard from the National Motorcycle Museum he'd sent them last year. It was the first time in fifteen years he had written anything more than just their names and street address. He'd told them he bought a used Harley, that "this bike's given me a new perspective." The postcard's tacked on C.J.'s cork board, the only one she's ever seen him display. Aside from presents for his birthday (hiking boots, a buck knife, a Camelbak) and the occasional FedEx envelope full of cash, Craig never offered his son anything more than a three-by-five glimpse of his latest surroundings. And while this may have been enough for her, she suspects C.J. may have found a future promise in Craig's postcards.

"I'm sorry, C.J."

"What's the difference?"

"No difference," Katie says. "I was just worried you'd be upset."

"Why would I be upset?" C.J. lifts his head and glares at her, his expression expectant. This is how he usually looks at her, as if waiting for a confession.

"I don't know," Katie says. "I'm concerned."

"He left us, right? There was nothing you could do, right? So why the fuck are we even talking about this?"

"We're not," she says. "We're done."

"You tell me like it's supposed to matter. As if Walter died."

"Don't get angry," she says, stepping away from him. "You're right, it doesn't matter."

A cold draft blows over her from his open window. She rubs at the goosebumps on her arms.

"What's for dinner?" he asks.

"Do you want to go out?"

He nods yes. "Anything else?" he asks.

"That's it," she says. "I'll see you downstairs."

C.J. shuts his door.

"Wear a coat," she calls through the wall.

Katie's legs are jelly as she climbs the wooden steps up to the third floor. Her mouth tastes like rotten oranges. She hears a loud bang from C.J.'s room and imagines another hole punched through his sliding closet door. "Jesus," she whispers, leaning against the banister, "another trip to Home Depot." For the sake of them all, Katie wishes Craig could have held on for a few more years, just long enough for C.J. to pass through this phase. She remembers asking her last boyfriend, Peter, what it was a teenage boy wanted. "To fight and fuck," he said proudly. "And unless you're doing one or the other, it's Hell." Katie never posed this question again, preferring to believe there was more to her son than sex and violence. Her sister, Caroline, told her it was dangerous to ignore the topic of Craig, that "you're asking for a world of shit one day," she'd said. But Katie felt the postcards were enough, the only connection C.J. could manage. "He hasn't asked about his father since he was a child," she told Caroline. "If he ever wants more, it's his."

In front of Walter's room, she stops to catch her breath. Katie hears Liberace's piano version of *Never on a Sunday* playing from the other side of the door. His polyester Harvard tie is looped around the doorknob, his signal for privacy. She knocks more than a dozen times until her great uncle answers.

"Craig's dead," she tells him.

"Well, that's something," he says, tightening the belt of his royal blue Polo bathrobe. Between the terry flaps she can see the rigid white scar on his chest from an old car accident. "Who's Craig?"

"C.J.'s father," she says.

"Oh, yes, of course." He lifts the needle from the spinning record, his right hand braced against his lower back.

Katie steps inside and sits down on the ottoman. The room reeks of mothballs and cilantro. She tells him about Carson City, the pod, her son's reaction.

"Let's go out to the widow's walk," Walter says, grabbing his camel overcoat from the back of the door.

She looks over at the short paneled door next to his bathroom, which leads outside to the small, four-person widow's walk. "It's freezing," she says.

"I need to take my medicine."

Katie helps him steer his feet into his moon boots. Only when he has to bend over does he feel dizzy, so she assists him with tasks below the knees. Once a stately physician on a six feet two-inch frame, Walter's since shrunk a few notches, though he's still remarkably nimble. He walks deliberately, airily, "like a model with a book on her head," C.J. once said. Walter's very conscious of his appearance, his impressively thick white hair carefully coiffed, slick and sticky with pomade, his smile the epitome of mischief. While he may look like the typical old man on the park bench, up close you're struck by his boyish glow, which he credits to a stockpile of Kiehl's skin products. Born and raised across the street from the naval yard in Marblehead, Walter speaks with a harsh Massachusetts accent, quick to point out the difference in tone between the North Shore and South Boston. From the few black and white photos she can recall seeing as a child, her great uncle was a peculiarly handsome man, like Richard Gere in *An Officer and a Gentleman*.

"What's the forecast tonight?" he asks, inspecting his vein-laden hands.

"Cold and shitty."

Katie watches as he carefully rubs Bag Balm over his frayed fingers, the tips especially dry and pruned. Most of his knuckles are enlarged and tender to the touch. Katie wonders how he can type, how he can even squeeze out toothpaste with such arthritis. Yet he still offers strangers a jock's handshake, a vice grip that lets you know he's damn glad to meet you. Seldom does Walter ask for assistance, as if concealing his pain will eventually arouse a healing.

For Katie, it's hard to imagine this room was once empty, that it was just she and C.J. until Walter moved in nine months ago—with a tackle box full of pills and a trunk stuffed with beach clothes, records, and a typewriter. Until he called to tell her he'd been evicted from his condo in Saint Augustine for staging an anti-war protest in the lobby, Katie hadn't heard from her grandfather's brother in ten years, not since her own father's funeral.

"It's depressing being old and retired in Florida," he'd confessed to her.

"Stay with us," Katie said. "We need the company." She told him he'd have plenty of space, his own floor, that no one would bother him. "It'll be handy to have a doctor in the house." He warned her that he only had a few years left, that his insides were failing, that the gun smoke from World War II was finally killing him sixty years later. When Katie ran the idea by C.J., her son offered to make up the guest room himself, he too welcoming some distraction.

Outside on the widow's walk, Katie zips Walter's coat up to his chin. A couple of long white hairs hang from his jowls, his lips purple from chugging cough medicine. "This and codeine are all that work," he says, lighting a medicinally prescribed joint. He passes it to her.

"I'm really worried about C.J.," she says. "I feel like he's going to burst."

Walter rocks back and forth on his heels and smiles deviously as he breathes in the cold sea air. A white ice line runs along the distant beach rocks, the memory of high tide. "So let him burst," he says.

"I swear it's like I can hear him ticking sometimes," she says. "God, I talk about him like he's hazardous."

A black hawk soars above their heads. Walter's eyes follow the arc of the bird's flight. He clears his flooded throat, then spits off the deck. Katie's fingers begin to numb. "To his dismay, I think C.J. has an artist's mind," he declares. "And he fights it. If he can make it through the next few years, if he can come to embrace himself, I believe he'll do something wonderful."

"If he can make it through?" she says. "Jesus, why do you have to put it like that?"

The cold shoots through the mesh on Katie's sneakers; her toes tingle. A wind chime is heard ringing in the background.

"I like being in a teenager's dungeon," Walter says. "No other time in life is quite so spirited. When C.J. and I play Halo, there's no age disparity. We're connected electronically." Walter removes his cap and runs a palm over his matted hair. "This government weed is truly inspiring." He extinguishes the joint on the wet and weathered wooden planks.

"It's getting dark," she says.

Walter rubs his hands together. "Let's try and wait for sunset."

Old snow drops from the roof and lands with a startling thud. Katie turns around expecting to find C.J., but all she sees is a rusty chaise lounge.

"What about you, Katie?" Walter asks, touching her shoulder. "What does Craig's death mean for you?"

She looks up at the crummy sky and sighs. She wishes she could grieve, could be stricken with frantic breath and frenzied sobs, but all she really yearns to do is pee.

"Trouble," she says.

CHAPTER 2

C.J. bangs on her bathroom door. "Where's the mail?" he shouts.

"Give me a sec," Katie says, thumbing through an old Victoria's Secret catalog.

"Is it in there with you?"

"Will you let me pee?"

He knocks again. "Just tell me. My ride to practice is going to be here soon."

"Nothing came from any schools."

"Are you lying?"

"No." She dog-ears a page for a pair of jeans she cannot fit into or afford. "Will you leave me alone? I don't bother you on the toilet."

He bangs on the door again.

"Godammit, C.J.!"

He walks away. She can hear him drag his heels. For a boy as strong and nimble as her son, she doesn't understand why it's so hard for him to lift his feet when he walks.

Katie throws the catalog in the trash.

Where on earth this prep school obsession came from Katie cannot figure. Since kindergarten, formal education has only inspired hostility in her son; he can't stand classrooms. Term paper assignments actually make him angry. So when C.J. announced he'd applied to six boarding schools, Katie wouldn't have been more surprised if he'd declared he wanted to wear women's clothes.

"With your grades?" she'd asked him. "Your only A's in art."

"I can get in with hockey," C.J. said. "The admissions guy at Farmingdale Academy said if I can keep shooting the puck into the net, my grades won't matter so much."

"But you hate rules," she told him. "Some of those places are very strict."

"Means to an end."

Never had she heard him use that expression. "Why do you want to go away?" she continued.

"If I have a shot at the NHL, this is the first step."

"The NHL? Since when do you want to play pro hockey?"

"Since forever."

Katie did not believe her son. Hockey or no hockey, she felt he just wanted to leave home. "Jesus," she said solemnly, "what else don't I know about you?"

From the bathroom window, Katie watches as C.J. throws his hockey bag and sticks into the back of Mr. Farquarson's SUV. He looks toward the house before he climbs into the car, their eyes catching for a second as he closes the door. Seeing them drive away, Katie broods over the potential of his looming departure. Even if they don't speak for weeks, she's feels contentment when he's right upstairs. The sound of his footsteps, the thud of dumb-bells, the blare of his stereo—he's close. Katie can't remember real quiet, the terrible anxiety of echoes and empty rooms. Often she's romanticized the future freedom, her parental parole, but in her bones she knows a sudden privacy will cut deep. With him, C.J. will take her understanding of consequence. Without him, there will no longer be a reason to hide.

HUNCHED OVER the easel in her studio, Katie frets over her latest painting—Isabel. It seems every time she picks up a brush, this piece tells her something new. Yesterday she tried to insert a ponytail, the week before a French braid, but no hairstyle seems to suit her subject. C.J. told her Isabel should be bald. The gallery in New Haven has lost patience, telling her "by Monday or no deal." And while she'd love to abandon this portrait, Katie has nothing else on deck, no inspiration elsewhere, which means it's Isabel or bust. Switching paints, she dabs Prussian blue over the background and paints around her subject, anything to distract her from Isabel's hair.

No painting has ever defied her like this one, a work that's been holding her hostage all winter. Three years ago, Katie garnered some minor acclaim when four examples from her recently discovered "faceless form" were shown at a gallery in Salem. A *Boston Globe* art columnist described her creations as "delicate stark white men and women with smooth blank faces like eggs. Fractured human souls who are just like us—ten fingers, ten toes, hopes and dreams, loneliness and dread." After that exhibit, Katie was able to leave the dreariness of landscape art behind, work which had always made her feel average. Her boss said her portraits reminded her of elegantly dressed mannequins. Peter thought her subjects looked like aliens. C.J. once asked her why she didn't paint faces, "the eyes, noses, and mouths." Katie told him she didn't really know, and suggested that she might not be very good with those kinds of particulars.

She turns up the space heater with her big toe and stares at Isabel until she blurs. Little curls begin to form in front of her eyes and she follows the vision by inserting wavy blonde strands along the base of the hair.

Even though she's sold several paintings over the years, she continues to introduce herself as a bartender, a job title which embarrasses her more with each passing birthday. On the brink of forty, it's hard for her to believe she's still slinging drinks—a single mother and a college graduate shaking your apple martinis. But it was her choice four years ago to leave her job as a production coordinator for the Lily Pad Theatre Company, her choice to pick up night shifts at Megan's Harborside Restaurant, her choice to commit to art. She's since tried hard to ignore detractors like her sister who say painting is no career. Caroline told her it was "financially reckless and selfish," and reminded

Katie to consider her child. "You can't live with someone who's stuck," she informed Caroline. "What nags me will nag him. Believe me, I'll be a better mom if I do this." What's more, her father had paid off the mortgage on the house before he died. All Katie had to worry about were the annual property taxes.

Katie continues with Isabel's curls, but all she can see is what's wrong. In the sink, she cleans her best brushes, then sponges up the crusty paint stains from the floorboards, Isabel's blank face glaring at her while she housekeeps. She pours herself a small Grand Marnier. "Fuck it," she says, turning the easel around.

In the kitchen, Walter's buttering a skillet. "I'm making ostrich burgers," he says as the pan spits grease all over his bathrobe collar.

Katie scowls at the stove. "For a sick man you have some appetite," she says. "Are you sure it's safe to eat an ostrich?"

"Ned at Whole Foods says ostrich is the new buffalo."

Behind his back, Katie transfers her drink into a coffee mug. She turns on the faucet so he won't hear the ice cubes clink.

"Oh, no," she says, covering her mouth.

"What?"

She points out the windows above the sink. "Look out there."

They watch as a large truck slowly backs into their driveway. The reverse alarm sounds louder as it approaches the house. The flatbed begins to descend, lowering a large white container onto the property. One side of the white pod is dented, the roof slightly caved in. The sight of it shakes her.

"How exciting," Walter says, eating a tomato like an apple. Little seeds stain the butcher block. "It's larger than I imagined. Maybe it's an elephant."

"It's a tomb," Katie says, finishing her drink.

A week ago, a FedEx from Carson City arrived containing Craig's placemat testament, which she hid beneath a pile of summer clothes in her walk-in closet. The placemat was from the Chum Line, a fishermen's bar in Gunnerside, just down the street from the town hall where Katie and Craig were hastily married fifteen years ago. The deputy had called a second time to let Katie know that Craig's mother flew to Nevada and arranged to have the body transferred to Cave Creek, Arizona.

"What about his father?" she'd asked.

"The deceased's father jumped off the Taos gorge some years back. Mrs. Hunter said it was an accident, but it was ruled a suicide in New Mexico."

"Does she know about us?"

"Your name never came up. She didn't ask about anyone. Mrs. Hunter just wanted her son. She said she hadn't seen him in more than a decade."

"Now what?"

"Well, it's over," the deputy said.

Katie wanted to ask about drugs, if he was trying to kill himself in Nevada. She wanted to know if he'd been alone when he died, what he was thinking about during the last minute of his life. She was curious about what happens when your heart stops, what it feels like to have a hollow chest. But when she opened her mouth to ask a question, Katie realized she didn't want to hear anything about Craig from a policeman.

"You're still getting the pod, Ms. Olmstead," the deputy continued. "Mrs. Hunter doesn't know about it. She doesn't need to. The placemat said it was for you and Calvin only."

"His name is C.J."

Calvin. She didn't even know who that was. Her son hadn't been Calvin since he was five, deciding in kindergarten that he wanted his initials instead of a name. Having never warmed up to Calvin anyway, Katie was glad for the change.

Two brawny young men in blue uniforms steady the pod, setting it on the left side of the driveway, allowing just enough space for her car to pass. When they approach the front door, Walter turns off the burner and scatters, his bones creaking as he hustles up the stairwell. He doesn't like outsiders to see him in his bathrobe.

The taller one hands Katie a key, telling her to call once she's unloaded its contents. "We'll then come and retrieve it," he says, his voice lower than she expected.

"I'll call you in an hour," she says. "I don't want this here when my son gets home."

They both wear gold wedding bands on their fingers. She wonders if these men are fathers and almost asks, but instead reaches into her purse and hands them each a ten dollar bill. Katie figures she has fifteen years on them, maybe more. She likes to imagine they think she's attractive for an older woman. "A hot mom" one might say to the other once inside the truck. Just last week a fairly cute Papa Gino's delivery boy said she looked like an older version of Abbie Cornish. When Katie googled the twenty-something actress, she was very pleased by the comparison. Sometimes she got Laura Linney, which was nice, but this was different. This was young. But here and now she finds no intention in these men's eyes. They see nothing lustrous before them, probably just lunch and pay day on their minds.

Outside, Katie circles the pod, rubbing the key between her fingers. Now that the men are gone, Walter reappears and presses up against the container, staring fixedly as if summoning x-ray vision, his camel overcoat buttoned over his bathrobe. She notices he's wearing C.J.'s red and black high-tops. "I don't hear anything," he whispers.

"Why would you?"

"If you have to guess," Walter says, "what would you say's inside?"

Katie looks out toward the ocean. A massive battleship pushes slowly past Hatcher's Island. She imagines the sailors are curious, spying on them through binoculars. "Relics of a poor ski bum," she says finally, her breath clouding in the wintry air.

Katie inserts the key, the padlock clicks open. She raises the pod door. Walter stands back. His teeth begin to chatter. "I thought there'd be more," he says.

"Me too."

Katie steps inside, thankful to be out of the cold. The pod is empty except for a large item concealed under a black tarp. No brown boxes, no knickknacks, no stuff piled on top of stuff.

"I have to urinate," Walter says. "Goddam Lasix."

"Why don't you go to the bathroom first?"

"Don't you dare uncover it without me." Walter speed-walks toward the front door, clumsy in her son's high-tops.

"Take it easy. You don't need to rush."

"Wait for me," he calls back.

Katie walks to the end of the driveway where she has a better view of the sea, and where she won't be tempted to pull off the black cover. Across the street, a rope line of little kids from Newquay Elementary make their way to the pier. They wave to Katie with their gloved hands. She waves back, offering her first smile of the day. Katie can't remember being that young. She just inserts C.J.'s childhood over her own, claiming she liked what he likes, hated what he hates. As the bells of Saint Joachim's ring three times, birds scatter from the rooftops. Crossing her arms, Katie looks back at her house, the brass historical placard next to the front door ruined by years of salt.

Locals refer to their home as "the tower," the only house in Newquay with three levels. Katie thinks of it more as a silo with post and beam. Her father once explained that it was originally designed as a cotton dye facility in the late 1800's, "built tall enough so they could hang wet products up to dry." He said the owners converted it into a red cedar shingle, two-and-a-half bath residence after they relocated the factory to Gunnerside in the 1930's. While the tower may be one of the tallest homes in strictly zoned Newquay, it's small compared to the McMansions on their seaside strip of street. The black and pointy roof (currently in need of patching) is marked at the tip by the bronze whale weathervane Katie bought her father one Christmas, his initials branded across the side, centered beneath the blowhole. Jutting out from the circular frame, the stairwell snakes around the house in candy cane fashion. When he was little, C.J. used to run himself dizzy up and down those steps, chasing the cat all the way from the kitchen to the widow's walk. He loved the nooks and crannies, the funny little spaces which made their house ideal for hide and seek. Since there's no basement, attic or garage, all their stuff is stored in the Tuff Shed at the close end of the driveway. According to the deed, the widow's walk was added in the 1960's by the Reeve family, who eventually sold the house to her father in 1983. Because there is no lawn—just an unkempt stretch of garden and no real land aside from the driveway to dwell in outdoors—the widow's walk has served as their backyard.

Inside the dark pod, Katie sits down and rests her back against the wall. As her belly pushes belligerently against her jeans, her mood shoots south. She hasn't been to the gym in weeks. No one's seen her body since November, since Peter.

"Hmmm," Walter says, poking his finger into the tarp.

"Go ahead," she says. "It's your Christmas morning."

Walter claps his hands, then tugs gently on the tarp. Katie closes her eyes. "Let me know when you know."

"Here we go," Walter says. He grabs the tarp and tries to draw it off like a tablecloth, but his grip is too weak and it catches. Katie would guess he's dropped ten pounds since he moved in nine months ago—maybe more.

"On four, we'll pull hard," Walter says breathlessly.

Katie stands up to help him. "How about three instead?"

Walter counts. They yank hard, falling back against the wall, their fists clenching the black nylon cover.

"Are you okay?" she asks, gently taking his hand.

He lets go of the tarp. "My, my."

"What the heck is this?" she says.

"This, Katie, is a Harley-Davidson Road King," Walter announces. "Man's great escape."

CHAPTER 3

Katie's always appreciated the need for escape, the lure of retreat, the thrill of shoving off, but she cannot accept the form it has now taken in her driveway. The second C.J. spots this albatross in front of the house she's screwed. Forever she's feared his yearning, this restlessness they share, dreading how and when it might hatch. If a motorcycle landed in her teenage lap, she'd have been long gone, California and beyond. With his angst, C.J. could wind up on Mars. But she isn't counting on him to settle what she once started, to be the relay on her own unfinished trip from home.

Only a week after her college graduation, with her father trying to convince her otherwise, Katie fled for Middleton, Vermont, telling him she didn't want to wear a business suit, that she didn't care to lose her identity inside the "starchy corporate culture." More to the point, Katie feared the real possibility of a drug test. She also worried she wouldn't blend well with that crowd, imagining an office full of people like her sister set on devouring her. "I belong in Vermont right now," she told her father. "Boston and New York don't want me." Her father said it was "a mistake, a great escape," that all she'd learn there was "progressive drivel."

Driving north in a used Saab with no windshield wipers, Katie felt inspired, believing the life she'd been searching for was finally within her grasp. Once in Middleton, Katie quickly fell into a routine, her days claimed by sleep, her nights cock-tailing for ski tourists. After the bars closed, she'd find the party, letting herself wander recklessly into the night. Her sister called her several times, telling Katie that "this is no time for a walk-about. You don't need to run away just because your art history major is useless. And there's certainly no need to hang around with half-wit pinkos." Caroline sent her a hardcover copy of Ayn Rand's *Atlas Shrugged*, which Katie used as a door stop, the book far too heavy to read comfortably in a bathtub. Katie told her sister she didn't understand "anything outside the norm," but the truth was after six blurry months in Middleton she was ready to go. The men she met in northern Vermont were loaded with ideas. Most, in fact, shared the same ones. The group she hung around with couldn't take a hike, go skiing, see a concert, or even cross the street without being high. Katie thought she might be better off out west, the Four Corners, maybe Port-land or Seattle. No matter the place, she decided once summer arrived she'd drive until she reached the Pacific, but that was before she met Craig on a cold Vermont ski lift.

With the middle seat empty, the two of them shared a triple chair up Powderkeg Mountain's challenging north face. As Katie fiddled with her jacket zipper, Craig lit a joint with a scrimshaw Zippo, blowing thick plumes into the white sky. She glanced his way, but all she got was the back of a red knit cap, his focus on the tall snow-sagged pines to their left. The smell of pot made her feel cozy, the perfect antidote to a frigid morning. If he offered a hit, she'd accept, but first Katie would pretend not to hear him, as if she hadn't been aware someone else was on this chair with her. But his invitation never came and they soon passed the KEEP SKI TIPS UP sign, which meant their ride was over. He skied to the left, she to the right.

Later that afternoon, at a run before closing, he was behind her in the singles line.

"You wanna double up again?" he asked, tapping her shoulder. His voice wasn't what she'd expected. It was very soft, almost feminine.

"Are you going to share this time?" she asked, pinching her gloved thumb and index finger together.

"If you ask," he said.

That night, over beers at the Ski Boot, they were exposed: no hats, goggles, or masks. He was thick, head to toe—sturdy—and as a result appeared shorter than his six-foot frame. She couldn't imagine what it would take to knock this man over, and wondered what he looked like under his clothes, a curiosity more scientific than sexual. He said he was thirty, but seemed older, his wind-burned face creased from a lifetime of alpine exposure. "Ruggedly handsome," she'd describe him to friends. "A mountain man."

With most men, Katie could see through their intentions, but Craig conveyed a concern beyond the immediate, a seeming indifference as to whether or not they ended up in bed. He said he was a journeyman ski instructor, born and raised in Cave Creek, Arizona. His drunken father put him on skis at four, then forced him down a hill against his will. "Only good thing he ever did for me," Craig said. No college, no corporate ambition, nothing beyond what he'd already found. Katie confessed she didn't know what she was doing with her life.

"Cheers to that," he'd said, clinking her bottle. He quickly downed his beer, then stood abruptly. "I gotta go." He reached for his puffy Gerry coat. They shook hands and exchanged phone numbers, promising to meet for drinks the following night. When he was out the door, Katie ordered another beer. Left uneasy by Craig's hasty departure, she stewed over what she might have done wrong. She pulled a cigarette from her purse, the guy next to her eagerly lighting it with a bar match.

Back at the Mogul Motel, Katie brought a chair and two mini-bottles of Baileys into the shower and steamed herself until the hot water ran out. Thinking about the next night, she doubted Craig would show up at the Ski Boot, and decided this wasn't the end of the world. After all, she wouldn't mind being by herself before returning to Middleton. And what could come

- 31 -

of this anyway, she wondered. How could she develop a relationship with a journeyman ski instructor? Nonetheless, she went to bed with a ball of regret wrenching inside her stomach. Around four A.M., she woke up thirsty and dry, her nose gushing hot blood. In the bathroom, she guzzled water from the faucet, then plugged her nostrils with Kleenex. Afraid to look at herself in the mirror, she shut the light, wishing she'd never left Middleton, as if she already knew how the next twenty-four hours would change her life forever.

The next night the Ski Boot was quiet. A couple of long-haired locals played darts, while three old men shared a corner table and a game of cribbage. The bored wait staff knocked back shots of Southern Comfort behind the order window. Craig was two hours late and Katie sat alone at the bar, accepting the fact that she'd been stood up. She drank accordingly, convincing herself it was for the best, that Craig was doing them both a favor, that she didn't need to get involved with a guy seven years older, a man who hopped from mountain to mountain, a person both Caroline and her father would certainly label a ski bum. But Katie couldn't deny the attraction. The need for escape she constantly craved had eased with the sight of this man. From a pay phone booth, she dialed her sister and told her how looking at him was like staring at the sun during an eclipse. "For fuck's sake, Katie," Caroline said just before hanging up, "sober up."

A half-full shot of Rumplemintz stood before her, but she was no longer inspired, she just felt heavy and tired. As she waved for a Jack and Coke, Katie felt a firm hand squeeze her shoulder. "Sorry," Craig said, brushing snow from his jacket. "I didn't get off the mountain until late. I got a little lost."

"That's okay," she said. "I just got here."

He was cuter than yesterday, his face less pointy than she recalled. As Katie arranged herself, she smelled the old men's cigar smoke in her hair. "Let's drink," she said, handing him her cocktail, ordering a light beer and a water for herself.

After a second drink, he confessed to her that his father didn't think teaching people to ski is a job.

"My sister says cocktailing's for trailer trash," Katie offered.

"My father's just pissed because I like what I do," Craig continued.

"My sister hates people," Katie said. "She's an extreme Darwinist."

"When I was working as a machinist in Flagstaff, I was miserable," he said. "My dad says to me, 'they call it work for a reason.' That really stuck with me." As Craig downed his beer, Katie followed his active Adam's apple. "Man, I hate him."

"I love my father," Katie said, "but he worries too much. He wants me to get married. He thinks that will cure me. My bet is he just wants a grandchild and he certainly won't get one from Caroline. I guess my life keeps him up at night."

Sensing the next morning's headache on the horizon, Katie reached for the water glass and drank it down. As she walked to the bathroom, she felt the surrender in her legs, the sweet softness in her mind. In the next stall were two pairs of boots. As Katie peed, she heard a girl throwing up, her boyfriend consoling her between eruptions. Had Craig been another hour late, this could have been them, their destinies altered. But they were headed somewhere else.

Back at the bar, Neil Young moaned from the jukebox. Katie grabbed the back of Craig's shoulders and sloppily massaged his back. "Who are you?" she said drunkenly, digging her fingers into his arms.

"What do you mean?" he asked.

"Tell me your mantra," she said, wrapping her arms around his neck.

He gently grabbed her hands and removed them from his body. She sat down, their legs pressed together. "To live right now," he said.

"Good one," she said, kissing him hard.

And they clung to his mantra throughout the night.

HE WASN'T next to her when she woke up. It took Katie a few minutes before she realized the shower was running behind the closed bathroom door. The sun was like saltwater in her eyes, but she didn't have the nerve to get up and close the blinds. Bits and pieces from the night before began to crash down like waves, a slideshow of horrors. Katie dug underneath the scratchy covers and felt her ache, the hangover pulsing through her pelvis. Her thighs were sore as if she'd gone ice skating the day before. Leaning over the bed, she begged for the sight of shredded condom wrappers, but all she saw was a half-empty Frito bag on top of her balled-up jeans.

Katie threw herself out of bed and stubbed her big toe on the end table, half-full bottles toppling onto the floor, warm beer spilling over her cold feet. She puked into the ice bucket, tasting him, tasting last night. Imagining an awkward breakfast, clumsy conversation and strained embraces, she frantically began to pack as blood pooled underneath her toenail. Katie buried her underwear in the trash and decided it was worth leaving her expensive moisturizer in the bathroom. She started a note, but couldn't get past *Craig*—. She snapped a photograph, catching the Polaroid before it fell to the floor. When the shower stopped, she was gone.

CHAPTER 4

"Our boys rode these in the war," Walter says, kicking the rear tire. "Mostly for scouting missions. My cousin, Irvin, was an Iowa postman and used one for his mail route. Cheaper than horses for the postal service. These are in our blood, Katie. Real Americana."

The black bike tarp covers their legs, like children sharing a warm blanket inside a dark fort. As breath clouds above their heads, Katie can see their blurry reflections in the motorcycle's glossy fender. An expired Arizona license plate peaks out from under a flat, square luggage mount. Hard black saddlebags are fastened on each side of the enormous seat, exhaust pipes like bazookas jutting out from beneath them. The seat is a wide open target, a catcher's mitt. The fattest of asses would be comfortable on such a throne. The bulk of the thick back tire is shielded by the dressy rear fender. Aside from the brake and signal lights, everything is black or chrome. Everything shines.

"It's a touring vessel," Walter says. "From here to eternity."

"I don't get it," Katie says, standing up. Her footsteps echo around them as she walks toward the bike. She brushes her fingertip across the coarsely stitched seat. The texture reminds her of snakeskin.

"It's a police style seat," Walter says. "There's air suspension underneath to keep a cop's caboose happy."

"He stole it from a policeman?"

"No," Walter says. "Harley manufactures police bikes. You can buy all sorts of police toys."

"Sounds childish," Katie says. "How am I going to keep this from C.J.?"

"I'll introduce him to the bike," Walter says. "I'll show him it's no toy."

Katie can remember Walter's motorcycle from the picture he sent when she was in college, but it looked nothing like this beast before them. His was more like Tom Cruise's in *Top Gun*, a ridiculously stylish ride for a man in his sixties. In the photograph, Walter leaned proudly against the bike's canary yellow fairing, a tight MARGARITAVILLE T-shirt hugging his skinny white arms. With a palm tree-lined Florida boulevard providing the backdrop, Walter offered thumbs up. Her roommates found it hilarious and insisted she display it on their fridge, where it remained throughout her freshman semester.

"This is a mistake," Katie says.

"I think it's yours, Katie."

She searches her pocket for a barrette, but all she finds is lint. "Is he trying to kill my son?"

Walter pulls his bathrobe collar to his mouth and coughs, his eyes bloodshot. Every load of wash contains a few of his rainbow-hued handkerchiefs. She delicately wipes his stubbly chin with her fleece pullover. "What can I do?"

"Nothing," he says, reaching for the small bottle of codeine in his jacket pocket. He winces as he drinks.

"Maybe you shouldn't smoke pot," she says. "It can't be helping your throat."

"It's my stomach," he says. "My throat has nothing to do with it."

"You swear no one can help you, right?"

"Only God."

Because Walter spends so much time in his room it's difficult for Katie to know the true extent of his misery. She'd love to know how he feels when he's alone, when no one's looking, but he hoards his pain. Often she wonders what else eats away at him besides his illness, what is really draining him.

"Does it hurt?" she asks him.

He grimaces. "Only when I'm not high."

Katie stretches her arms to the ceiling, begging the tension to ease from her neck. Lately, she feels as if she's slept on a floor. "I'll bring you back some hot water and honey," she says, skirting past the bike as if it's poisonous. "I'll also call Nevada and make sure we have the right pod. Are you warm enough out here?"

"I'm burning."

Inside the house, she ignores the early hour and pours herself a petite Grand Marnier. From the third floor, she hears Walter's cuckoo clock screech, a keepsake he claims to have found during the war inside an abandoned Nazi headquarters. The shrill sound of the cuckoo unnerves her as she drinks. The first few sips sting as she makes her way to the tumbler's icy bottom. Once there, Katie calls Nevada.

"You sent me the wrong box," she tells the deputy.

"Pods sent it to you, Ms. Olmstead. Not us."

The cat pounces on the mail as it falls from the door slot. Katie's close enough to see a letter from Choate Rosemary Hall.

"You sent me the wrong box," Kate repeats. She burps away from the receiver.

"What's the number on the container?" he asks impatiently.

She reads it from the pink invoice. He says he'll call them for her.

"I don't have to do this," he says. "What's inside, anyway?"

"What's your first name, Deputy Ward?" she asks.

"Donald," he says, clearing his throat.

"What's inside is the death of us, Donny."

In the studio, Katie refills her tumbler to the brim. She's lost all desire to go back outside.

A little while later, Walter calls from the other side of the studio door, "Are you all right, Katie?"

"I have a headache," she says, trying to conceal the liquor from her tone. "I'm just lying down for a bit. Are you all right?"

"I'm all right," he says.

Katie turns Isabel around and scratches the back's surface with her nails. Because she can't paint properly after more than two drinks, Katie must face another day's passing without finishing this piece. New Haven already canceled her; they were in fact rude enough to say they'd grown tired of her work.

"Unfortunately, you've been churning out more of the same. Now's the time to reinvent yourself," the coordinator said.

"And what do you paint?" Katie asked, venomously drunk. "Oh yeah, you can't so you work in a gallery." Of course she later regretted her little tantrum. After all, he wasn't the first person to voice this concern. It wasn't the criticism that bothered her—other people's input often fueled her best work. What really ate at her was the dark suspicion that she might never finish Isabel—that she couldn't, that this was it.

WHEN KATIE comes to, she finds herself in a ball on the studio love seat. By the timid nature of the light, she guesses that it's late afternoon.

"C.J.?" she calls.

She pushes herself up from the love seat, her bladder so full she can feel it in her teeth. She moves like she's been in an accident. In the bathroom, Katie flosses until her gums bleed. When she braves the mirror, she sees the cushion patterns stamped on her forehead. Her cheeks are fleshy and red, the jowls of drinking. Like Peter once told her, "There's nothing uglier than a drunk woman." He'd been referring to a celebrity socialite's misbehaviors caught on tape, but she knew this truth applied to her as well.

"C.J.!" she shouts.

Saint Joachim's bells ring five times. A slew of awful hours remain until she can go to bed properly. God, it's been over a month since she drank away an afternoon. And like every time before, Katie swears this will be the last occasion. Eyes firmly shut, she prays she isn't full of shit.

The motorcycle stands in her driveway. It looks more like a science exhibit than a weekend ride. Through the kitchen window, Katie watches as they circle the bike, Walter pointing out areas to her son, C.J. nodding. Katie can't get over its size, like a fat black insect too plump to step on and squash. She turns away and sorts through the mail, but can't find the letter she saw earlier from Choate. Peeking inside the cabinet, she detects only a splash of Grand Marnier left in the bottle. Half a shot at best. She slams the cabinet shut, too little being far worse than none at all.

"We sent Salvation Army away," Walter says, stabilizing his lower back with his hands. "I gave them a pair of trousers, though."

"We can sell it," Katie says, closing the front door behind her, the screen still in need of repair. The wind is sharp against her skin. "The deputy told me they're very popular now."

"No," C.J. says, marching toward her. "I want it."

"What happened to your hand?" Katie asks, reaching for his palm. Blood speckled his knuckles. "When did that happen?"

He yanks his hand away. "I hit it against a tree by accident."

"Oh, bullshit."

"I walked by a tree," he repeats, concealing his bad hand with the other. "The bark was sharp."

"Please tell me you didn't hit somebody."

"I didn't hit somebody."

"You make me crazy," Katie says. She turns her attention to the motorcycle, resolving to revisit the hand later. "You're fifteen, C.J. You're too young to ride it," she continues, stepping toward the bike. "It must weigh a thousand pounds. You're not big enough yet."

"Seven hundred and twenty pounds," Walter says, leafing through a very thick silver service manual. "Found this handy item in the saddlebag. The title's in there too."

He reaches inside the left saddlebag and hands her the document. She looks at it, but doesn't read anything. She gives it back to Walter. "Just please leave everything alone for now," she says. "We need to figure this out."

"We can't sell it," C.J. says. "It's mine too. You said the pod is for us."

"But I didn't think a deathmobile would be inside. I'd rather he left you a loaded gun."

"Walter knows all about these," C.J. pleads. "He can teach me."

"We have nowhere to put it," Katie says. "We have no garage."

"The shed," C.J. says. "There's only crap in there anyway. I'll clear it out. I'll make room."

"I don't need this now."

"Well I do," C.J. says.

Too run down to argue with her son, too unbalanced to gain ground, Katie's forced to surrender. His energy will only bulldoze her.

The sky darkens a shade. She's suddenly very cold. Katie reaches for the wooden shovel handle which peeks through the snow bank by their walkway. She tries to pull it out, but it's frozen inside. Yesterday, she watched from her studio as her son cleared their entire driveway, doing the plowman's work with fury.

"There's plenty of space in the shed, Mom," he continues.

"We're done discussing this today. You haven't even aired out your equipment yet." She kicks his blue hockey bag. "Plus, you have homework."

"I already did it during study hall."

"Just put the bike back in the pod. I don't want to hear any more about it tonight."

Walter's knees buckle as he leans into the motorcycle.

"I don't like you moving that thing around," she says to him, as they pull the bike upright from the stand.

"Exercise will keep me around longer," Walter says, struggling with the weight, his frailty pronounced next to the motorcycle.

"Just leave it in the driveway then," she decides. "No one's going to steal it from here."

As C.J. heads for the house, she catches up to him.

"Did you open the letter from Choate?" she asks.

"The one from Taft too," he says.

"Well?" she says.

"I need to take a shower."

"Come on, C.J."

He sticks his tongue out and shows her thumbs down.

"Damn," she says. "I'm sorry, honey. I'm sure—"

The motorcycle erupts, Katie swerves. Thick black smoke shoots out the pipes as clouds materialize over the driveway. C.J.'s face lights up, which jolts her even more than the engine's thunder. Walter grins at them as he twists the throttle. He talks, but she can't hear anything over the bedlam. She yells at him to stop. Across the street, Mr. Kashgarian steps out his front door and stares at them like they're naked. Walter revs the engine and waves his free hand. As Katie swallows a mouthful of exhaust, C.J. reaches for the handlebars.

CHAPTER 5

"What are you doing here?" C.J. asks.

Katie spatulas the omelet onto his plate. Steam rises from the fluffy yellow heap.

"What's this?" he asks, squinting at the table.

She spoons a dollop of salsa on top of the omelet. "Breakfast," she says. "There's ham inside. Enjoy."

"Where's Walter?" he asks.

"He's writing."

"Writing what?" C.J. rubs his eyes with his knuckles. His bangs are almost down to his nose.

"Short stories," she says. "You should ask to read some."

"What's your deal this morning?" he asks.

"No deal. I just thought I'd make breakfast for once." Katie pulls out a chair for him and places a glass of orange juice next to the plate. "I even added a spoonful of that muscle potion you like."

He smirks, then shakes his head. "It's creatine powder," he says. "Why are you being all weird?"

"How am I being weird?" she asks. "Just sit down. I'm not poisoning you."

"Why are you up so early?"

"Can't I make breakfast without an inquisition?" she says.

He sits down; the chair creaks. With a fork, he scrapes the salsa from the omelet, then digs in. "It's good," he says, his mouth full.

She sits down across from him. Under the table, the cat figure-eights through their legs. Because she's a stranger in the kitchen at this early hour, Katie can sympathize with her son's confusion. Being awake, sharing the sunrise with him, she's suddenly shamed by her usual absence. Up until seventh grade, Katie regularly saw him off to school, but that all changed when C.J. began to shower on the third floor. She no longer wakes to the ding of water pipes, or to her son's lumbering noises from the small shower stall just behind her bathroom door. Sometimes she'd hear him talking to himself. She misses those sounds.

"Tell me about your hand," Katie says.

"I already told you," he says.

"Tell me the truth or that motorcycle is going to the pawn shop."

"You don't sell motorcycles at pawn shops."

"Tell me about your hand," she repeats.

"Christ, Mom," he says. "I'm fine." He wiggles the fingers on his cut hand.

"I'll sell that bike, C.J. Don't think I won't."

"It better still be out there," he says.

She points her coffee spoon in his face. "Did you punch someone?"

C.J. groans and shakes his head. "I punched some glass. It's no big deal." He leans back and looks toward the window, away from her.

"What glass?" she asks. "Someone's window?"

"No."

"Then where?"

"My room."

"What glass in your room?"

"The seashell picture frame," he shouts.

"Why?"

"I was trying to frame the postcard from the motorcycle museum." He wipes his mouth with his arm. "The postcard from him."

"So it was an accident?"

"Sure," he says.

"How did it break, C.J.?"

"I don't know," he says. "Can't I just eat?"

"You never tell me anything anymore."

"You never tell me anything either," he says.

"What do you want to know?"

"Nothing," he says.

Katie finishes the last of her coffee, the day a downhill slope from here. "What do you do with the postcards?" she asks.

He takes a large bite from his omelet. "I chuck them," he says, dropping a piece of ham on the floor for the cat.

"Why'd you punch the frame?"

"I guess I was pissed."

"What were you hoping for?"

"Can we please fucking drop it?"

"Did you think he might—"

"Mom!" he shouts. "Just stop." C.J. stands up and kicks his chair into the table. He looks at her savagely. "Why are you deciding to be a mother today? Huh?" He leans hard on the tabletop, pushing it into her gut. The veins in his forearms thicken and rise. He looks strong enough to Frisbee the table across the room. Katie braces herself for the worst.

"I have to finish my social studies homework," he says calmly, letting go of the table.

"I'm sorry, C.J."

"I hate this class."

"I'm as confused as you about all this," Katie offers.

He runs his hands through his still wet hair. "I'm not confused."

Now wishing she'd just stayed in bed this morning, she watches him stomp upstairs, the Hilfiger logo on his underwear band visible above his low hanging pants. Walter passes him on the stairwell and gives a salute. C.J. pats his shoulder. When he gets to his room, Katie waits for her son's door to slam, but it doesn't.

"You two getting to know each other again?" Walter asks. He sits in C.J.'s seat and picks at his unfinished breakfast.

"Why did I decide to be a mother today?" she asks. "That's a fair question."

Walter reaches into his bathrobe and places a small collection of pills onto C.J.'s plate. He takes them in between sips from C.J.'s juice.

"Any painkillers for me in there?" she asks.

"What were you fighting about?"

"Everything."

"Teenagers are terrified," he says. "I can still remember that anguish."

"He's so damn closed up."

Walter takes a spoonful of C.J.'s untouched salsa. Each time he swallows, Katie catches him scowl. "You can't expect him to open up like a flower," he says; "and if you're going to get into it, you have to be willing to get hurt some of the time."

"I always wanted to believe there was some connection underneath our silence," she says. "I guess that was wishful thinking."

"His father just died. He's struggling."

"What does he tell you when you're playing video games?"

"Our time together is mostly silent. I hear what he doesn't say."

"What does that mean?"

"I read his expressions," Walter says pensively. "He's obvious."

"But he acts as if Craig's no loss. And I believe him when he says he doesn't care. I mean, he never knew Craig. Craig was never here."

"Do you believe him now?" Walter asks.

"No."

"This is an important year in your lives," Walter continues. "We've all got to be careful."

Katie stands up from the table. "Why do you have to say it all doomsday-like?" She collects C.J.'s plate and glass, then drops them into the sink. When she throws the silverware on top, the glass shatters. Walter coughs, then covers his mouth with a paper towel. Brown liquid seeps through the porous cloth. His eyes redden. The cycle starts, his cough like an old car struggling to start.

Katie rushes over to him with a glass of water. "Are you all right?"

He waves his free hand, his eyes sealed with tears. In between coughs, he forces a blue pill down his throat, washing it back with water. "I should go to the bathroom," he says hoarsely. Katie helps him up from the table, reaching under his arms like a child. From behind, she grabs him tight as they walk toward her bathroom, her fingers snug between his ribs. The back of his neck is wrinkly and brown, a shade darker than his face, the bones of his spine stretching the skin. Up close he smells like a Band-Aid tin. And though he has no trouble walking, he's sweet enough to let her hold on, to let her believe she's easing his pain.

"Do we need to take you to the hospital?"

"No," he says. "I just need to vomit. And I like to do that in private. You go back and finish your breakfast." Walter closes the bathroom door. The faucet turns on. Katie waits outside, crouched down, her ear pressed to the door. He blows his nose, clears his throat, blows his nose, clears his throat. Then she hears whimpering, the awful sounds of an old man crying. Tears begin to well in her own eyes. She wishes he'd just throw up, but all he does is wail. Katie picks herself up off the floor, not wanting to eavesdrop on his agony any longer.

In the mudroom, she opens the windows and lights a cigarette. She sits on C.J.'s lumpy hockey bag, the smell from his pads stronger than her smoke. She sprays it with Febreze. For a mother, a future in hockey means a busted nose and broken jaw, dentures at thirty, her son's face spoiled with scars. She worries the game will ruin him. Before high school, he used to draw every day, sitting himself down at the kitchen table before dinner and working while she painted a room away. He had an artist's concentration, the ability to remain still for hours. When C.J. would run in and show her what he made, Katie would offer suggestions—finer points to consider—to help his drawings come alive, to convince the viewer the creations existed beyond the paper. "You want them to startle people," she explained.

Now, if and when he draws, it's upstairs in his room. C.J. shows her nothing, his sketch pads guarded like dirty secrets. More than a year has passed since he's shared his work. When he offered her a pick from his collection for her thirty-ninth birthday, Katie broke down, hugging him until he pushed her away, telling her to "get a grip." She chose a transparent wild turkey, its bloated insides exposed, a decrepit fetus budding in its stomach. She told him it was lovely and she'd meant it. Peter told her it was "crazy," warning that she'd better watch him closely in the years to come. "Good art is crazy," she said.

Katie pulls a jersey out from C.J.'s bag, the black mesh Bruins shirt he wears during practice. When he was in the children's league, she remembers being the only woman in the boys' locker room. The players were all too young to dress themselves for the ice, their fathers and older brothers helping them into their gear. Katie taped his sticks, fastened the garter belt to his socks, snapped his helmet shut, but she couldn't tie his goddam skates, her fingers too weak to get them tight. She reluctantly had to ask a man to help her, her son red and quiet as a stranger laced him up.

"It smells like cancer in here," Walter says, fanning his nose. His eyes radiate exhaustion.

Katie flicks her cigarette out the window. "I don't smoke that much," she says, lifting herself from C.J.'s hockey bag. "Are you better now?"

"Oh, yes," he says. "Much better now."

She leans down and picks up C.J.'s hockey stick. She notices a crack running down the heel of the blade. She fakes a slap shot.

"I heard you crying," she says.

"I've heard you cry too."

"Touché," she says, opening the sliding window. From the driveway, the motorcycle's exhaust pipes aim at her like gun barrels. "Where the hell's the pod?"

Walter approaches the window. "The driveway sure looks a lot bigger, doesn't it?"

"What happened to it?" Katie asks.

"C.J. must have sent it away."

CHAPTER 6

C.J. booms down the stairs, his hair grungy with Walter's pomade. She can see that the rugby shirt she bought him in the fall is already too tight, his arms stretching out the blue and white striped sleeves.

"You look nice in collared shirts," Katie says. "Very handsome."

He grabs his laptop from the butcher block and stuffs it into an already crammed book bag.

"You should wear more blue," she adds.

"Mommm," he groans.

"You should."

He zips his bag shut, dropping it hard on the table. "I'm late."

"Did I do something wrong?"

"What are you talking about?" he says.

"If you don't tell me, I can't fix it."

"There's nothing to fix." As he walks past the butcher block, he knocks over her mug. Coffee splashes across the floor. "Fuck, fuck, fuck," he says, picking up the mug.

"You swear too much," she says. "It doesn't make you sound cool, you know. It makes you sound like a dipshit."

He maneuvers the book bag over his broad shoulders. The bus driver honks the horn. "I don't have time to clean this."

Katie grabs a clump of paper towels and blots up the spill.

C.J. pushes open the front door. "Later."

"Bye."

Katie watches him climb onto the bus and walk down the aisle toward the back. He sits down next to a girl. Their faces mash together. All she sees is their hair. As she heads outside for a better look, the bus drives away.

Back inside, all she unearths beneath C.J.'s bed are dirty socks and old magazines—*Rolling Stone*, *Maxim*, *GamePro*. She lifts up his mattress, digs through his messy desk drawers, pulls his clothes out of the bureau. She even splits his globe apart at the equator. Pot, rubbers, steroids, long strands of a young girl's hair, any little secret will do, but she should have known C.J.'s too careful to leave tracks. Of course his laptop is password protected; she's tried hundreds of names since last year. As Katie lies down on his bed, she wonders if he'll figure out she was here, if he arranged his room in such a way as to sniff out her trespass; but he's been begging her to snoop the way he behaves. Caroline once told her it was her maternal duty to ransack C.J.'s room, that she should seriously consider a surveillance system. "You can watch him like a movie," Caroline had said. "That's parenting." Katie explained she didn't need to spy on her child, that they had an "open door policy"; but that was long before he started punching glass. Sitting on C.J.'s bed, Katie finds she misses Caroline's calls, actually misses the sound of that pompous voice telling her what to do.

Before she moved to California, Caroline phoned them a couple of times each year, usually on C.J.'s birthday and Christmas, which she consistently spent in London. Every summer she sent him a collection of stock certificates, which he'd immediately cash in, amazed at how much money could be contained in just fifty shares. After she talked to C.J., he'd hand the phone over to his mother, to give Caroline the opportunity to pass judgment on her younger sister, to offer her Orwellian take on parenting.

Caroline was born in charge. Right out of law school, she'd landed a job at an elite Manhattan tax firm, earning her way to the high six figures before her thirtieth birthday. Four years later, she had a tantrum: she'd told off her boss—and his wife, apparently—during a charity wine dinner in Chelsea, later informing Katie and her father over dinner that she'd never work "for Harvard chicken shits again." From there, Caroline moved to the Upper West Side for a MBA at Columbia. While she wasn't in class, she ran a three employee consulting firm from her cramped home office in Queens. What they consulted about, Katie had no idea. All she knew was that her sister intimidated people enough for them to want her on their side. One night in Brooklyn, Caroline informed the family she'd never marry, preferring a life uncompromised. Their father worried she was a lesbian, which he told Katie would be "even worse than your situation," her *situation* being that of a single mother. Katie figured her sister was just asexual, having somehow learned to push away the inconvenience and distraction of lust. "Or maybe she just uses a vibrator," said Peter. "Done and done."

Nothing in Caroline's life was any surprise to Katie. Having lived on top of each other for Katie's first fourteen years, Caroline's choices weren't remarkable to her, as Katie's weren't to Caroline. They shared a very small room: bunk beds, a single desk, a solitary closet, a room for one. Katie's convinced this childhood arrangement, in part, led directly to the sisters' current demand for distance—Caroline on the Pacific, Katie on the Atlantic. Her sister was a frantic child, "crazy with credentials" their mother said of her one Thanksgiving, explaining to the table how in nursery school Caroline resisted nap time, throwing "shit fits" whenever they tried to sit her down on a cot. One Fourth of July at Doyle's Beach, a holiday Caroline hated for its "lazy excess," Katie recalls her thirteen-year-old sister spending most of the afternoon in the car doing her homework. She didn't even bring a bathing suit. "It's like sleeping all day," she said of the summer sunbathers. "Yeah, it's nice out, but get over it. Can't they *do* something? I hate the beach." And Caroline did hate—she had a list—and it consisted of everyone who couldn't keep up with her, who got in her way, who dared to challenge her understanding of things.

As little girls, Katie was deathly afraid of her, and made no complaints when Caroline laid claim to every available space in their tiny room, Katie's mission to remain unnoticed and unharmed. The sisters seldom played together and rarely confided in each other, which forced Katie to turn inward for companionship. They could go days without a word. Their father immersed himself in work, their zombie mother in an alcohol- and pill-induced stupor, the four of them orbiting like astronauts around each others' lives. So Katie spent a lot of time in her top bunk, her mattress slab the only place Caroline chose not to conquer. And there, underneath the covers, her father's flashlight shining next to her, Katie discovered the treasure of privacy. In this dim place, while her sister studied diligently at her desk, Katie read books like *The Bell Jar*, *Go Ask Alice*, and *The Catcher in the Rye*. She drew pictures of dogs and porcupines, scripted Valentine's Day cards to crushes. Under the covers, she discovered the reward and bounty of solitude. It was there in the dark that she learned to be an artist.

Three years ago, Caroline had the nerve to inform Katie she needed help raising her child. "You can't work full-time and really rear this kid. He's what, thirteen now?" In the background, Katie heard anxious voices and busy printers.

"Twelve," Katie corrected.

"Well, those are formative years. With all due respect, you don't want to fuck this up."

"I work part-time, not full-time," Katie corrected. "And I'm starting to sell paintings. Plus, C.J.'s happy. You don't know what it's like to be a single mother."

"Let's not have a big pity party," Caroline said. "I'm simply calling to offer my help. I believe my nephew needs me."

"My son needs you? You mean the nephew you've never met?" Katie said. "What's this about, Caroline?"

"It's about being human," she said.

Katie laughed into the phone, carrying it into the studio where she lit a cigarette. C.J. wouldn't be home for hours.

"Look, Katie, I'm serious. I'm cutting my hours, maybe down to forty, forty-five a week before I head out west. You're not that far away from New York. I could come visit for a bit before I go."

"Why not go somewhere interesting, Caroline? If I were you, I'd be in Bali, not northern Massachusetts. What do you want from me?"

"I want to take your son out to dinner, to baseball games, clothes shopping. I want to meet him. God, I'm just asking to be his aunt a few hours a week for fuck's sake." Katie heard the flick of a lighter, then a heavy exhale. It comforted her to know they were both smoking. "Once I move to California, Katie, I'm gone."

As much as she wanted to reject her sister's presumptuous invitation, as much as she didn't want Caroline to think she needed any help, the offer was too tempting to refuse. Most of C.J.'s friends had two parents, twice the childhood. Being alone, she was handicapped.

"Katie?" Caroline said. "Are you still on the line or what?"

"Look, Caroline, he's not a little boy anymore. Don't expect someone you can push around."

"We'll be fine," she says. "I deal with men all day long. Is there any father figure in the picture?"

"I just got a brochure for Big Brothers, Big Sisters."

"Oh, don't do that," Caroline said. "That's for welfare mothers."

"I have to go now."

Katie waited for her sister to hang up, but she never did. Listening on the line, Katie heard Caroline barking orders to her staff, typing furiously on the keyboard, making calls from what she imagined to be an arsenal of telephones. Katie twirled the phone cord around her finger, taking in the sounds of her sister making money.

CHAPTER 7

When Katie opens her eyes, she's surprised to see C.J.'s ceiling. His pillows clutched in her arms smell like Axe body spray. She could fall back asleep in a flash, but the thought of waking up in her son's room again creeps her out. Katie fluffs his pillows and smoothes out her body dent from the bedspread. The light coming through his window looks like noon. She refolds his clothes and places them back in the bureau. His desk drawer she leaves open an inch, the way she found it. As she opens the window to air out any trace of her scent, a chilly wind slaps her face. She sticks her head outside and sees an empty black driveway below. Craig's motorcycle is gone.

Pacing up and down the front walkway, Katie cracks her second Michelob Ultra. The fingers on her drinking hand are frozen. Just as she decides to dial the Newquay Police Department, Craig's motorcycle pulls into the driveway. She shoves the beer bottle into a rain gutter.

"Are you insane?" Katie shouts over the engine.

Walter shuts down the bike. The sharp stink of tire rubber invades her brain. "I was only gone twenty minutes," he says. "I left you a voice mail."

"A voice mail? Why didn't you wake me up? Why not a note on the butcher block? What the fuck?" The plaid-uniformed arborists across the street pretend not to listen as they fuss over the crippled cherry tree on Mr. Kashgarian's lawn. She's embarrassed she swore. "How are you even able to ride it?" Katie asks in a quieter voice.

"Momentum," he explains. "Even corpses like me can brave the open road." He unfastens C.J.'s hockey helmet from his chin and loops it over the brake handle. Over his body he's wearing her brown pleather Gap jacket.

"I thought you were asleep. Jesus, I thought C.J. took it," she screamed. "I was out of my mind!"

"I didn't want to wake you," he says.

Katie lights a cigarette. "I can't handle this, I can't," she says, exhaling smoke. "You know I almost reported it stolen?"

Walter eases himself off the bike. Katie holds his arm as he maneuvers his leg over the seat, his slacks hot from exhaust. "I'm sorry, but I never rode a Harley before."

"Look, I don't need to worry about you *and* C.J." Katie grabs the keys from Walter's hand and throws them toward the rotting wood pile. "I hope you enjoyed it because that's it."

"Oh, yes. What a machine," he says, holding his crotch. "I'm still trembling."

WHEN SHE calls the Chesterfield Academy athletic department, Peter Boyardee doesn't seem surprised to hear his ex-girlfriend's voice. Even though they haven't spoken in ages, he says he'll be glad to help her move the bike into the storage shed, that he's free until wrestling practice at three. Peter is a dutiful man, pleasantly corny, the type of person who pulls over to assist strangers with car trouble in the rain. And the truth is, she didn't know who else to call, her address book utterly devoid of capable men. Aside from her son, Katie knows no one who can muscle Craig's motorcycle into the Tuff Shed. She doesn't want to wait for C.J., preferring that the bike be well out of everyone's sight before her son comes home from school. This is what she told herself as she dialed the familiar phone number. What Katie won't admit is that she's lonely, that one hundred and thirty days have passed since she's been touched. The last time she saw Peter was four months ago when she cut him loose over a dreary lunch at Friendly's. When Peter asked her what he'd done wrong, she simply said the relationship had run its course.

"What course?" he'd asked, digging a straw into his low-carb vanilla milkshake. "What does that really mean?"

Katie wasn't prepared for the cross-examination. Most men she'd known never questioned that reason. When she was dumped, Katie didn't dare probe for answers, preferring not to hear her defects voiced aloud.

"You want more," she said to Peter, her eyes on the Friendly's counter waitress. "I don't."

"When you're drunk you want more," Peter said.

"Well, I'm not drunk now."

"You want to go to the Chum Line?" he asked.

"I'm serious, Peter," she said. "We have to cool it."

"I can't believe you dumped him," Megan said to her later that night. Katie and her boss were sharing a bottle of Pinot Gris after the restaurant's closing time, Katie often the last employee to leave Megan's Harborside. "A man asks to be part of your life and you freak out. Most women in your position would be thrilled."

"My position?"

"Most men retreat from kids," Megan said.

Katie refilled both their glasses. "Well, those are the men I prefer."

"What are you worried about?"

"C.J.," she said. "I won't screw him over again."

"He might want someone like Peter around."

Katie shakes her head no. "Let's say I bring in some man and C.J. gets attached. He'll blame me forever if we break up. Or what if they hate each other? I don't want to be the referee."

"Fair point," Megan said, igniting a cigarette.

"I like Peter, but I don't love him," Katie said. "And he certainly doesn't love me. I'd have to be head over heels to take that risk."

"When's the last time you felt like that?"

"Middle school," she decided. "Slow dancing to 'Stairway to Heaven' with Dan Winterson."

Katie took a thoughtful drag from Megan's cigarette. She chose men for the moment, for satiation. Katie picked them despite her desire to be alone, to prove she wasn't abnormal. Eventually, she revealed a woman they didn't want—a head case or a hassle, a dead end. So while the guys she grabbed never lasted, they were hardly mistakes.

"Head over heels is for kids," Katie continued, extinguishing the cigarette. What she didn't share with Megan were the headaches of starting over, figuring out fresh ways to present herself—the invention of new lies, the retelling of old ones. The process exhausted her, but after a few months it wouldn't matter anyway because no man made it past C.J.

Peter and Katie dated for three months before her alarm went off. "Shouldn't I meet your kid?" he said, when he asked to accompany her to one of C.J.'s hockey games. But like all her past unions, her son and her home were off-limits to their relationship. One night after hours of karaoke and expensive tequila shots, Peter said he was "dying to bang" her in the tower. When she announced in the cab that she'd never had sex inside her house, they were all surprised, the taxi driver included. Even when C.J was away at school or at a friend's house, even when Walter was sequestered in his room, she refused to bring men inside. Not one of her past boyfriends has met C.J., a condition she established for both their sakes. When he was younger, he'd cringe when she told him she had a date. He said he didn't like the word "date," that no one used it anymore, that it wasn't meant for mothers. Katie could tell it made him uncomfortable to see her dressed up—the makeup on her face, the special flair in her appearance—the blatant display of his mother as female.

When he was nine, C.J. asked where she went with "these men."

Katie had stood over the stove cooking hamburger, rice, and scallions, his dinner to be microwaved later by the babysitter.

"We go out to eat. Sometimes we see a movie or go to a museum exhibit."

"Why can't you eat here?"

"Because it's nice to be served once in a while."

"Do you fool around?"

"C.J.," she said, blushing. "Try and think of it like you and Matt Hyde. You guys play together, right? You build forts. You trap bees. That's all dating is."

"How come I can't come with you?"

"You wouldn't have any fun, C.J."

"Are you going to get married again?"

"No," she told him. "Don't worry about that."

"Are you going to have another baby?"

"God, no," she said. "Listen." She walked over and kneeled before him, reaching for his hands. "You and I come first. Do you understand that?"

He nodded, pulling on her hands. "I don't want to see them," he said.

"Who?"

"The men," he said, squeezing tighter. "Don't bring them inside."

"Okay, I won't."

"Promise," he said.

"I promise, sweetie."

PETER'S WEARING his grey Chesterfield wrestling sweatshirt, the same hoodie she used to don whenever she was cold inside his apartment, which was often since he was too cheap to push his thermostat past sixty-five degrees. A light and misty rain falls, the air unseasonably warm for a winter morning. The snow wall formed by the plows is a foot shorter than yesterday, a puddle of black sludge at its base. Beyond Mr. Kashgarian's seawall, the current is frantic, a storm on the horizon. Waves crash the red and green signal beacon on the point. Katie can hardly fathom that soon Newquay will be clambakes, ice cream, and beachcombers.

"Man, I can't believe you got this for free. I wish I had a dead relative leave me something decent," Peter says, fingering the bike grips. "Your cousin left you this?"

"Third cousin," Katie lies. "Very random."

"My father had a Fat Boy until he sold it to pay off my brother's tuition. He'd let me ride it on my birthday, but other than that I couldn't go near it."

"I can't let you ride it," Katie says.

He rolls his eyes. "I know, you've mentioned that a million times." Peter leans over and uses his scarf to wipe mist from the gas tank. "What's so funny?" he asks.

"Fat Boy," Katie says, shaking her head. "Who comes up with these names? I doubt many women would want to own a bike with the word fat in it."

"Women ride Sportsters."

"What makes this one a Road King?"

"Read here," he says, pointing to a chrome ornament shaped like a football, ROAD KING printed in black. "That's the air cleaner cover."

"Road King sounds like a lot to live up to, like you have to be conquering all the time."

"You're over thinking it," Peter says.

He circles around to the other side of the bike and leans heavily against the seat. When the motorcycle shifts, she can hear the gasoline splash from inside the tank. Crossing his arms like a tough guy, she catches Peter enjoying his reflection in the left side mirror.

Watching him pose by the Road King, Katie recalls how he loved to show off his body, how he pounced on any opportunity to model his black and yellow Iowa Hawkeye wrestling singlet. Stuffed in that outfit he was her "tidy little bumblebee," a moniker he didn't appreciate. A former one hundred and forty-one pound college champion, Peter lived to flaunt his uniform, and though he'd gained twenty pounds since college, he still looked good in that tight suit. In bed he'd demonstrate the fireman's carry, the Russian drag, the hip-heist, showing her how to maneuver out of each wrestling move, letting her pin him every time. His bedroom reeked of gym class, the stink of tiger balm stuck to his sheets.

When they met he told her Brazilian jujitsu was his latest obsession, a martial art which left him perpetually bruised, especially the interior of his biceps. His ears were somewhat cauliflowered from grappling without headgear, from "rolling with guys half my age." Often he walked around with a slight limp due to recurring foot sprains, his toes constantly wrapped together in white medical tape, explaining how his pinky got caught on an opponent's kimono during practice. She could tell he got off on the injuries, was proud to display his warrior scars to his lady. Most of his DVD collection was comprised of fight tapes, UFC showdowns which sickened her because of all the blood. The few movies he owned centered around combat. Katie figured physical confrontation was his way of feeling young, his stand against the approach of forty. And she really couldn't tease him about his taste in programming since she herself was addicted to *The Hills*.

"How do I look next to it?" Peter asks, winking.

"You need to be six inches taller," Katie surmises. "Forty pounds fatter. And the Burberry scarf has to go."

"Nope, not anymore." he says. "Bankers, soccer moms, prep school wrestling coaches, they're the Harley guys now." Peter sits on the bike, his feet nearly flat to the ground, his right hand releasing the front brake lever. Wind sweeps sand into the driveway. A brown dust settles over the motorcycle's chrome.

"Are you growing a goatee?"

"Maybe," he says, rubbing the black stubble on his chin. "It'll probably last a week. Then I'll get self-conscious and shave it off."

"Good idea. Only bald people grow goatees. Short and fat guys also."

"Well, at least I'm not fat or bald. Not yet."

"You still look good."

He yawns, but it's a fake, a nervous habit which used to drive her batty. It was his way of stopping momentum, slowing down a scene. "You're scared of the bike, huh?"

"I really can't see beyond the danger."

Peter waves her off and reclines in the seat. His hair's a bit longer, stringy in the salty wind. When they were a couple he'd kept it army short, often asking Katie to shave the portion below the neckline he couldn't get to with his barber clippers. She doesn't mind it grown out, though she hopes he doesn't plan on getting silly with it. Guys with ponytails irritate her. Jock exterior aside, Peter is really a pretty boy in disguise. With a Mediterranean nose—broken twice—and olive skin, Katie can easily imagine him in a tunic, a head wreath and sandals, walking through a dusty downtown square in Pompeii. His best feature by far is his back, the groovy ripple trail from the lumbar to the shoulder blades. As for Katie's body, he said he'd "probably go with the tits" if it came down to one choice. Though short for a man—five feet seven like her—Peter seemed taller because of his confidence. In bed, he was more than she'd anticipated, more than she really wanted. It took Katie a while to accommodate his presence within, to learn how to make it work for her; and he was patient, aware of his endowment, sensitive to her predicament. And though she'd be sore for days afterwards, Katie took a perverse pleasure in knowing she'd been really fucked.

"Are you still bartending at Megan's?"

"Only one or two nights a week," she says. "I need to pick up more shifts."

"How's the art selling?"

"It's not," she admits. "I've been stuck on the same damn piece since we were together."

"No shit," he says, stepping off the bike, holding it steady. "Irene?"

"Isabel," she corrected, lamenting the topic. "Are you working this summer?"

"I may go to Martha's Vineyard and dig clams. My brother has a place there. Or I might coach a summer wrestling program somewhere."

"Martha's Vineyard sounds nice," she says. "I haven't been there in years." Katie imagines cold Sauvignon Blanc and warm summer breezes, the smell of hot butter and steaming lobsters.

"We better get this going. It's starting to come down," he says, grimacing at the grey sky.

Peter pushes the bike up the driveway, his fists tight on the grips, his bulbous calves muscling the motorcycle forward. Katie follows him closely. "Be careful," she says. "It's real slippery over there." Peter stops before the shed. He holds the brake.

Mice scatter as she pulls open the rickety door. "My son cleared a space." The inside smells of damp woodchips. She spots the inversion table Walter bought on eBay stacked upright against the wall.

"I'm going to need a running start to make that incline," he says, rubbing the cement ramp with his boot. "This thing must weigh a thousand pounds."

"Seven hundred and twenty," Katie says.

"My ass is gonna be sore tomorrow."

"Maybe I'll massage it for you when you're done."

He looks at her like she's trash.

"I'm just screwing around," she says, kicking a clump of brown snow from the shed doors. Her cheeks are boiling. "Sorry."

Peter eases the bike backwards to level ground. He stops and wipes the gas tank again with his scarf. Ducks laugh from the distant harbor. He takes a deep breath and holds it. "Here goes."

Steering the bike uphill, his legs move slowly, deliberately, as if he's running underwater. A cluster of veins emerges from his neck. Katie squats like a tennis player waiting for the serve. Over the hump, Peter roars as the Road King wheels reluctantly into the shed. He kicks down the stand.

"Man," he says breathlessly. "What a beast."

"Thank you so much."

He holds out his palm. "Now let me have the keys."

"For what?"

"So I can shove them up my ass. Why do you think?"

"It's staying put," she says.

"I just want to hear what it sounds like. I'm not taking it anywhere."

Katie looks over the bike—switches, buttons, levers, controls as unfamiliar as an airplane's. "It's too damn loud."

"Come on," he pleads. "I did you a favor."

"Fine." She hands him the keys. "Don't take it out of neutral."

"No kidding." Peter sits on the bike, turns the key and flips the run/stop switch. "And liftoff," he says, pressing the red start button—*BOOM!* The engine growls as if waking from a grouchy slumber. The flimsy shed walls begin to tremble. Katie inches between the Road King and an old mattress. She runs her hand back and forth across her neck, shouting for him to shut it down, but Peter proceeds to twist the throttle, which makes the motorcycle scream even louder. Katie grips the seat, her hands inches from his body. Her fingers go numb. Like a thousand angry chainsaws, the bike sounds like it's headed for explosion, the belligerent engine ready to leap out of the frame.

She watches Peter sit where Craig has sat, touch what Craig has touched, moved by the moment, the blend of lives. When Katie and Craig were together there was no motorcycle, no hint of two wheels in their future. Back then it was on skis where he sought risk. And while she knew he was reckless, Katie didn't worry when Craig crossed the orange boundary lines and ventured into a mountain's abandoned back country. Being so young, she was spared the wariness that has come with age. Fifteen years ago she wasn't afraid to fall asleep. Fifteen years ago she didn't wake up nervous. All she wondered then was what she might be missing by being too scared to follow Craig past the perimeter and onto the lonely side of the mountain. The few times they skied together, they never lasted the entire day as a pair. Skiing groomed trails bored him and he'd eventually flee for the untouched. Katie preferred long, tortuous alpine runs, her focus on form and style, Craig's on adrenaline and survival. When they'd meet for après-ski, he'd show up with a torn jacket, scraped cheeks, wheezy breath and jubilant eyes, a glow she envied.

Peter shuts the bike down. Katie embraces the silence, an enhanced quiet after all that noise. The bike begins to cool down, the ticking sounds of hot oil dripping inside. When she breathes in, she smells burnt fuel.

"I love that smell," Walter says from outside the shed. He's wearing C.J.'s black TAPOUT sweatshirt, the hood strings tight around his head. "Did you take it to the red line?"

"Almost," Peter says, stepping off the bike, careful to avoid the exhaust pipe. "I think I took it to 5,000 RPM."

"Walter Olmstead," he says, extending his arm. "I'm Katie's great uncle."

Peter timidly takes his hand. "Peter Boyardee."

"Like the chef?"

"Yes," he says.

"Ahhh!" Katie shouts, yanking her left hand away from the engine fins. "Son of a bitch."

"It's still hot," Peter says.

"No shit." She pushes past him, past the motorcycle. Outside the shed, she waves her hand through the cool, wet air.

Walter inspects her palm. "Just a little burn. Minor."

"Why'd you have to start it?" she says, glaring back at Peter. "I don't understand any of you."

Peter shrugs his shoulders, then looks at Walter as if waiting for an answer. "I didn't tell you to touch the cylinder heads," he says defensively.

"I don't even know what the cylinder heads are," she wails. "I don't know anything about this mess."

"It's okay, Katie," Walter says. "We have Neosporin."

She rubs the burn with her middle finger. Fire shoots through her fingertips. Peter lumbers toward his truck. "See ya," he says, opening the door.

"Aren't you coming inside for lunch, Mr. Boyardee?" Walter calls. "I'm boiling yams."

He cleans off the windshield wiper with the sleeve of his sweatshirt. "That's up to her."

Katie suddenly feels like a bitch for yelling at him, for sending him off like cheap labor. She'd just wanted to scream, burnt skin her chance to act out and complain. The frustration and disappointment had nothing to do with her hand. In fact, she was grateful for the injury.

When Katie glances at C.J.'s window, she doesn't feel the panic she expected, having a man so close to their home. What she feels instead is the rush of a teenager about to break the rules.

"Why don't you come inside, Peter?"

CHAPTER 8

As C.J.'s team takes the ice, Pam Delaney, a Viking mom, pounds the glass with her well-manicured hands. The home crowd boos over the Viking applause. A few rows behind them, a group of nubile high school girls hold up a VIKINGS' PRIDE banner. The man in front of them rings a cowbell.

"These people are crazy," Walter says, tugging on his turtleneck. "You'd think Elvis was in the building."

"The playoffs are nuts," Katie tells him. "It's win or go home for both teams."

In between sips from a thermos full of Baileys and Swiss Miss, Katie explains the ice to Walter. "They face-off in those circles there," she says. "The red line divides the ice in two. The blue lines represent zones, one for them, one for us."

Katie waves and smiles to other Viking parents. A few come over to say hello.

"They seem surprised to see you here," Walter says.

"I normally sit with the opposition's supporters."

"Why's that?"

"Because I'm usually here alone."

Katie doesn't have to explain why it's more comfortable for her to be alone amongst strangers, how she only really minds her solitude when others take notice. A sick old man who cries in the bathroom probably understands her need to hide. When Viking parents ask her why she sits with the enemy, Katie lies, explaining it's "just a silly superstition I've followed since C.J. was in the children's league."

Katie tucks the blanket ends under Walter's legs, securing the wool cover over his lap. She holds his tea cup as he sprinkles in his special Chinese herbs. While she'd warned him it would be frigid inside the arena, Walter insisted on coming, saying he must see C.J. play hockey before he "disappears." Her last guest was Caroline three seasons ago, who found the parents' enthusiasm to be "crude."

"Remember," Katie tells him, "the Vikings are crimson."

"Like Harvard."

"The Nighthawks are blue," she says. "They beat us twice during the regular season and knocked us out of the playoffs last year."

"Welcome to the Jungle" by Guns N' Roses cranks over the loudspeaker. The girls holding the banner begin to dance. Katie wonders if one of them might be C.J.'s secret friend from the bus. When she asked Walter about him having a girlfriend, he said "C.J. probably wouldn't play video games with me on Saturday night if he had one." Katie used to be aware of all his friends, but since she bought him a cell phone, none of them call the house line anymore.

One minute to face off, bellows the announcer. *One minute*. The crowd claps and screams. Katie grabs Walter's frail arm. "I hate this," she says.

"What's the matter?"

A shiver runs up her spine. "I just wish I could enjoy the game like everyone else," she says, "but I'm always a wreck until it's over. It doesn't help that it's freezing in here." Katie twists open the thermos and drinks. It seems she's often colder than everyone else.

Surveying the crowd, she locates the prep school hockey scouts: conventionally handsome, sporty men in their forties who sit high in the bleachers. One wears a blue and red Farmingdale cap. As they rise for the National Anthem, Katie focuses on these men and hopes her son will show them what they want to see.

C.J. stretches his legs against the boards, pulling on his skate tucks for leverage. At six feet, he's taller than many of the boys on the ice, a battleship in his pads. "Your kid's gonna be a brick shithouse," Coach Gardner once said to her, which Katie took as an insult until C.J. explained it was slang for massive. Unlike his teammates, C.J. never looks at the crowd during a game, playing as if the arena is empty. It bothers her when she sees other players wave to the stands after they score, saluting those who came to watch them. When C.J. scores, he just punches his fist and skates back to the bench, which makes her wonder if he even wants his mother there.

The buzzer sounds. Five boys from each team line up at center ice. The referee signals each goaltender; they wave back. The puck drops.

"What's his number again?" Walter asks.

"Forty-four," she says. "Right wing."

They watch as C.J. crosses over into his own zone, the crisp sound of slashed ice rising from the frozen surface. Dark strands of hair shoot through the breathing holes on his helmet. He holds his stick like a weapon.

"He skates beautifully," Walter says. "Very elegant."

Katie watches C.J. collect the puck in the corner and pass to the breaking center, but the play is dismantled before the red line. The Vikings back-check into their zone, C.J. circling toward the play. All ten players are in motion, the game in a constant rhythm, a masterpiece of choreography. As C.J. hurdles the boards, his replacement jumps onto the ice, a boy she doesn't recognize. From the bench, her son lifts his mask, showing his face, the blue in his eyes. C.J. squirts water over his cheeks and passes the green bottle to another player. She's warmed by the camaraderie and sharing.

With his teammates pinned in their own zone, the Nighthawks play keep away.

"Are the Nighthawks showing off?" Walter asks.

"Yup," Katie says, biting her fingernails. "Get used to it."

Coach Gardner shouts from the bench, his thick hand megaphoning over his mouth. The Viking net is swarmed. Katie feels their panic.

"Nighthawk goal!" the announcer shouts. "Kane scores, assisted by Jokl and Downs."

"Dammit!" Dennis Magnotti shouts from his seat three rows behind them. "God, we suck."

"Who's that?" Walter asks, twisting around.

"His son, Colton, plays center for us," Katie whispers.

"Is anyone playing defense today?" Dennis asks.

"Give it a rest, Dennis," Owen O'Malley shouts, the father of a Viking defenseman.

"I'm just saying," Dennis says. "We can't score if we're stuck in our zone all day."

"What a ghoul," Walter says.

A pigeon flies over the ice and comes to roost on the metal support beams. Katie wills it to shit on Dennis's head.

"We need your boy out there," Owen says, tapping Katie's shoulder. "We need some presence."

"Yeah, but we don't need penalty minutes," Dennis interjects.

"Just shut up, Dennis," Pam Delaney shouts, offering Katie a sympathetic smile.

"Your son gets penalties too, Dennis," Katie says, her eyes on the ice.

"Well, look who's here," Dennis says. "Someone decided to sit with the masses today."

Walter pats her knee, a touch of caution and understanding. Katie bites her tongue. From the bench, Coach Gardner shouts *dump and chase.*

"What does that mean?" Walter asks.

"They're supposed to shoot the puck into the opponents' zone and chase it down," Katie says. "It's kind of a desperate option."

"Ice it!" Dennis shouts.

"That won't solve anything," Pam replies.

Katie watches the Nighthawks set up in the Vikings' zone. Their passes are tape to tape, their positioning spot-on, the defensemen orchestrating plays with militaristic precision. The Vikings play as if they're shorthanded.

"They're maestros," Katie admits. "Very pretty."

"Get it out!" someone shouts.

"Clear the zone!" screams another.

From the middle of the blue line, an enormous Nighthawk stick handles the puck. Katie watches as he fakes the pass to his wing, then blasts a low shot on net. The puck deflects off a Viking's blade and swiftly changes direction, zipping past the goaltender.

Two – zero.

The Nighthawk fans rise and rejoice as the Viking goalie slams his fat stick over the crossbar.

"That poor boy," Walter says.

"We scored on our own net," Dennis says. "Perfect."

The referees squeegee excess water from both goal creases. The Vikings surround Coach Gardner as he holds out a clipboard marked with plays. A whistle blows for the face-off in the corner. The Nighthawks win the draw. A defenseman fires a high slap shot—*smash*, the puck cracking the glass above the boards. A crew is called out to replace the pane. The teams return to their benches. An organ plays "When the Saints Go Marching In."

"C.J. just needs to sell his game," she tells Walter. "It doesn't matter if we get clobbered. He can separate himself from them."

Walter starts to speak, then coughs. He covers his mouth with his hands. The woman on the other side of him wrinkles her nose and turns away. Inside his fanny pack, Katie finds a small water bottle full of codeine solution wrapped in a red bandana. She sets it in his lap.

"Godammit, I wish you'd see someone," Katie says.

Walter takes a swig from the bottle, then another, and instantly calms down. "The elixir," he says, exhaling deeply, his turtleneck now spotted with purple drops.

"A second opinion besides your own might help," she says, dabbing his chin with her sleeve. "You make it very hard for us this way."

Walter clears his throat and spits into an abandoned Dunkin' Donuts cup. "What you want is a magician."

They watch as the rink staff struggle to situate the new pane of glass into the slot. Walter sips Aquafina; Katie finishes the thermos.

"I wish you'd just humor me then."

"I know what I'm doing." Walter removes his coat and pulls up the sleeves. Liver spots and freckles cover his forearms. "I'm getting hot."

Katie reaches into her purse and hands him another bottled water. "What's it like for you?" she asks.

"How do you mean?"

"When you feel down," she says. "What's it like?"

"I just sleep when I feel crummy."

"What about when you can't sleep?" she presses.

"Then it's shrill."

"Shrill?"

"Noises," he explains matter-of-factly, "screeching sounds. Like fingernails against a blackboard. Some days it goes on for hours. That I can't sleep off."

"It's probably all these meds," she says, shaking his fanny pack.

"No, the drugs help drive it away."

She leans into him. "How long have you been hearing it?"

"Three or four years."

"And the sounds make you break down?" she asks. "Make you cry?"

"No," he says. "A high pitched wind makes me cry. A telephone ringing. Running water. I bawl over bullshit."

"You know," Katie says, "I think the only reason I cry is to show off, to remember that I can, but the truth is my heart's never really in it."

The buzzer sounds. *Game on*, the announcer shouts. The referees lead the teams to the face-off circle just outside the Vikings' zone. C.J. stands up from the bench and removes his helmet, wiping sweat from his forehead with a familiar beige washcloth from their linen closet. When the puck drops, both centers rush each other.

"Fight!" someone shouts.

Walter stands up with the crowd; Katie clutches her seat, feeling years' worth of hardened bubble gum beneath. In the far corner, both teams hold each other back as two boys drop gloves.

"Why do they remove their gloves?" Walter asks. "They're going to break their hands on each others' helmets."

The boys stay on their feet, each trying to pull the other's jersey over their heads. The referees stand around and wait for them to fall.

"Rip his head off!" Dennis shouts.

The boys punch madly, their skates digging into the ice. Both teams lean over their benches and cheer on their boxers. Katie relaxes knowing C.J.'s still on the bench.

The boys fall to the ice. The referees move in and carefully untangle them. Each boy raises his arm in victory while both benches tap their sticks against the boards.

"Does C.J. fight?" Walter asks.

"Yup. He leads the team in penalty minutes this year. A dubious distinction."

It was after a November morning practice when Coach Gardner told her C.J. was starting to play mean. "A bit too rough lately," he'd said, "even by hockey standards. If he really wants to move on to the next level like he says, C.J. needs to channel that temper." Just to prove her son wasn't some thug, Katie was tempted to show Coach Gardner some of C.J.'s drawings from his flower phase in seventh grade. One look at his tulips and he'd see her boy wasn't all mean. But Katie agreed with the coach, believing he could put his rage to better use. "C.J. has trouble receiving a hit without hitting back. He takes each shot against him personally," Coach Gardner said. "He's starting to go after people, which worries me." While he was polite enough not to ask *is everything all right at home*, Katie could see the accusation in the coach's eyes.

Just a month after that little conference, C.J. received a ten-minute game misconduct for spearing an opponent in the gut with the butt end of his stick. "Could've been a two or three game suspension," Coach Gardner said. "I'll be benching him one for sure." Katie shivers whenever she recalls that hideous sound, that awful human howl which silenced the arena. As the kid dropped to his knees, he punched the ice with his gloves, fighting for his wind. His teammates came out for C.J.'s blood, but the referees had isolated her son and quickly escorted him off the ice. One outraged parent just missed his head with a full can of Sprite, the soda exploding into the boards. Katie shot out of her seat and hid in the women's restroom. The stall was gross and the seat was cold, but she didn't come out until the game was well over, until C.J. phoned her from the empty parking lot.

Miles away from the rink, parked outside a Chelmsford McDonald's, she asked her son if he was okay.

He nodded.

She asked him what made him so angry at that boy.

C.J. said she wouldn't understand.

"Why did you do that, C.J.?"

He groaned, then kicked the glove compartment. "On the ice it's different," he said. "Something flips when I put on that helmet."

"Then why do you play?" she asked. "You draw wonderfully. You have talent. You can do other things."

He bit into his Big Mac and chewed over her question. "I like the action," he said.

"But your actions are dangerous. Look what happened tonight. You could have really hurt that boy."

"He just got the wind knocked out of him. He was making a show of it for the audience."

"Did you want to hurt him?" she asked.

"I don't know," he said, his mouth full of fries. "He was bigger than me anyway."

"But you're going to outweigh them all soon. With your size will come responsibility."

"Was Craig responsible?"

"Yes, he was," she said, puzzled by the question. "And you're already his height."

"What did he weigh?"

"230, 240. Maybe more."

"Good," C.J. said.

It seemed whenever he asked about Craig, she'd end up talking about muscles. C.J. knew what his father weighed, he'd asked countless times, yet he never grew tired of hearing her say the heavy number. Katie figured it was his way to see what was coming, to imagine himself grown. And as long as they were having a conversation, Katie didn't really care what they discussed. Last summer, when she showed him a picture of Craig posing in front of the Mount Frost Ski School, C.J. only mentioned his father's shoulders, how he hoped his would be as broad. When she told him they had the same eyes, he said he didn't give a shit, then handed Katie back the old Polaroid snapshot. Yet as a child, her son openly wondered about Craig—what he was like, how they met, why he left. Back then, mother and son weren't so damn suspicious of each other.

"Six feet, two hundred and thirty pounds. That's thick," C.J. continued, plunging a McNugget deep into barbeque sauce.

A young family crossed in front of their car, a little boy swinging between his parents' hands. He turned and smiled at them. Katie waved.

"Are you taking steroids?" Katie asked. "I saw on *60 Minutes* how—"

"—Mom," he said, laughing. "No."

"Are you sorry about what you did?"

"Sure," he said, rubbing his mouth with a napkin.

Katie felt as if she'd picked up the wrong kid, that her son was still at the rink waiting for a ride. She didn't want to know this child. This child spooked her.

"Can't we just go home?" C.J. said. "The cat's probably starving to death. Walter fed him Beefaroni last time."

"Promise me no more violence," Katie said.

"I'll try."

She rubbed her son's sweaty hair. "You know I love you, right?" she said.

He slurped his Cherry Coke to the bottom.

"Right, C.J.?"

"Yup."

She put the car in drive. "Good."

The morning after the spearing incident, Katie phoned the school's counseling office, but hung up each time they answered. When she mentioned the idea to C.J., he told her every kid sent there came home with a prescription for Ritalin. "They're all hooked," he said. "I don't want to end up at rehab."

Around this time, Katie's drinking went up a notch—a touch more than she intended—but it was also getting chillier outside and Grand Marnier was like a Snuggie. With her blood so warm, she didn't have to turn the studio thermostat up so high, which helped her feel financially responsible and justified. And like clockwork, the edge eventually dulled, the severity of C.J.'s assault softening as weeks passed. Once again, Katie could convince herself that she had overreacted to C.J.'s emotional state, had needlessly panicked over her maternal shortcomings. What's more, he didn't want drugs, a stance she found encouraging. Then she stopped drinking so much. Six straight nights without a drop. No cold sweats, no shakes, no cause for concern. Then one night Katie woke up short of breath, hunched over the side of the bed begging for air, stunned to discover that she was a liar.

THE ANNOUNCER indicates both players have been ejected from the game for fighting. Four additional penalties have been doled out for roughing. The referees have cautioned both teams to keep themselves in check. The announcer issues the same warning to the crowd.

As they face-off in the Nighthawk's zone, Katie looks up at the rafters and notices the pigeon is gone.

"This sport is too violent," Walter says. "He should try diving."

"It's a better game without the hitting," Katie says. "When they're little, there's no checking. No trouble at all."

In the corner, players push and shove over the puck. A Viking kicks it free and C.J. follows it up the ice.

"He has the puck," Walter shouts, standing up.

Instead of watching C.J., Katie focuses on the scouts, hoping it's a positive sign when they type furiously into their laptops. Her son's strength is his skating—his fierce acceleration, his speedy stops and starts, his seamless transition from forwards to backwards. She can remember when he learned to skate, when he was five years old and pushing a chair across the ice. He'd wave to her as he went by, his smile shining through the face mask. No other sport captivated him like hockey. He simply liked being in skates and holding a stick.

As C.J. charges through the neutral zone, his arm is hooked from behind. He loses the puck and the Nighthawks take control.

"Call the penalty!" a parent shouts.

"Are you blind, ref?" another calls.

Katie spots a speedy Nighthawk maneuvering through the middle. The Vikings' coverage breaks down. The Nighthawk splits the defense pair and skates into a breakaway. He shoots high on the goalie's blocker side: Three – zero.

"Godammit!" Dennis shouts.

The Nighthawk fans chant *sieve-sieve-sieve* toward the Vikings' goalie.

"What does that mean?" Walter asks.

"They're being cruel. They're saying the goalie is like a sieve. The puck passes right through," she explains with her hands.

Katie spots Ted and Valerie, the goalie's parents. Ted, a Boston College sociology professor, stands up, adjusts his V-neck sweater, and purposely heads toward the Nighthawk crowd. Two obese security guards impede his progress. "You goddam yobs," Ted shouts, shaking his fists over the guards' meaty shoulders.

"This is better than Springer," Walter says.

"They need to end this game," Katie says. "I can't handle two more periods." She reaches for the thermos: empty. Katie places it to her right, away from Walter.

One minute remains in the first period, the announcer says. *One minute.*

C.J.'s line takes the ice. Her son conferences with the centerman. She imagines the scouts honing in on him. Her son and the opposing winger battle for space along the hash marks. A referee splits them apart, forcing them to maintain their position until the puck drops.

The Nighthawks' centerman wins the face-off and quickly draws it back, but the puck misses the mark, gliding between the two defensemen and into the Nighthawks' defensive zone. She sees C.J. hustle through center, knocking over the winger in the process. The boy drops hard. C.J. snatches the puck before the lumbering defensemen. He speeds up. The crowd rises, the noise peaks, and Katie waits for them to let her know what's happened.

"They fouled him," Walter says, pinching her elbow.

The ref sweeps his arm, indicating the trip.

"Penalty shot!" Dennis roars.

"Oh, shit," Katie says.

"What's happening?" Walter asks.

Katie sits on her hands. "C.J. gets a breakaway. Just him and the goalie."

"Well, that's good," Walter says.

"Not if he misses."

C.J. skates to center, circles the puck twice, then stops. Both teams remain on their bench. The crowd is muzzled. The referee waves to the goalie, then to C.J. Katie's heart pounds as if it's her shot to take. Burying her face in her overcoat, she pleads: *Please let him have this. Just this.*

"He'll make it," Walter says.

The whistle blows. Walter places his papery hand on top of hers.

C.J. attacks the net, a full speed charge. The goalie quickly backs up. Katie expects him to shoot between the legs, but the goalie reveals no promise between his pads. C.J. suddenly draws his stick back, faking the high slap shot, but the keeper doesn't bite, holding his position deep in the net. Desperate, her son tries a left to right fake-out, but the goaltender has already called his bluff. Now it's the goalie's advantage, his play to make. The puck beams the right post—*ding*.

Circling away from the net, C.J. slams his stick into the boards—*BOOM*. The glass wobbles from the wake. Black friction tape streaks the white surface. As he skates toward center ice, he raises his stick like an axe, smashing it over the Nighthawk logo: *Whack, Whack, Whack, Whack*. His stick shatters, the splintery heel flies across the ice.

"Who is that?" she hears a woman say.

Skating toward the bench, C.J. javelins the broken stick into the crowd. The fans scatter.

Oh, my God . . .

What's wrong with him . . .

Where are his parents . . .

As the crowd follows the soaring stick, Katie keeps her attention on her son. At center ice he rests on one knee, his mask propped open. He finds her eyes.

The stick lands by the snack bar. "Oh, my," Walter says.

A fan throws C.J.'s stick back onto the ice. The referee carries it over to Coach Gardner.

Amidst the referees, C.J. leaves the ice through the corner doors. Katie tries to picture her son's expression and while she'd like to believe he's distraught, his cheeks wet with sweat and tears, she suspects he's numb underneath that mask.

She hands Walter the keys. "Meet me in the car," she says.

"Why?"

"C.J. has nowhere to hide," she says. "Someone should be waiting for him in the car."

"What about you?"

"I'm staying for intermission." She leans over and kisses his cheek. "I need to clean up his mess."

Braving the glare of the crowd, Katie walks toward the Viking bench, her legs quivering as she descends. She knocks on the glass behind Coach Gardner. Without a word, he hands her the fractured stick, his bewildered eyes asking why. The crowd boos her as she carries the shattered Titan back to her seat. Pam Delaney rubs her arm and tells her it's all right, that the game's been out of control since the puck dropped. Holding the hockey stick tight, Katie keeps her head up and ingests the crowd's wrath, accepting all the blame for her son.

Dennis stands in front of their section, raises his arms to the sky. "It hit a little girl!"

CHAPTER 9

As fans flock to the concession stand, the players skate back to their locker rooms. Under the fluorescent lights, the ice is shredded and yellow. Katie can see the gash at center ice where C.J. slammed his stick.

"Come on, Katie," Pam says. "Let's move."

"I'm going to find the little girl."

Pam squeezes her arm. "Look, Katie, you can't fix this right now."

"I can't just flee the scene."

"Dennis said she just spilled a little hot cocoa on her shirt. She's not hurt."

A dirty snowball explodes a few feet in front of them. Another one hits her in the chest. Wiping the crusty snow from her jacket, Katie watches a pack of boys retreat under the bleachers.

"Now can we go, please?" Pam says.

"This is so wrong."

"Do you want to get in a mommy fight? Because that's what'll happen if you go over there. Now come on," Pam says, tugging on her arm. "We'll go through the Zamboni garage. And leave that stick here."

Katie props C.J.'s broken hockey stick against the outside of the boards, giving it a pat before she lets it go. As the two women near the exit, the crowd begins to boo. "Just ignore them," Pam says. "We're almost there." Katie leans into Pam's shoulder and lets her lead. She keeps her eyes down on the rubber mats until they reach the door.

Outside, the boos are replaced by singing birds. Puddles of melting snow spot the parking lot. The air smells like fabric softener.

"It's like spring," Pam says. "Look at the sky color."

"Persian blue," Katie says, shielding her eyes from the sun.

The Zamboni emerges from the rink and dumps its snow collection onto the gravel. The driver leans back in his chair and lights a cigarette. If she were alone, Katie would go over and ask him for one.

"Are you going to the hockey dinner this year?"

"I'm sure I'll have to work." Katie says. "I bartend in Essex."

"Oh, how fun," Pam says. "I waited tables all through college."

Katie stops when she sees her old Volvo station wagon parked alongside the far curb. Inside, C.J. taps his fingers on the back window, his head bobbing to the beat of his iPod. Walter sleeps in the front seat, his head hung like a hostage.

"Well, thanks for helping me out of there, Pam. Please tell everyone I'm sorry for all the drama."

"Where's your car?"

"It's just a few rows down," Katie says. "I can take it from here. You should get back to the game."

"Oh, I don't mind."

"I can go by myself, Pam."

"You're right," she says. "I apologize."

"No, I apologize," Katie says. "It's just C.J. will be embarrassed to see anyone right now."

Pam wrinkles her mouth. "Is he all right, Katie?"

"Oh, yeah." Katie smiles and flips her bangs, trying to shoo away the concern, but the apprehension in Pam's eyes won't soften. "His father just died," Katie confesses.

"Oh, jeez. I'm sorry."

"It's fine," she says. "We're dealing with it."

"Is he an only child?"

"Yeah."

"Do you two have a good relationship?"

"For the most part," Katie says, suddenly feeling as if her motherhood is on trial. "C.J. just lost it today. That's not how he is all the time. Doesn't your son ever act out?"

"Sure he does," Pam says. "But we keep Jason on a very tight leash. My ex-husband, Michael, is very involved. He has a zero tolerance policy."

"How come Michael is never at Jason's hockey games?"

"Michael gets baseball, I get hockey."

"Well, I get everything," Katie says. "The good, the bad, it's all mine."

"Do you want Michael to talk to C.J.? He's very good with both our boys. It might help."

"Oh, no," Katie says. "Thank you, but no. My boyfriend, Peter, is close with C.J. I wouldn't want to confuse him by adding another man."

"I understand," she says. Pam reaches into her purse and pulls out a business card from her wallet: PAMELA DELANEY, SENIOR VICE PRESIDENT, KILLINGTON INVESTMENTS. "Look, Katie, if you ever need anything, just call. Use my cell." She writes the number on the back of the card. "I better get back inside for the second period." Pam hugs her quickly. "Take care."

She watches how Pam walks awkwardly in her Chanel shoes, careful to avoid the gritty puddles. Looking down at her dingy Reeboks, Katie notices the ugly mustard stain on the toe from a pre-game pretzel. She kicks her sneaker into a snow bank and rubs until the yellow is gone. Leaning over, Katie makes a snowball with the grimy residue and throws it at the back window of her car, but C.J. doesn't flinch.

"What took so long?" Walter asks. "I thought they might have lynched you."

Katie fastens her seat belt, then drinks an entire bottle of water. She turns to C.J. *"Boo, Boo, Boo,"* she chants.

"What?" he says, removing his headphones.

She reaches back and points in his face, her fingertip brushing his nose. *"Boo, Boo, Boo,"* she repeats.

He slaps her finger away. "What's wrong with you?"

"What's wrong with you? You made me feel like Hester Prynne in there."

"Who?"

"You embarrassed us," she says. "Why would you do that to yourself?"

"Coach already chewed me out."

"I don't care," she says. "I just want to know why you're so goddam mad."

"I'm not mad."

"What do you call jettisoning your stick into a crowd full of people?"

"It was a crazy game, Mom. You weren't on the ice. You don't understand."

Katie puts the car in reverse. "Oh, bullshit," she says, pulling away from the curb. "Why play if it makes you act like a maniac? I mean, what's the point? Are you trying to warn everyone not to come near you?"

"You should count to ten, C.J.," Walter offers. "Process before you react. And if you find out that's not possible, then we should really try and figure out why."

C.J. squints out the window, his eyes on the passing trees.

"The answers aren't outside, C.J.," Katie says. "You can't tell me you're happy about what happened this afternoon."

"The season's over anyway," he says. "It doesn't matter."

"Oh yes, it does matter. What about next season? How are you going to top this? Are you going to stab someone with your skate?" C.J. laughs, rolls his eyes. "You say you want this as a career," she shouts, "but you'll be in jail with a job like this."

"Christ, Mom, ease off."

"That's all I've done and it's obviously not working."

Katie follows a large red Hummer onto the highway. BE KIND TO ANIMALS, HUG A HOCKEY PLAYER reads the bumper sticker on the rear fender. She used to think that was funny.

"How do you think those scouts viewed your performance today? You think you helped your cause? Boarding schools don't like liabilities."

"Maybe I won't go to boarding school," he says. "Maybe I'll go somewhere else."

"Oh, really," Katie says. "What does that mean?"

"I can live in Alaska for a year or something."

"With no high school diploma, you'll be working in a cannery," Walter says. "Balls deep in salmon guts."

"You need to see someone," Katie says.

"I'm not talking to Dr. Phil."

"Can you talk to anyone?" she says. "*Do* you talk to anyone?"

"Will you please let me handle it?"

Katie pulls off the exit. At the intersection, she watches two teens make out conspicuously in front of Pizza Hut. Only kids kiss like that. "Do you have contraception because I'm not dealing with a teen pregnancy. Do you understand me?"

"What the hell, Mom?"

"You know what I'm talking about."

"No, I don't."

"Your little girlfriend on the bus."

He looks at her like he's offended. "We're just friends," he says.

"Do you kiss all your friends?

"Yeah, I do."

"Does your friend have a name?"

"Roxy."

"Sounds promiscuous," Katie says flatly.

"Relax, Mom."

Walter unbuckles his seat belt, then lowers the headrest behind him. His body groans as he sits up and faces C.J. "Don't fuck yourself over, C.J."

"A-men," Katie says, switching on the radio. When she hears NPR, she turns up the volume and tries to lose herself in a story about peak oil. Except for the nerdy sounding reporter, no one says a word the rest of the drive.

Back home, C.J. airs out his hockey equipment in the mud-room for the last time this season.

"Where's your stick?" Katie asks. "Oh yeah, it's in pieces."

"Ha, ha," he says, heading upstairs to his room.

She pours herself a glass of Shiraz. While Katie couldn't wait to get home and decompress, she's dismayed she can't sit still and settle in, can't read a sentence without grinding her teeth over C.J.'s on-ice tantrums. Surrounded by a year of unfinished chores, Katie quickly downs her glass and declares war on her mess. She removes the couch cushions and vacuums the debris from the cloth. She sponges the hardwood floor free of cobwebs and cat hair, her fingertips grimy and grey. Had she more nerve, Katie would organize the sloppy nest of cable cords beside the television set, but she's suddenly very tired. Plopping down on the couch, she hates to think what Pam Delaney would see, what a strong, corporate woman would make of this mayhem. Of all the smart girls she went to college with, Katie bets none of them is living like this. Had her father not paid off this house, their life wouldn't appear half as credible, but James Olmstead knew his younger daughter wasn't cut out for a rich man's mortgage, knew she couldn't handle it like Caroline. And he was right, because most years she's forced to borrow money just to pay the property taxes, just to keep pretending they're like everyone else on the block.

Katie pours another Shiraz, a half glass, and carries it out-side. A snow plow roars down their street, dumping sand onto the melting black ice. Her cat drinks from the thawing birdbath, tapping its paw against the thin layer of ice. Katie reaches out her hand and catches the water that drips from icicles decorating the shed. When she looks up at C.J.'s room, she sees him eyeing her from the window, but he's gone before her next blink.

Back inside, Katie knocks on his door. She hears him grunting through a set of what she imagines to be sit-ups. When she says dinner is ready, he says he isn't hungry. When she asks what he's doing, he says none of her business. When she tells him the house is on fire, he says good.

"Godammit, I'm trying to help you," she shouts.

"Then go away."

A man wouldn't let him hide in his room, Katie thinks. A husband would kick that door open. A father would grab him by the neck and holler. A man would do something.

In the kitchen, Walter boils water for tea, the *Boston Phoenix* fanned across the butcher block. "We should all go see *Blue Man Group*," he says. "Some much needed levity."

"C.J.'s going to kill someone," she states. "That's what's next."

Katie opens the refrigerator and frowns. Nothing makes her hungry. She reaches for a beer. "You know, when he was little, I didn't believe the older mothers. I remember Vivian Shipley said to me, 'no man will ever crush you like your son.' Well, she was right. They were all right. I should call Vivian and see what became of her kids. Maybe I'll listen now."

"Have some tea," Walter says, commandeering the Sam Adams from her hands. "You're beginning to slur." He pours the beer down the sink. Katie doesn't fight him. In an hour he'll be asleep and there'll be no one to stop her.

"I'm with you," he says. "Therapy's the best option."

Katie loads the coffeemaker for tomorrow's batch. "What did he say to you outside the rink today? Before I got in the car."

"I asked him why he did it," Walter says. "He told me he didn't know. When I asked him what he felt, he said he felt nothing."

"I don't believe that," Katie says.

"I told him I didn't think that was the real C.J. on the ice today."

"What did he say to that?"

Walter blows on his tea. "He assured me it was," he says.

CHAPTER 10

"It's getting nasty out there," Peter says, setting his peacoat over the corner barstool. "A real nor'easter."

She hands him a freshly laminated menu, glad to see his goatee has vanished. She notices long blonde hairs stuck to the back of his coat. "Do you still drink Shipyard?"

"Sure do." Peter sits down and rubs the chill from his arms, showing off his muscles. A celebrity poker match plays on the television above his head. With a coaster, Katie clears the excess foam from the beer glass, then hands him the sloppily poured pint.

"Sorry," she says. "Something's wrong with all the kegs."

"No matter," he says, wiping away a beer mustache. "Man, it's quiet in here tonight."

"There's only one waitress on. This crap weather keeps everyone home."

Peter picks up the menu and squints through the listings. Frozen rain begins to rattle the rooftop. She hears the wind tear through the marshes outside. "Looks like nothing's changed here," he says.

"Same menu since Megan opened in 1995." Katie looks up at the TV and sees an actor from *Seinfeld* grin as he rakes in a pile of red and blue poker chips. "Since when is gambling shown on ESPN?"

"It's a fad," he says. "So how was your kid's playoff game?"

"Heated."

Katie turns away from him and rips an order ticket from the printer. From the refrigerator, she pulls out two Michelob Ultras and sets them on the waitress's tray. Even though it's slow, she's grateful to be away from home, especially after the galleries in Westport, Rochester, and Newton called to reject her most recent submissions, a couple of her older works from years past. "While we have always appreciated your intention," Westport had said, "we're trying to be a more accessible gallery now." Rochester asked her "to try and fill in those blank faces. Allow the buyer more insight into the artist." Newton wondered if she "might consider something more germane to the region."

Last night on the widow's walk, Katie disclosed to Walter that the art world was on to her. "My day has come and gone," she declared.

"Don't be so dramatic," Walter said. "Why didn't you send them something fresh?"

"Because I have nothing."

"What about Isabel?"

"Fuck her," Katie said. "She's sinking me."

"You know, there's weeks when I have loads of short story ideas. So many I can't contain myself. Then there're mornings I can't craft a decent sentence. That's art."

"Yeah, but this is my so-called career," she said. "You were a doctor, not a writer who treated patients on the side. You fought in World War II. You laid railroad track to pay your way through Harvard." Katie walked toward the edge of the balcony and lit a cigarette. "You're my goddam hero," she said, exhaling smoke.

"Do you not like the bar anymore?"

"Not when I'm sober," she said. "It's just getting harder. Grey-haired men look natural tending bar. Sophisticated even. A woman over forty pouring drinks brings everyone down."

"Right now you're in an artistic rut," he told her. "When you start to create again, you won't mind your job so much."

"It's not a safe environment for me," she confessed, hoping he'd ask why, but he seldom meddled with her vices, rarely probing beneath the surface, which disappointed her.

Walter sat down on the snowy deck chair. She saw he was wearing an old pair of C.J.'s snow pants, the tear in the knee from one of C.J.'s many sledding mishaps. "Do you have to paint, Katie?" he asked.

"What do you mean, *have to?*"

He cleared his lungs and swallowed. "Do you feel you must paint or else?"

"I think so," she said. "Yeah."

"The poet Rilke says that your life, in even the most mundane and least significant hour, must become a sign, a testimony to this urge."

"So what?"

"So you shouldn't complain about what you must do."

"Okay," she said, "but just because you have to paint doesn't mean you can. What does Rilke say about that? What happens to those people?"

"You let me know," Walter said.

KATIE SALTS four margarita glasses as the blender churns noisily. From the podium, the hostess changes the TV channel to the Bruins game. She turns it up.

"What do you want to eat?" she asks Peter over the sudden clamor.

"A bowl of chowder," he says. She takes the menu from his hand. "How's your Harley burn?"

Katie holds up her palm. "About healed. I snagged some of Walter's Vicodin for the trauma."

"What about the cigarette burn on your thigh?"

"Jesus," she said, glaring at him. "Don't be a dick."

"I'm just asking."

"I already told you."

"I think you're full of shit."

"I was drunk when that happened."

"Uh-huh."

"I missed the ashtray. You do stupid things when you're drunk, too," she says, pointing in his face.

"I don't harm myself."

"Oh, shut up."

"At least you're not a cutter."

"I'm not a burner either. It was an accident, okay?"

Katie pours the margaritas from the pitcher, but there's only enough slush for three-and-a-half glasses. "I'm a shitty bartender when it's slow," she says. She blends another batch and adds extra for herself, which she pours into a Dunkin' Donuts coffee mug. The cold drink rushes her brain, an instant ice cream headache.

"How's the Road King?"

"In the shed where you left it," she says, pressing on her forehead. "I had a locksmith secure the door."

"What's your plan?" he asked.

"God, what's with all the questions?"

One of her many major complaints with bartending is being stuck, trapped behind the bar, on trial before the customers. Katie snags a rag and wipes down the grimy bar sink. A cluster of lemon and lime wedges clog the drain. The fruit flies scatter as she picks them out. She turns on the hot water and lets it run. "Sorry," she says. "The bike makes me bitchy. All I want to do is sell it, but I'd never be forgiven."

Katie sets up a row of cosmos for the five shiny women at the round table. She overhears them discussing their ladies' weekend to Palm Beach.

"Does Megan care if you drink on shift?" Peter asks, pointing to her Dunkin' Donuts coffee cup.

"A few cocktails make me a better bartender. And I pay for every single one," Katie says, savoring the limy margarita taste. "Besides, she's in St. Barts."

"Wow," he says, dipping bread into his chowder bowl. "How much money do you think Megan has?"

She pours him another beer, herself a half-shot of Grand Marnier. "More than us," Katie says. "Cheers."

"Take it slow," Peter says, pushing his beer away. "You're outpacing your only bar patron."

She downs the shot. "Whatever."

"Are you going to shut that water off?" Peter asks.

Katie reaches for the faucets. All three sinks are filled with hot, milky water. She bends over and unplugs the drain. Her apron is soaked.

"Yuck," she says. "I'm filthy."

"I prefer you dirty."

She rings out the water from her apron. "No," she says, "you prefer me easy."

"That too." He leans over the bar, his face inches away. Katie sees a black patch of hair he missed with his razor. His periwinkle T-shirt shows off the blue in his eyes. "Do you wanna come over tonight?" he says slyly.

"You have a girlfriend, Peter," she says, hiding her face behind the beer taps.

"That didn't seem to bother you last time."

"Last time I was a drunken slut."

Peter finishes his first beer. "Well, I liked that floozy."

When he came over to move the bike the other day, Katie hadn't meant to seduce him, but once Peter came inside for lunch she seized the chance to right her ship, to cross sex off a nagging list of things-to-do. After lunch, when Walter went upstairs to nap, she invited Peter into the studio, the blood zooming through her veins as he opened the door to her private space. Katie poured them each a snifter of Grand Marnier, her fourth drink counting the three glasses of Shiraz she downed with lunch. She showed him her easel and brushes, her favorite colors and blends. Peter looked over the studio as if trying to find Katie's secret, the reason he was never allowed inside when they were dating.

"I always pictured it bigger," he said. "This is more like an office space."

"If I painted in the toilet I'd call it my studio."

"What happened up there?" he asked, pointing toward the black scuff marks on the ceiling.

"I use a hockey stick when C.J.'s music gets too loud," she said. "The divide between us is porous."

When he asked to see Isabel, Katie let him touch the canvas. "It looks done to me," he said, draining his drink.

She sat him down in her father's chair. "Look through these," she said, handing him a gigantic photo album which displayed some of her sold paintings. "This is what *done* looks like." As Peter patiently flipped through her catalog, Katie provided a brief synopsis of each piece, momentarily recapturing the triumph she experienced during those final brush strokes.

"Do you see the difference now?"

"Not really," he said. "Who's this?"

"That's my sister, Caroline."

"You should paint her," he said. "She's kind of hot."

"She's also kind of crazy."

"What's this one?" he asked, pointing to a grainy Polaroid.

"That's the motel room where my son was conceived."

"What's that all about?"

"Memories," she said.

"Do you have shots from the conception too?"

"Stop," she said.

"The room doesn't exactly look like the Ritz."

"More like the Shitz."

"It must have been a special night."

"It was very special," she said. "I made my son in a blackout."

"Just like a fairy tale," Peter said, closing the book.

Katie flipped it back open. She'd forgotten there was a fireplace at the Mogul Motel and was shocked to see a faux-glass chandelier above their old bed of sin, wondering how such an obvious ornament could have escaped her memory. Fortunately the photograph had darkened over time, too blurry to dwell over and get stuck. "It wasn't a good way for C.J. to start off," she said, shaking her head. "Things might have been different for him if I was more connected that night."

"Why do you think his dad killed himself?" Peter asked, emboldened.

"Oh, shit," she said, blushing.

"What is it?"

"Craig didn't kill himself," she confessed, scrunching up her face in shame. "I only told you that so you wouldn't be so eager to approach C.J."

"Wow," he said. "That's twisted."

"It is."

"So is he alive then?"

"No, and while I'm being honest, I should tell you the Road King belonged to Craig, not my cousin."

"It was your third cousin."

"Not my third cousin either," she said. "Anyway, Craig left it to us in his pseudo-will. He had a heart attack in February."

"Holy shit," he said, standing up, "what else don't I know?"

"That's it, I swear. I guess when it comes to Craig, my first instinct is to lie."

"Apparently so," he said, firmly closing the photo album again. "So why are you coming clean now?"

"I think because you're here," she said. "It's hard for me to lie in my own space."

"God, I wish I'd come in here before. Or maybe I don't." He pulled his coat from the back of the chair. "I gotta get back to school for practice. We have a big match against Avon Old Farms on Saturday. Thanks for the booze."

"Hold on."

"What is it?"

"Just hold on."

"What?"

"Come here." Katie pulled on his shirt and kissed his face, his sporty Right Guard scent rushing her nostrils. She grabbed his hand, pressing it against her breasts.

"You're nuts."

"Come on," she said, rubbing against him, feeling his rising interest.

"What do you want?"

She licked his neck. "Just stay for a little while longer."

"Why?" he said.

Katie yanked off her sweater.

"You sure?" he whispered.

"Yeah."

"I don't want any drama," he insisted.

"Me neither."

"You've had a few drinks."

"A few is nothing."

He wrapped his arms around her shoulders. His fingertips tickled her back. She was trembling.

"No strings attached, right?"

"None," she said, pulling off his shirt.

"I should tell you I'm seeing someone," he said.

Katie unzipped his pants, ambushed by the fresh yellow Hawkeye tattoo on his upper left quad. "Just stop talking."

THE BAR phone rings for take-out. Katie hands it to the hostess, Kayla. Peter smiles at the young woman. Katie admires her ass and laments her own passing youth. The Bruins score from the television above.

"I'm so sick of hockey," Katie says.

"Did your kid play well Saturday?"

"No, he went berserk." She tells him about the penalty shot, the hostile crowd, her getaway with Pam. As Katie runs through the mortifying details of that afternoon, she's surprised by her willingness to share such a shameful story with someone like Peter. In the past, she wouldn't have revealed her son's hair color without a fight.

"Maybe he didn't mean to throw it into the crowd," he says.

"I don't think he *means* anything."

"Is the little girl okay?"

"Yes, thank God," Katie says, wiping down the sticky beer taps. "You know, every time he's blown a gasket, I've felt sorry for him. I've felt sorry for me. But that just made me mad when he threw that stick. He can dump on me all day, but I can't stand for anyone else to be hurt because of us."

Katie tells him how they drove all the way to East Long-meadow to apologize to little Molly Ashe, to show her they weren't brutes. "It was rough at first," Katie says, shuddering. "The father's in Iraq and the mother is an admin at a chiropractor's office. You could tell they were pretty broke. Molly's brother plays defense for the Nighthawks. God, I've never seen C.J.'s face so red, but he told Molly he was sorry and he seemed to mean it. He didn't fight me on this one. They were so damn kind to us."

Katie had been touched by C.J.'s sincerity, a remorse he hadn't revealed in ages. She felt the whole awful event was almost worth it just to witness this tiny moment of grace. While Katie said sorry over and over ad nauseum, it was C.J. who earned their forgiveness with silence and solemnity. Before they left, her son gave Molly a present wrapped in the *Newquay Daily Times*. When that little girl kissed C.J.'s cheek, both mothers' eyes softened, and Katie was heartened to see a familiar vulnerability on another woman's face.

"That was very sweet of you," Katie said as she pulled onto route 128. "What was in there?"

"A squirrel," C.J. said.

"What?"

"It's a drawing of a squirrel racing up a tree with acorns shoved in his mouth. It was the only one I could find that seemed right for a kid."

"I'm very proud of you today."

"Yup."

"It was nice to see you express yourself."

"Uh-huh."

"God, why can't you talk to me like you talk to strangers?"

He plugged his ears with his iPod, pressed play. "Because you're not a stranger."

What Katie doesn't tell Peter about is the sand bucket full of blood-stained glass shards she found under C.J.'s desk when she dropped off his laundry. Underneath the bucket were three old postcards from Craig shredded to bits. As Katie rubbed her fingers over the broken glass, she gathered he left this wreckage out on purpose, that he wanted her to see his rage on display. And although the sight of his blood upset her terribly, Katie felt strangely encouraged by the exhibit, as if he was letting her in on a secret.

When she sat down at C.J.'s desk, she wondered what a daughter's room would look like, if his Megan Fox picture would be replaced by Johnny Depp, his hockey players by ballerinas, his blood-stained glass by diaries. What she really wondered was if a girl would have made any difference at all.

KATIE UNLOADS the dishwasher. She stands on the ice bucket to hang the wine glasses. "Do you want more chowder?" she asks Peter.

He shakes his head no.

"I'm sorry about jumping you last week."

"Don't worry about it," he says.

"I was selfish and gross."

He hands her his credit card. "Relax, don't be such a woman about it."

"Was I okay?"

"You're freaking me out," Peter says, shifting his focus to the hockey game. "Man, the Bruins suck."

An old couple shuffles toward the bar. The man pulls out the stool for the woman. Katie smiles beyond her normal range as she hands them menus. She takes a singular pride in ensuring that elderly patrons' visits to Megan's are special.

"You sure you don't want to come by later?" he asks.

"We'll see. Maybe I'll call you," she says. "God, what are we doing?"

"Keeping it carnal," he says, standing up. Peter puts on his peacoat, which fits him perfectly. He waves from the door. "Goodnight, bartendress."

"Drive safely," she calls.

After she takes the couple's order, Katie walks to the other side of the bar and brushes the bread crumbs from Peter's warm seat, then pushes in the chair. Four dead hours loom ahead until she's free. Outside the window, she watches him sit in his truck, knowing how he likes to let it warm up five minutes before driving anywhere. She bets he's on the phone, probably with the woman with blonde hair. It's uncharacteristic for her to project, to wonder who he's talking to and why. When they were together Katie harbored no jealousy, no concern over his whereabouts. He could have shown up reeking of sex and she'd have kissed him anyway. What baffles her now is the greed, how she suddenly wants this man badly.

"Here you are," Katie says, handing the white-haired couple their food: haddock sandwich and a cup of chowder, a dinner for one. She brings them two more cherry-filled Manhattans. "Enjoy," she says. From the television, the crowd boos, the Bruins down by three goals. Standing on the ice bucket, she changes the channel back to celebrity poker. As she watches the elderly couple share their meal, Katie wonders what they make of her behind those old eyes.

SPRING 2007

CHAPTER 11

With a cold bottle of Heineken Light wedged between her legs, Katie parks at the far end of the mouth of the river. She kicks off her grimy bar sneakers and throws her socks into the backseat. After a ten hour shift, her feet look like two cartoon hams. Across the causeway, she hears sand grinders and swearing, the sound of men working the late shift at Lee's Boat Yard. A group of boys a few years younger than C.J. fish for stripers along the river's railing, their flashlights shining over the wavy water below. Over a dozen cars spot the marshy landscape, many of them occupied by teenagers. For all she knows, her own son is a couple of parking places away steaming up the windows.

Katie takes a swig of the beer, wishing this was her first pop of the night, something special and earned. She can't remember exactly when shift drinks turned from treat to necessity, how the simple courtesy of saying hello to a customer became so unbearable. Once upon a time she waited until after closing to unwind. One season she promised no drinks before last call. Last summer she allowed herself only beer before ten, liquor after midnight. Now there are no rules.

She hurls the empty bottle at a graffiti-marked granite wall— *SMASH!* The kids on the pier point her way. Katie waves to them as she reverses out of the parking lot and floors it onto route 133, a month's worth of ATM receipts flying out the car window. Turning up the radio, she sings along to Mötley Crüe's "Home Sweet Home," remembering the massive crush she had on Vince

Neil in ninth grade, her crazy obsession with his platinum blonde hair. The one time she saw them live Vince insisted on wearing a black and orange bandana over his locks, which spoiled the show for almost every girl in the audience. Shortly after, she abandoned glam metal for alternative music, falling in love with freaky men and their pretty voices.

Katie taps the brake as she passes C.J.'s high school. She sticks her head out the window and tries to make out his building, the ugly blue door, remembering the cheaply carpeted homeroom where she sat for parent-teacher conferences last December. There Mrs. Timlin told her "your son's attention is lacking. C.J. seems to be somewhere else. I know he's very good at art, but that's not exactly a reliable career path."

"Tell me about it," Katie said.

"It's just a lot harder to get into college than when we were in high school, Ms. Olmstead. Prep school might help, but I think we both know that's a long shot, even with a strong hockey season."

Katie wished she'd prepared for Mrs. Timlin the night before. She could have spat out some rehearsed action plan to improve C.J.'s focus, some Internet method to address his restlessness. Sitting at a high school student's desk, Katie felt like she was the one being chided, that all fingers were pointing at her. She didn't know what to say to Mrs. Timlin besides "thank you" because she couldn't see anything wrong with excelling in one subject. She should have told her C.J. was lucky to be good at something, even a subject as *unreliable* as art. She should have said how proud she was to have a creative son, that she was overjoyed to have borne an artist.

Red and blue lights flood the back window. Katie hits the brake hard, then releases, letting the car glide. She has no idea how fast or how slow she was driving. Rummaging through her purse for gum, all she finds are empty wrappers. She pulls over into a marina parking lot and waits, hoping the cop will pass by in pursuit of someone else. When he turns into the marina, her stomach free falls.

"I'm sorry—was I speeding?" she asks, her foot still pressing on the brake.

The officer turns his flashlight on the car, then shines it in her eyes. All she can see is the brim of his chauffeur-style hat. "You were swerving," he says, eyeing the back seat. "Have you been drinking tonight, ma'am?"

"Oh, no," she says. "I work at a bar. That's why I smell."

"Smoking anything?"

"Just a few cigarettes," she says.

"I'll need your license, registration, and proof of insurance." He slaps at a mosquito on his neck. "Will you turn down the radio, please?" he says, inspecting the bug smudge on his hand.

Katie hands him everything from her glove compartment except for the small ice scraper. "The registration and insurance are in there somewhere," she says. "I'm sorry it's such a mess."

"I don't need your Rage Against the Machine CD," he says, handing the disc back to her.

"Oh, that's my son's. Sorry."

"Your license is expired," the officer says, quickly shifting his scrutiny between the photo and her face.

"I know," she says. "I was going to do that tomorrow."

"Also, your windshield is smashed," he says, thumbing the spider-web crack in the glass. "Were you going to do that tomorrow as well?"

The officer shuts the flashlight and places it in his holster. Katie's eyes adjust. The moon is almost full, the sky bright and clear. As he stares at her, she doesn't move, allowing him to figure out what he must. He's startlingly young, someone she'd certainly card at Megan's. His goatee is a blonde glimmer. It annoys her to be scolded by someone his age.

"Wait here," he says, walking toward his car.

Katie shoves a handful of pennies into her mouth, a trick she learned from Craig sixteen years ago. "You suck on them like candy," he once explained to her, "and you can beat a breathalyzer." She doesn't remember him driving anywhere without a beer in his hand, the sound of the ignition followed by the pop-top of a can.

She used to keep a baby picture of C.J. taped to the horn, a reminder of why she shouldn't drive buzzed. Standing in the sink, his goofy little body covered in suds, Katie would recall the nostalgic scent of Selsun Blue she scrubbed into his scalp to soothe his cradle cap. Of course, the photo never altered her careless course—the image only made her romanticize the past, the longing to go back in time and start over. Usually Katie wouldn't even know she'd been driving drunk until the next morning, until she experienced the hangover; because the night before she'd felt glorious, certainly not impaired, a woman way too confident and secure to be surrendering keys. In that state, Katie could saw off her feet and still insist on driving, all the while swearing she wasn't handicapped. The truth only occurred to her later, after the fact, when it was too late to make life and death adjustments.

The officer steps out of his squad car with the radio still in hand. The patrol lights remind her of a pinball machine. Katie tries to decipher what he's saying on the CB, but the wind is too strong. She knows he won't find any tickets or warrants, no past problems with the law. And while Katie doesn't know exactly how many drinks she had—three, four, six tops—she does know she can drive. There were a few blender leftovers, a Grand Marnier in between. One customer bought her a shot of Bushmills. There was a glass of champagne with the chef before she left, the Heineken Light by the river—but all this consumption over several hours with many glasses of seltzer in between.

The officer puts down the radio. The pennies in her mouth taste like silt. Katie spits them out and reaches for an empty water bottle, hoping for a miracle as she taps the hollow bottom. From the trunk, the policeman retrieves a set of orange cones, setting up pylons on each side of a long white line. She looks forward to the challenge, eager to embarrass him. Maybe then he'll turn off those obnoxious lights.

"Will you please exit the car, ma'am?"

As she steps out of the car, she realizes she's still wearing her apron. Her legs are dog-tired.

"Where are your shoes?" he asks.

"I've been on my feet all night," she says, grabbing her sneakers from the passenger seat.

"It's illegal to drive barefoot in Massachusetts."

"For fuck's sake," she says, tying her sneakers.

"What's that?"

"Nothing,"

"Listen up," he says. "I want you to walk this straight line." He points toward the white paint delineating the parking space. "If you haven't been drinking, it shouldn't be a problem."

"Just so you know, I have bad knees. I was a softball catcher in college," she lies.

"Please, ma'am," he says. "Just try."

"Can I at least get my coat?" she asks. "I'm freezing."

"I'll get it for you."

"It's in the back seat," she calls.

A ragged American flag blows steadily from the harbormaster's hut. Vacant lobster traps decorate the rooftop. She notices two men watching her from the stern of a docked Hatteras. They have beer bottles in their hands. When Katie gives them the finger, they move back inside the spacious cabin. The light goes out.

The officer hands her the coat. She sees that his nametag reads, DEPUTY MIKE ROLLINS. "Go ahead," he says.

Katie warms her hands in the furry fleece pockets. Amongst the loose change, she detects one of Walter's pharmaceutical joints. She quickly zips the pocket shut. Katie can't bare to imagine C.J.'s reaction if he were the one to answer her call from jail. Neighbors will see her name and address printed in the *Newquay Daily Times* police blotter. She'll be labeled a drunken wreck, an unfit mother. The Department of Social Services will pay a house visit. Like the elderly, she'll have to take cabs to the grocery store. Walter will encourage her to do the work she fears, to turn this trouble into some valuable life lesson. C.J. will destroy her.

"Let's go, ma'am," the officer says.

"Is this okay?" she asks, holding her arms out like a tight-rope walker.

"As long as you walk straight, I don't care what you do," he says. "Just go."

A loud pickup truck slows as it drives by the marina parking lot. The tires look almost as tall as she is. Five or six kids are in the back of the truck, a row of baseball caps. Hip-hop music blares from the cabin. "Go, lady!" one of them shouts over the music. The horn honks. When the officer walks toward them, the driver peels out.

"Forget about them," he says. "Just walk."

As Katie closes her eyes to summon confidence, she loses her balance, her right foot tripping over her left. She staggers off the line.

"I had my eyes closed," she says. "Let me start over with them open."

"That was enough to disqualify you."

"Please," Katie pleads. "Give me another chance."

"One more shot," the officer says. "Hurry up."

Katie steps deliberately, focusing on the toes of her dingy black sneakers. Each time her foot covers the line, she pauses and takes a breath. Whenever she feels like dipping, she takes another step and her balance is restored. Never has walking been so complicated, but if she can just place one foot in front of the other, if she can manage a toddler's chore, she can make it home without real consequence.

She hears the truck again. Katie stops, her right foot directly in front of her left. She holds her position.

"Give her a body cavity search!" a boy calls. Katie untangles her pose and turns toward the truck. All she sees are white faces and preppy windbreakers. They shine a LED flashlight on her. "No way," she hears the driver say, pointing right at her. The officer makes a call on his CB radio. "Let's go!" a boy calls. The truck speeds away.

From the car, she hears her cell phone. Katie recognizes the ring tone she set up for Peter. She guesses it's three A.M., a booty call.

"You can get back in your car, ma'am," he says. "I'll be right with you."

She puts on her seat belt and cranks the air vents. An oncoming headache presses behind her eyes. All she wants to do is brush her teeth. If C.J.'s still up when she gets home, she'll tell him she had to stay late to do inventory, that she wanted to call but lost track of time, that her phone had no reception downstairs where the liquor is stored. Katie will promise it won't happen again.

"I know you've been drinking," the officer says, leaning into the window. "But I'm not going to bust you."

"Thank you so much. I only had—"

"—Quiet," he says, holding up his hand. "A woman your age shouldn't be driving around drunk. You say you have a son? I'd be horrified if my mother was out and about like this."

Katie swallows the lump in her throat. "I'm sorry," she says.

"Get your license renewed tomorrow." He hands her a pink speeding ticket. "I've been working this route almost a year. I've seen you before. Next time it's serious, Mom."

Katie takes a right out of the lot, the officer a left. Hunching over the steering wheel, she follows the speed limit home. An eighteen-wheeler zooms past in the opposite lane and rattles her car. When she looks in the rearview mirror, the patrol car is out of sight. Katie would like to show that little shit she isn't drunk, that's he's too young to cast judgment. If only she asked for the breathalyzer, she'd never have been subjected to such ridicule. In Katie's mind she was only drunk if she *felt* drunk and she expected people like Officer Rollins to understand this distinction. Four cocktails can be a wild night for some women, yet a simple warm-up for others. She thinks sobriety tests should be scaled, individualized, catered to each person's tolerance and DNA. A fair and balanced assessment unlike the indignity she was subjected to this evening. Tomorrow she'll call the Essex Police Department and complain.

Katie cranks the steering wheel and skids into her driveway, the seat belt keeping her firmly in place as the car comes to a sudden stop. Quickly she rolls up the windows as the stink of burnt rubber competes with low tide. Once she locks the car door, she realizes the headlights are still on, the beams shining over the Tuff Shed, the doors split wide open.

"Oh, shit," she says.

CHAPTER 12

Katie dials the police, but hangs up once she sees one of C.J.'s hockey sticks wedged between the shed door hinges. She yanks it free and chucks it into the pachysandra, which instantly quiets the crickets. For the first time tonight she can humbly admit she's drunk, for had she been sober it would not have taken high beams to spot such an obvious break-in.

Inside the shed, Katie finds C.J.'s corduroy jacket hanging from the Road King's handlebars. The engine is cold, the mileage unchanged. Nothing is missing. She shuts the doors and sets a cobblestone against the base to keep them from opening. As she heads for the house, her son's light turns on.

"I can't believe you," he yells from the stairwell.

"I can't believe you," Katie says, dropping her purse on the butcher block. "Here." She tosses his corduroy jacket onto the marble table. "You forgot this at the crime scene."

"You're the criminal," he shouts.

"Shhh," she says. "You'll wake Walter."

C.J. storms downstairs. He's wearing the plaid Banana Republic pajama bottoms she bought him for Christmas.

"Why is that shed door open, C.J.?"

"Why was it locked?" he says.

Katie pours a glass of C.J.'s fuchsia colored Gatorade, washing the penny taste from her tongue. "Take a wild guess."

He charges her. "What the fuck is wrong with you?"

"Excuse me?"

"Are you crazy?" he asks, his spit spraying her cheek.

She backs away. "What are you talking about?"

C.J. pushes her into the refrigerator. Katie holds up her arms in surrender. He raises his hand.

"What are you doing?" she shrieks.

Katie shuts her eyes and waits to be hit. In the darkness, she pictures split lips and chipped teeth, the startling taste of blood in her mouth. A pain strange and new. Raising her chin, she dares him to put her down.

"Jesse Miller called me," C.J. says, shaking his cell phone in her face. "She said her boyfriend and a bunch of his friends saw you doing the drunk walk."

"Jesus," she says, remembering the monster truck full of teens. She reaches for his shoulders. He swats her hands away. "Listen, I wasn't drunk. The cop was just testing me. I didn't even get arrested. You can tell them that."

"Bullshit." C.J. cocks his fist and punches the refrigerator; she jumps. Walter's Pellegrino bottles crash behind the door. C.J. fans his hand as blood rises from old scabs.

"Would you please calm down?" she says.

"I won't calm down," he says, pointing in her face. "I won't."

"Nothing happened."

"You're such a fucking liar."

"Why do you always have to hate me?" she yells. "Can't you take a day off?"

"They saw you," he says. "The whole school's gonna find out. First thing Monday everyone will know my mom's a lush."

Katie slaps at his face, but he blocks the shot before it reaches his cheek. She tries again with her right hand. C.J. catches it and clutches it tight.

"You're hurting me," she says.

As he squeezes tighter, his fingertips redden. The cat flees upstairs.

"Please, C.J.," she whispers. "Walter's going to hear us."

C.J. keeps his grip. As she tries to yank her hand away, his nails dig deeper into her skin. His eyes look more puzzled than angry, as if he can't believe he's doing this, either.

"Tell me what you want," she says.

He smothers her face with his palm. His skin smells like bread. With his other hand, C.J. mashes her fingers together, cinching the circulation.

"Please let go."

"Are you going to stop?" he asks.

She drops to her knees. "Stop what?"

"Stop pretending," he says, twisting her wrist, the pain turning white hot.

"C.J.!" Walter shouts.

His hand springs open, freeing his mother. As C.J. backs away, Katie's fingers slowly unravel. Walter clings to the banister, inching his way downstairs. "What the hell is the matter with you two?"

C.J. points at her. "She's drunk."

"I'm not drunk."

"Some hospice," Walter says, shuffling across the kitchen floor. Without his Velcro slippers he looks brittle, his feet dry as a desert, his toenails petrified. It occurs to her she's never seen him barefoot.

"I'm going upstairs," C.J. says.

Walter grabs his arm. "You sit down. You're not checking out now."

"I'm going," C.J. insists.

"Just sit a minute," Walter says, pointing toward the round marble table. C.J. rolls his eyes, but follows Walter's order. Katie remains on the floor.

The red stove light tells her it's four A.M. Regular people will be waking up soon. At the counter, Walter squirts honey into a soup spoon. He swallows it down, wiping his mouth with his bathrobe collar.

"I was just eating myself in a dream," he says, licking his lips. "Actually chewing on my own ribs. Quite the metaphor. Or is that symbolism?"

"I'm sorry we woke you," Katie says.

"Do you two know what scares me most about dying?"

C.J. holds his head in his hands, working his fingers through his hair. He won't show his eyes. Katie blows on her palm. Her skin still tingles.

"Either of you have any idea?"

"No," C.J. says.

"It's you two left alone again." He sits down next to C.J. at the table and exhales, his breath a faint whistle. "But maybe that's what you deserve. What do you think, C.J.?"

"I don't know."

"Doing calisthenics all day doesn't seem to help, does it?

"Help what?"

"Our house is turning into your own private hockey rink."

"What are you talking about?" C.J. asks.

"Tell us why you're furious," Walter says.

"I'm not."

"This can all get real bad fast, C.J."

"You need an outlet," Katie offers. "Without mountains, Craig would have been somewhere real bad fast."

"I don't like to ski," C.J. says matter-of-factly.

"I'm just saying he found a way to live in his own skin."

"I'm happy for him."

"You need to find a way out of your head," Katie says. "A better channel."

"I'll join a drum circle and free Tibet. Will that work for everyone?"

"Do you even want to feel good?" Walter asks.

"Why am I on trial?" he demands, pointing at his mother. "She's the one who drove home drunk."

Katie fights the urge to explain to him that she wasn't drunk, that she would have passed a breathalyzer, but she doesn't want to spoil a rare chance between them.

"It will never happen again," she says.

"Swear it."

"I swear. Now you tell me never again," Katie says, holding up her injured hand.

"Never again," he promises.

Katie stands up and walks over to the table. She hugs him cautiously. With his forehead against her belly, she holds his face, his cheeks warm beneath her fingers. Walter pats his shoulder. C.J. remains seated, docile. Bound together her son doesn't feel so strong. When she lets him go, he reaches down and picks up the cat, setting him in his lap. Katie can hear him purring.

"I want the motorcycle," C.J. blurts out.

"How are we talking about this now?" Katie asks. "Jesus, let's all just go to bed."

"It was sent here for me too," he presses. "I'm almost sixteen. Walter can show me how to ride. How to be safe."

"This can be his catharsis," Walter adds.

"Oh, bullshit," Katie says. "I'll show you a website full of motorcycle crash pictures. It won't be so cathartic when you have no skin."

"Those guys are all on crotch rockets, not Harleys," C.J. says.

"Do you think it's fair that I'll be waiting up every night worrying?"

"You mean like I did tonight?" he says.

Katie sighs, defeated. "I really don't want to talk about this now."

"Figures." C.J. stands up and gets a Hot Pocket from the freezer. He places it inside the grungy microwave.

"Look, I'm exhausted," she says. "I've been on my feet all night."

"We should all go to bed," Walter says.

"If you had a job in an office your feet wouldn't hurt," C.J. says, pulling silverware from the drawer.

"Believe it or not, I make more money than a lot of people in offices."

"Hardly any of my friends' mothers even work. And none of them work in bars."

"Your mother's a painter," Katie explains. "Things are a little different for us."

"Why don't you just paint then?"

"Because the refrigerator would be empty and you eat like a barbarian."

"What if I got a job after school?"

"You can work at the Cheesecake Factory," Walter suggests. "Then we'd get a family discount."

"That's sweet, but if you want to work that's your money. I didn't pay my own way as a kid and you won't either." Katie stretches her arms to the ceiling, relishing the expansion of her backbone. "Listen, Megan's isn't some nightclub. It's very safe."

C.J. opens and closes the microwave door. He adds thirty more seconds to the cooking time. "Will you need to bartend even more if I get into boarding school?"

"They'll give you financial aid."

"What if they don't?"

"They will," Katie says.

"Didn't your dad pay off the mortgage or whatever?"

"Yes, but not the property taxes. Those alone kill us."

"What if you went back to work at the theatre in Waverly?"

"What if you went back to seventh grade?" Katie wipes down the marble table with a wet paper towel. Using her fingernail, she scrapes away a crusty ketchup stain. "We can't go backwards."

"It was better when you had a regular job."

"No, it wasn't," Katie says.

"You weren't coming home at two A.M. You weren't getting pulled over."

"I was very unhappy, C.J.," she says, changing the trash bag. An inch of dark liquid coats the bottom of the bin. Tomorrow she'll make the kitchen sparkle. "Look," she continues, "it's hard for you to understand now, but when you get older and find you're not doing what you feel you're meant to do, it runs you down. Makes you mean."

"A-men," Walter says. "It wasn't until I became impotent that I decided to write seriously. Before that I was merely dicking around, no pun intended."

"The night you fell through the mooring stone," she tells C.J.

"What about it?"

"That's when I stopped dicking around."

"That was like four years ago," he says, opening a jar of tomato sauce. "What's that have to do with painting?"

She remembers frying him a cube steak with Rice-A-Roni, taking their dinner into the living room so they could watch *Survivor: The Amazon*. Because she was out of wine, Katie had to mix a Tanqueray and tonic. Cabernet managed to settle her into a lovely trance, but the gin fueled the uneasiness she normally drank to restrain. A few weeks away from her thirty-fifth birthday and with Caroline's first visit looming, Katie had felt an increasing obligation to make their home lives more wondrous. Suddenly shaken by their sluggish routine, Katie shut off the television and ordered C.J. to put on his hat and gloves, his turtleneck and the one-size-too-large waterproof Timberland boots Craig had sent for his birthday. Back then he actually liked doing what she told him.

"We're going out," she decided.

"But the show's not over."

"Are we prisoners of *Survivor*?"

"I don't know," he said, tying his laces.

When she opened the front door, C.J. darted outside like an excited dog. As they walked, he aimed the flashlight through the sky, pointing out stars she couldn't see. She eventually let go of C.J.'s hand so he could chase toads down the footpath. Standing in the middle of the street, Katie noticed that every house was aglow, television light beaming through each living room.

She climbed over the Seton's small granite wall and tiptoed through their tomato garden. She could hear C.J.'s gravelly footsteps from the path, his delighted voice reaching her in the wind. Katie leaned against the Seton's house, her face inches from the windowpane, and watched as the family stared helplessly at the TV, their faces flush with boredom, their bodies cumbersome and tired. As Katie jumped up and waved, no one noticed her. She was about to knock on the glass when she heard C.J. scream. Two yards over, she found her son frantically trying to free himself from the hole in the Llewellyns' mooring stone.

Every other house on Cape Mary displayed a mooring stone on the property, but the Llewellyns had the only one aglow with Christmas lights. Katie grabbed his gloved hands and yanked him loose, their bodies falling hard onto the damp grass. C.J. was on top of her laughing, his pants torn from knee to ankle. He tried to pin her down by tickling her into submission and Katie let him until she burst out laughing, pushing him from her chest. When the Llewellyns' front door opened, they both took off, racing each other home, slip-sliding along the frozen sidewalk. After she tucked him in that night, Katie dug out her art supplies from the Tuff Shed and painted through sunrise. Her technique was sloppy, her ideas clumsy, but for six hours she felt something close to honesty.

C.J. mixes a blender full of peanut butter, bananas, and creatine powder. It's barely morning and he's already ingested a day's worth of calories.

"I want you to see someone," Katie shouts over the noise.

He shakes his head no.

"If you do, the Road King is yours."

He turns off the appliance. "Deal," he says, holding his thumb up. "But I'm not taking any drugs."

He drinks from the blender, his lips smeared with sludge.

"Okay," she says. "Good."

The microwave dings. C.J. bobbles the hot Hot Pocket. Katie curiously eyes the stack of mail at the base of the stairs. She hadn't noticed it before.

"Did anything bad happen today in the mail?" she asks. "Anything from schools?" She poses this question wishfully, hoping for a tangible reason to explain her son's outburst, one far removed and disconnected from her own failures.

"I only have one more shot," he says, pouring Ragu over his Hot Pocket. "All rejections so far except for Farmingdale. I made their waiting list."

"That's pretty good, right?"

"Screw it," he says, stuffing his face, eating faster than he can swallow.

Watching him devour his meal, Katie's stomach growls, but she doesn't have the heart for food. "I guess I'll go to bed," she finally says.

"I'm going to Shawn Lynch's house tonight," he informed her. "I might stay over."

"Leave his number and his parents' numbers on the butcher block for me."

Katie stands up, her calves achy from her shift so many hours ago. She refills her Gatorade glass and swallows two Aleve. As C.J. carries his plate to the table, Katie sneaks a beer from the fridge, shoving it deep into her pants.

"When Walter's done in the bathroom, tell him there's plum flower and reishi mushrooms in the pantry."

"What the hell's that?"

"The stuff from Whole Foods he likes." Katie opens and closes the pantry door. "Well, good night, C.J."

"Good morning, Mom."

In the studio, she lights a cigarette, then strips off her grubby clothes, wrapping herself tight in a faux cashmere blanket. Reclining on the love seat, she downs the beer, and rolls the cold empty bottle across her forehead.

She wakes up at nine thirsty for water, at eleven anxious to pee. At some point in the afternoon Lewis claws at the door. Outside her room, Katie finds the cat and a fake red rose from Cumberland Farms, C.J.'s usual Mother's Day offering. She brings the cat and the felty flower with her underneath the blanket. From the driveway she can hear Walter's hacking cough, C.J.'s clapping hands, the Road King rumbling to life. Katie presses on the tender spots of her palm, the bruising memory of her son's fingertips. Alone in the dark, she misses that savage embrace.

CHAPTER 13

Katie pulls her hand from the lobster pot full of ice, careful not to drip water on her father's brown leather chair. Her fingertips are corpse-white and pruned, the fat of her palm still sore when she squeezes. Above her head, she hears C.J. jumping rope. Even with the rubber mats she insisted he lay over his floor, he still makes a racket. When she offered to buy him a fitness membership for Christmas, he said he wasn't going to "lift with a bunch of Guidos." She told him it was mostly old people at her gym, but he stood by the privacy of his room.

As his weight plates clank, she falls back into her father's chair and rereads Walter's short story from the *Cape Mary Literary Review* about a family of six who take in a homeless person. When they discover he'd been the mother's sixth grade math teacher, she doesn't tell her husband and children how he was fired in the middle of the school year for repeatedly using the women's restroom. One afternoon while shopping for spring linens, the mother sneaks her old teacher into the ladies room at Target, telling him he should pee where he's comfortable. While sitting in neighboring stalls (he in the spacious handicapped unit), the mother confesses that she doesn't love her husband anymore, that she wants to vomit when he's on top of her. He reveals that his second wife left him when she caught him wearing her underwear. Several pages later, the story ends with them getting married in a Las Vegas bathroom. Walter's stories are about fresh starts, middle-aged men and women who decide to take one final risk. When she told him he should write a book, he said he wasn't a novelist, that it would be like her trying to paint with chopsticks.

As the volume rises from C.J.'s stereo, Katie taps the ceiling with her hockey stick. When he finally turns it down, she finds she doesn't actually want the sudden silence. She snaps her fingers, waiting on his next exercise, but all she can hear is her own jittery breath. The muse has left the building, her studio now a dismal reminder of past triumphs. All her paint tubes and brushes are hidden away in the bottom desk drawer, her easels and canvas shut behind the closet door. The unfinished Isabel lies under the love seat wrapped in cellophane, while her smock remains buried inside the clothes hamper. The one benefit of her artistic slump is that her fingernails have never been cleaner. She didn't even want to come in here this morning, but she missed her father's chair, the one place she can read without falling asleep. And when she woke up this morning, Katie swore she wouldn't cave in to another afternoon watching television in bed.

On this same soft cushion where she now sits, James Olmstead drank Dewar's while poring over his company's scrap metal contracts. Even though their mother told her daughters not to bother him when he was in his office, her father left the study door open a crack, which enabled Katie to spy on him from behind the den curtain. She envied her father's privacy, wishing she could have the same sort of hideaway. She liked to believe that he knew she was there, that in fact he counted on his daughter's company. When Katie tried to explain this to her mother, Martha Olmstead told her six-year-old daughter to "keep your nose out of other people's asses." Katie has no pictures from their old house in Haverhill, no real mementos passed down to her besides this chair and her mother's sewing table.

Because their mother couldn't stand clutter, she threw away all her children's keepsakes. Unlike her friends' houses, the Olmstead refrigerator door was blank. Even Caroline's perfect test scores couldn't be displayed under a magnet. "We'd have to search the landfills for something we made in elementary school," Caroline would say. At their neighbor's house in Haverhill, that family's basement was overcrowded with the children's schoolwork, their kids' entire lives saved and catalogued by the mother. Katie was shocked to see the children's nursery school doodles framed in the bathroom, family photos decorating the mantel, board games left in progress on the coffee table, a refrigerator stocked with Capri Sun, a pantry full of Fruit Roll-Ups.

Meanwhile, Katie's mother didn't put out one cigarette in the ceramic ashtray she made for her in the third grade, telling her daughter she simply preferred the disposable aluminum kind from McDonald's. In the seventh grade Katie waited for weeks, but her mother never hung up the watercolor she painted of Bass Rocks, saying it was "a bit too florid for the living room." Martha didn't even protest when Katie took back the flowery Mother's Day gift and donated it to a children's gallery in Stony Neck. If it weren't for the bedroom Caroline and Katie shared, a visitor would never guess a kid lived inside the Olmstead home. "She was Joan Crawford crazy," Caroline said years later. "But at least we weren't ever starved or raped."

By Katie's fifteenth birthday, the earth shifted as her father closed his first major business deal with a metal refinery in Turkey. Overnight, he upgraded their 1,000-square-foot home in Haverhill with an oceanfront property in Newquay. He paid for Martha's three-month "spiritual accumulation" to India, and financed Caroline's Ivy League transfer to Princeton. He sent Katie to a private high school where the girls dressed in plaid skirts and the boys wore ties. For the first time in her life, she owned new clothes from stores like the Gap and J. Crew, Caroline's crummy hand-me-downs finally boxed off to the Salvation Army. When her acne began to clear, Katie believed it was Newquay's ocean air that fixed her face. She grew three inches her sophomore year. Her legs went from stumpy to slender, her breasts from A to B. All of a sudden she was pretty.

But with Caroline away at college and their father constantly traveling, the split between mother and daughter only widened in Newquay. In the old bungalow house in Haverhill they bumped into each other like pool balls, but in Newquay everyone was liberated by three floors. While Katie cherished the fresh start, Martha's depression only darkened. When the weather was pleasant, her mother spent her time reading on the widow's walk, but when it was foul she refused to get out of bed. In the new house, Katie chose to be downstairs as much as possible, alternating between her bedroom and her father's study. She did her homework in the study, using his fancy office phone to call boys. Many nights she fell asleep at his desk. One night as she microwaved her dinner, it struck Katie how she was no longer so frustrated with her AWOL mother, her contempt fading as she learned to give up. When she could forget they shared the same blood, when she could ignore the personal affront, she was somewhat free to forgive. Living separate lives under one roof actually pushed them closer because, like Martha, Katie was growing up to be a woman who just wanted to be left alone.

A brain tumor killed her mother at fifty when Katie was a freshman at Hobart. Her father told them it was all a result of their mother's chronic exhaustion. "How can someone who slept all day be exhausted?" Caroline asked. When they went through her closet, Katie found a fire safe full of narrative poetry written in her mother's shaky handwriting. Many of the stories revolved around an old widow who lived on a farm sanctuary in New Hampshire. The writing was bad and the stanzas didn't seem to connect. Right away she felt sorry for her mother, but as she read on about two handicapped cows discussing Schopenhauer's philosophy, suddenly she was mad at her, angry that she wrote hundreds of pages without telling anyone. And even though it was drivel, she wished Martha could have shared this one secret. She couldn't understand how her mother could go out of her way to hide her silly poetry, but when it came time to showcase her dementia she revealed no shame.

"I always believed we'd have a relationship after I grew up," she told Caroline one Thanksgiving. "I'd come visit with my husband and kids, and Martha and I would drink tea or something on the widow's walk."

"That's Disney nonsense," Caroline said.

"It just bums me out that she'll never know who we are."

"Fuck it, we have no idea who she was either."

"At least she saw you graduate from Princeton," Katie said. "That's something."

"Well, I don't know how much she saw that day after polishing off four Bloody Marys at the dean's breakfast reception."

"You don't give a shit, do you?"

"Not really, no."

"You don't want to remember a nice time?"

"For what?"

"Well, I'm going to remember Mom driving me to soccer games. She hated to drive and we routinely got lost; it was a disaster, but she did it anyway. That's what I'll keep."

"And I'll keep the many times Mom left us in the back of the station wagon while she drank at Blowhards when Dad was at work. She was kind enough to leave the windows open a crack in the summer, I'll give her that."

"I still don't remember that," Katie said.

"Because you were eternally off in la la land."

After her mother's funeral, Katie saw even less of her father; and it wasn't until James Olmstead's health began to decline that he decided to play catch-up in his final few years. Her father never really accepted C.J., never approved of her unorthodox "situation," but nonetheless Katie chose to believe he found a semblance of peace knowing he had a grandson to carry on his name. The last time she saw him alive was during a typically awkward and unsettling visit to Newquay, just months before she became the unlikely owner of oceanfront property.

"You have to color inside the lines," her father told C.J., taking her son's hand and placing the crayon on the coloring book. "Inside the lines now," James repeated. C.J. wiggled away and drew a pair of purple horns on Oscar the Grouch's head. He filled them in with orange. "Oh, well," her father said, flipping to the next page. "Let's try it again. What color is this Big Bird character supposed to be?"

"Yellow, Dad," Katie said.

"Use yellow then, Calvin," he said impatiently. "Why is his chin so red?"

"Eczema," Katie reminded him. "He's been itchy since birth."

"You should see a dermatologist."

"It'll go away," she explained.

"Do you have proper medical insurance?"

"Dad, he'll look fine in a week. Children's skin is resilient."

He took a sip from his drink and gasped. "Well, you girls never had rashes."

To keep herself still, Katie sat on her hands. The house reeked of Joy perfume, their family's smell long gone. In Katie's old room on the first floor was a Stairmaster and two yoga pads, a shrine of stinky candles and a gigantic wooden Buddha. "As you can see, my lady friend is very California," her father explained. On the third floor, inside her mother's dresser, were the clothes of a younger, tackier woman. Most of the familiar furniture in the house had been replaced with more modern, uncomfortable pieces. Katie couldn't find a family picture, not one single photograph of James's wife and daughters on the premises. She felt as if she were at an open house, the layout an obvious stage for strangers.

"Yellow, not red, Calvin," her father repeated.

"Just let him do it his way, Dad."

Annoyed by her father's intolerance, Katie got up and washed her hands. James Olmstead wasn't well, he'd be dead in a year, and the uneasiness he showed toward his grandchild was too depressing for her to watch. He positively glowed when talking about nonferrous metals or the current price of stainless steel, but when it came to showing affection, both her parents had been abject failures.

"Oh, well, he'll learn as he gets older," her father said, licking the whisky from his lips. "We all do somehow."

"He won't learn *somehow*," Katie said. "I'm actually raising him, Dad."

"He's going to need a man," her father continued. "You can't raise him in a broken home."

"Why do men think they're so damn essential?" Katie asked, topping off her tumbler. "What difference do you really make?"

C.J. banged on the piano keys, her father cringing with every harsh note. "Please make him stop," he said. "That piano is beyond expensive."

"Calvin!" Katie shouted, pointing in his direction. "No more piano, sweetie."

"Noooooooooo mooooooooore!" he shouted back.

Her son slammed the keyboard hood shut to the shrill cry of piano strings. Pushing off the high bench, he ran toward the center of living room and plopped down on the floor into the midst of his coloring books. Her father eyed his grandson warily. He wasn't used to the energy of a boy.

"You weren't really around," Katie said. "Don't you think we turned out all right?"

"It's presence, Kaitlin," he said. "You're shortchanging this boy without a father figure. How old is he now, four?"

"Five," she corrected, "and times have changed, Dad. The family model has adapted."

"Where's the ski bum? Why can't he be involved?"

"I hate that term," she said, Scotch streaming through her veins. "You sound like Caroline. You never even met him."

"He has a responsibility to that child."

"Calvin's my responsibility," she said. "Craig and I both decided that. We were good enough to be honest with each other."

"But you're married."

"Technically, sure."

"So where's your wedding ring?"

"You're worried about a ring?" Katie asked, holding up her finger. "No rings, no bouquet. No vows. Sorry I couldn't give you the country club routine, but this is your daughter."

"Are you going to divorce?"

"I guess, if we see each other again. But it's really not relevant."

He grabbed her arm and escorted her forcefully toward the bay window, away from her son. Shaken by his touch, Katie allowed him to lead, unaccustomed to such direct attention from her father.

"Godammit, why did you have it?" he whispered.

"Because *it* is mine. Calvin is mine."

"What are you trying to prove?"

She pulled her arm away from his grasp. She craved a cigarette and wanted to go outside and smoke on the widow's walk, but Katie still felt like a child in her father's presence. She couldn't enjoy a butt in his house. "He's part of me, Dad. This is what you don't get, what most men can't seem to understand."

"How can he not want to see his own son?"

"Where was all this concern five years ago?" she asked. "Why are you so interested in us all of a sudden?"

"Because I don't like what I'm leaving behind."

"That's your problem," Katie said.

C.J. tore a yellowed page from the coloring book. Folding it into a paper airplane, he threw it toward their feet. At the bar, Katie added a splash of water to her drink.

"Your mother and I stayed together. That was our sacrifice to you and Caroline."

"Are you kidding me?" Katie shouted. "You weren't together. There was no marriage in that house."

"Martha and I thought we wanted a family," her father said solemnly. "We truly did." He bent down and picked up the paper airplane, grimacing as his knees buckled forward. He threw it back toward C.J. who clapped as it flew. "But after you two were born," he continued, "we found out we had no clue about what we desired."

"Why didn't you ever help her?" she whispered.

"I had to work," he growled, tapping his glass.

"You knew she was shot, but you left me with her anyway."

"Christ, I didn't know she was passed out all day. She lied to me all the time. She stopped taking her medication. I didn't know that until it was too late. My uncle Walter, a doctor mind you, told me there was nothing I could do about her, about her so-called affliction."

"It's called depression, Dad."

"I had to step to the side. Christ, I didn't want to make her worse. Then what?"

"You didn't have to step to the side when it came to your kids. We had to grow up by ourselves. And I'll tell you right now, I'll never leave Calvin like that."

"Call me in ten or fifteen years and then lay your blame," her father said. "We'll see how idealistic you are then. Believe me, you have no idea what you're talking about yet."

"I don't want to lay blame," Katie said, "I don't, but you have to trust me for now, no matter how you see my life."

He finished his drink. "Fair enough."

Katie took her father's tumbler to the bar. She poured him two more fingers' worth of Scotch. With a damp cocktail napkin cupped around the bottom, she handed him the glass. "What was she like before we were born?" she asked.

He took the drink. "Like nothing you or Caroline ever saw," he said.

"This place is so boooooooring," C.J. moaned. "Boring, boring, boring, boring."

"I'm sorry for you, Kaitlin," her father continued. "Both you and Caroline have no one."

"Neither do you," she said.

C.J. lumbered into the den with a stack of music books in his arms. Katie placed her drink on the bar and picked up her son. "Tell Grandpa we'll be fine, Calvin. Tell him we're a-okay."

C.J. kicked from his mother's grip, his little hands pushing on her shoulders. James Olmstead reached out and touched his grandson's warm cheek. "Shhh," he said, brushing his papery thumb over his grandchild's skin. C.J. stuck out his tongue and began to cry. Katie felt terribly sorry for her father, a man too old to learn anything new.

The studio door bangs open. Katie bolts upright from her father's chair. "Where's my blue Under Armour shirt?" C.J. says.

"Don't you knock anymore?"

"I really need it."

"Well I didn't touch it. Go look somewhere else." Katie stands up and draws her hair back into a ponytail. "What time is it anyway?"

"Maybe it's in my hockey bag," he says, ignoring her question. He pulls an old picture nail from the wall. "Where's all your art stuff?" C.J. asks.

"I lost it."

"What's up your butt today?"

"The usual."

"You need to see someone," he says mockingly.

Katie dunks her hand back in the ice. In the darkness of the studio, C.J. looks withered, older. Rarely has she imagined him past eighteen, past this teenage trench.

"Do you think you're going to have children one day, C.J.?" she asks.

"What?"

"Do you think you'll have kids one day?"

"What do you mean?"

"Do you want a family is what I mean."

He laughs. "I told you," he says, "Roxy's just some girl."

"I'm simply asking if you want children."

Chewing on his fingernail, he eyes her suspiciously. "I guess it depends on what happens."

CHAPTER 14

The smell of burning garbage tells her it's Wednesday. Katie pushes open the curtains and finds it's earlier than she imagined, the sun just peaking over the eastern horizon. She watches old Mr. Kashgarian poking an ashen trash heap with his cane. He covers his mouth with his tie as embers pop over his white orthopedic shoes. While Walter has gone over there a few times to play cribbage, Katie has yet to step inside her neighbor's home. She doesn't attend the semi-monthly community meetings at the town pier. You won't find her amongst the crowd handing out water to the runners who pass down their street during the Newquay Marathon. The closest Katie has come to the summer cookouts is inhaling the hot dog scent that breezes through her windows. The truth is she'd love nothing more than to show up at one of their parties as Caroline, to flaunt her prowess all over their lawns. Despite an entire decade passing since Katie moved into her father's home, she still can't help feeling like James Olmstead's flaky, teenage daughter.

Twenty-five years have passed since she's listened to The Smiths under black lights in this room, the same place where she snuck beers, gagged on her mother's Kool Filter Kings, and practiced making out with grapefruits in front of the mirror. Here she stewed over the banality of her body, her boring butt and bland thighs, her head to toe lack of flair. Here she sweated over algebra problems and chemistry formulas, convinced the right side of her brain was damaged. She fretted over the boys who didn't call, the boys who did. Every problem was massive and dramatic, all emotions spiked. If she could just tap into that long gone heat of adolescence—feel what she once genuinely felt—Katie could provide her son with some useful advice. But that teenage girl's vanished, ditched this place years ago.

Rummaging through the hamper, Katie manages to extract a gym outfit. The only sports bra she can find reeks of cigarette smoke. While the black spandex makes her ass look somewhat tight, the elastic manages to inflate the jelly through her middle. The actress, Catherine Deneuve, warned that "after forty, it's your ass or your face," implying a woman must choose between the two, that improving one means losing the other, a point well illustrated by aging, red carpet celebrities. Frowning at herself in the mirror, Katie pinches the flab she'd like to work off before summer, digging into the trouble spots with her fingernails. Last year during a free training session, Katie blushed when a kid not much older than C.J. said how "smoking your bod" could be with the right regimen. That same afternoon she bought a cute fitness bag and spent a hundred dollars on Hydroxycut Hardcore and Lipo-6, but when she got home C.J. told her "that crap is for fat people who don't exercise."

Since she's joined the gym, Katie spends most of her workout in the steam room, soaking up the eucalyptus mist that shoots intermittently from the wall vents. Many women her age are saddled with toddlers and way too busy for sports clubs, their bodies plummeting fast. Peter said she looked "better than most women pushing forty," but Katie only heard the insult implied in such a declaration. If only she had more patience for the Stairmaster, more incentive to climb nowhere in front of a close-captioned TV screen. If only she'd substituted protein powder for potato chips, white rum and Diet Coke for Grand Marnier. With a little more sweat and effort, she might not be so haunted by her slutty exhibition in front of Peter last month.

Parading her nudity in his face, Katie traipsed about like a stripper, like Demi Moore in *Striptease*. Peter kept his eyes closed throughout the ordeal, which at first she attributed to pleasure; but as they progressed Katie became apprehensive, wondering who he imagined, what woman he really craved as he came inside her. For her part, Katie exaggerated her enjoyment, but she couldn't get past the sudden weight of her mistake. As Peter plodded along, she grew sorrier, sickened by the woman who'd invited this pounding. If she hadn't been so weak, Peter would have still been outside in the cold. After he left (within minutes of the final thrust), Katie sat in the tub and sulked, noting how yet again sex had disappointed her, bummed her out like a heavy meal.

Turning away from the mirror, she quickly covers her spandexed legs with running pants and throws on C.J.'s old Bruins sweatshirt. In the kitchen, she pours herself a cup of coffee, but no sugar. She starts Walter's tea and sets aside two eggs for his breakfast. Instead of a glass of Tropicana and a blueberry Eggo, Katie chooses tap water and a stale rice cake. At Megan's, she'll cut back on the high calorie shift cocktails. No more clam chowder and rolls. She can help the bussers run food to the dining room. Hector from Guatemala says he tracks three miles on a busy night.

"You training for a marathon?" C.J. asks from the stairwell.

"Hardly," she says, pushing against the butcher block to stretch her calves.

"You should try Pilates. It's really good for your core."

"If by core you mean hips and thighs, then I'm in." Katie kicks off her sneakers and socks. "I already have blisters," she says, inspecting her heels.

C.J. opens the refrigerator and pulls out a deli pack of turkey pastrami. "Are you up because of the sirens?" he asks.

"What sirens?"

"You didn't hear the cop cars going by this morning?"

"I guess I did. I was already up, though." Katie looks outside at the four large wild turkeys huddled by Mr. Kashgarian's gazebo. "Do you want me to make you breakfast?"

"I'll just have a sandwich." He sits down and reads through the classifieds.

"What are you looking for?" Katie asks.

"A job," he says.

As Katie drops the used coffee filter into the trash, she spots an art catalog from Dick Blick she doesn't recall throwing away. She picks it out, brushing the grains from its cover. "I see a lot of kids your age working at Star Market."

"I'm not bagging groceries."

Katie's phone rings. "Who calls now?" she asks, pressing the *ignore* button.

"Probably Mothers Against Drunk Driving," he says.

"Don't start." Katie pages through the desk calendar by the blender. She has to see the dentist on Friday. "Hey," she says, thumbing the date, "Monday's your appointment with Dr. Brown." She grabs a green apple from the fruit basket. As she bites down, Katie can't remember the last time she ate a piece of fruit. "Did you hear me?" she asks, her mouth full of sour skin.

"Yup."

"Do you know where his office is?"

"On the same floor as the principal's."

"This is a good thing, C.J.," she says.

"Sure." He circles an ad with a Sharpie. She can see it's under MISCELLANEOUS. "I think I'll have an Eggo actually."

She pulls the yellow box from the freezer. "Would your creatine help me lose weight?"

"Just the opposite."

C.J.'s phone rings. "That's mine," he says, digging into his pajama pocket. He eyes the screen. "Restricted number. Screw that."

Lewis jumps up on the table and sits on the newspaper. C.J. reads around the cat's tail.

"So what do you need the extra money for?" she asks.

"You don't want me to work?"

"I just don't want you doing it to help me out."

"Don't worry about it."

Katie spits the rest of her apple into the sink. "What about a fishing boat? You might like that kind of labor."

"Maybe I won't be near the ocean this summer."

"What do you mean?"

"There're jobs all over the country."

"Like where?"

"Like all over," he says.

"You're too young for a walkabout." Her phone rings again. "Dammit already," she says, squinting at the display screen.

"Just answer it," C.J. says.

She presses *send*: "Who is this?"

C.J. scratches his earlobe with his shirtsleeve. When he pulls his arm away, Katie notices a tiny black stud in his left ear she's never seen before. "Where did that come from?" she whispers, cupping the phone receiver. He shrugs his shoulders, playing dumb. "It's cheesy," she says.

"Cheesy? What about that Journey tie-dye you wear in public?"

Katie waves him off. "What are you talking about?" she says into the phone.

"Who is it?" C.J. asks.

"I can't hear you," she shouts into the receiver. "You're all static."

"Pull up the antenna and move toward the window," C.J. tells her.

"You're mistaken," Katie says, shaking her head back and forth. "Well, check again," she orders.

Securing the phone between her shoulder and ear, she scrubs away coffee rings from the counter as she listens. "You're crazy," she says, pressing the cold wet sponge to her forehead. "No, I'm hanging up now." Katie yanks the phone away from her ear as if it bit her. "I'm hanging up, I said."

She throws the phone into the sink and turns on the water, tilting the lever toward hot.

C.J. stands up and holds out his hands as if she's about to fall. "What's wrong?"

"I need to think."

"Tell me," he says, grabbing her shoulders.

"Let go of me."

"Just calm down."

Katie pushes the phone into the sink's waste disposal and flips the switch.

"Stop it," he says, over the sound of the clamoring motor. He turns off the switch. Reaching into the drain, he pulls out the chewed up phone.

"Chill out," he says.

"Go upstairs and wake up Walter."

"Who was on the phone?"

"Do it, C.J.!"

C.J. puts her mangled phone in his pocket. He eyes her suspiciously, then darts upstairs. She turns on the faucet and drinks until her mouth's full.

"He's not answering," C.J. shouts from above.

"Go inside and wake him up," she yells.

He opens Walter's door. "He's not in here," C.J. calls. He leans over the banister, his face a mile above hers. Katie hears the cuckoo clock start to squawk. "Will you just tell me what's going on?"

"I'll be back," Katie says.

Outside, pebbles wedge into the heels of her bare feet as she runs down the walkway. The wild turkeys are now in her driveway. She jerks open the shed door as the birds lumber away.

"Son of a bitch," Katie says, rubbing her toes over the oil stains the motorcycle had once shadowed.

C.J. catches up to her and grabs her sweatshirt hood. "Where's the Road King?"

A police car pulls into the driveway. The reds and blues flash silently.

"What'd you do?" C.J. asks accusingly.

With the engine still running, the cop steps out of the car. His partner remains in the front seat.

"Ms. Olmstead?" he says.

"What do you want?" C.J. shouts at him, stepping in front of his mother.

The policeman removes his hat and presses it to his chest. "I'm sorry, folks."

C.J. turns toward his mother. "What's he sorry for?"

Katie rubs her son's back, then points at the squad car. "Please shut those damn lights off."

CHAPTER 15

Katie inhales one of Walter's government joints, her mind unraveling as the sticky smoke rushes into her bloodstream. She watches as sea gulls swarm an incoming fishing boat, their bratty squeals carrying all the way to the widow's walk. Beneath the salt and dust, Katie can still see the little black stains on the wooden railing from her mother's cigarette butts. Thrilled she was no longer putting the Dunhills out on her legs, her father didn't bother his wife with talk about ashtrays and house fires when she was hiding out on the widow's walk.

"What are you doing out here?" C.J. asks.

"Jesus, you scared me," Katie says, cupping the joint in her palm. "Why are you sneaking around?" She steps back into the rusty Weber grill.

"I'm not," he says. "I'm just looking for the Road King manual."

"Why would it be on the widow's walk?"

"I was checking Walter's room and heard you out here."

An orange and white Coast Guard helicopter roars above the point. The swatting sound of the propeller rings in her ears. "Heard me what?"

"Just heard you," he says.

"I'm just getting some fresh air."

He wrinkles his nose. "It stinks like a dead skunk out here."

"Well, maybe I like that smell."

"I'll leave you alone," he says, walking off.

She rubs the joint out on a broken white Frisbee. Reaching into her pocket, Katie shoves a handful of cinnamon tic tacs in her mouth. Her hands smell like a campfire.

Inside, C.J.'s bent over Walter's bed, his hand pawing underneath the frame.

"What's down there?" she asks.

"I told you I'm looking for the Road King manual."

"Can you give me some more time in here?" she asks. "I'm not done sorting."

C.J. jumps up. Dust bunnies cling to his T-shirt. "Why are your eyes so red?"

"Allergies," she says, rubbing her nose. "Maybe you can go downstairs and get me a Claritin."

"More like Visine," he mumbles.

"What was that?"

"I didn't say anything," he says.

She picks up the two foam pillows from Walter's bed and hugs them to her chest. "C.J., I need to clean up in here, alone."

"Fine, just let me know if you find the manual."

"What's with the manual?"

"The mechanic at the Harley dealership in Everett said the damage is mostly cosmetic, that with a manual and a semi-decent set of tools I can fix it myself." C.J. reaches for the yellow happy face stress ball on Walter's desk and squeezes. "Really all it needs is a new front tire and rim. Brakes too," he says. "I just need someone with a truck to pick it up and bring it back here."

"Hold on," she says, wishing to God she hadn't smoked that joint. "When did you go to a Harley store?"

"Jimmy drove me," he says, juggling the ball.

"Jimmy who?"

"Jimmy Tew," C.J. says.

"I don't know him."

"Mom, he's been in school with me since like fifth grade. His father used to own Christine's Variety, remember?"

Katie toes a bunched pair of Walter's argyle socks toward the trash bag full of donations. "I just want to know where you're going from now on," she says. "Period."

"I did tell you."

"Well, keep telling me."

"Anyway," he says, rolling his eyes, "as soon as I find someone with a truck, I'm gonna bring it back home."

"Why are you pushing this?"

"Because it's mine."

"Even after what's happened?"

"Don't get all hysterical," he says.

"We should go over what's going on here," Katie says, brushing the hair from her eyes. "I don't think we're grieving the right way. We haven't talked about Walter at all."

"Getting the bike back is my way."

"Yeah, your way to get what you want."

"Don't take it out on me because you don't know how to grieve or whatever."

Katie lets out three quick sneezes. Blowing her nose, she feels the instant crush of a sinus headache. "Tell me you really don't think it's the least bit dangerous," she says in a quieter voice.

"I'm not gonna crash."

"You have no idea what's going to happen."

"Walter was old and out of it. He was crazy to ride it," he says.

"This isn't about him."

"Sure sounds like it is."

She throws Walter's pillows back on the bed. "Fine," she says, "go crash."

"You'll die before me."

As he opens the door, the cat darts inside. "Where are you going?" she asks.

"I have homework."

"You can do it up here," she offers, scooping up the cat.

"You just said you wanted to clean, alone."

- 134 -

She presses her ear into Lewis's purring chest. "Why do you think I'll die before you?"

"Oh, man," he says. "Look, forget it. I'm not going to crash."

"Well, I do hope I die before you."

"Do you want me to leave the door open?" he asks, gripping the knob.

"Either way, I guess."

"I'll just leave it open," he says, "in case the cat wants to get out."

She listens to him walk downstairs, the sound of his door clicking closed. Sitting on the edge of Walter's bed, Katie wishes there was more to do, but she already stripped the sheets, scrubbed the bathtub, and bagged up most of his clothes for the Salvation Army. His unfinished stories she'd filed away with C.J.'s school papers, his typewriter left on his desk as an ornament for the next guest to admire. Walter's turntable and records are now in C.J.'s room. Aside from his will, a few wishes were scribbled out on a sheet of notebook paper Katie found in a silver-plated box containing his passport, birth certificate, and baby teeth. What was left of his money was donated to the Coconut Grove Playhouse charity in Florida, except for a twenty-thousand-dollar bond provided for C.J.'s education. When Katie called Pit-Bull Software Security to deliver the news, she was told by her sister's assistant, Renée, that "Ms. Olmstead" was on business in the Far East and wouldn't be back in California for a few weeks. So with only two relatives in attendance, Katie threw her great uncle's ashes off the widow's walk while C.J. read aloud from William Blake's *A Cradle Song*, a poem Walter typed out on the back of his will. After the three minute service, C.J. picked up a chunky piece of Walter's ashes and placed it inside an empty blue Skoal tin. Katie searched for her own remnant, but the rest of his ashes had already blown away.

WALTER HAD been riding thirty-five miles an hour when he crashed into the granite seawall on Back Beach. The front tire of the motorcycle absorbed the brunt of the impact, but Walter shot over the railing and dropped fifteen feet onto the exposed rock and seaweed of low tide. When they found him, crabs were crawling over his belly. "A helmet might have saved him," a policeman said. "He died from the head trauma." The cops told her the road was clean—no salt, ice, sand, or potholes. There was no fog, no traffic. "This shouldn't have happened," one of them said.

"What do you mean by that?" Katie asked.

"He didn't brake," the policewoman said. "No skid marks. No last second swerve. No evidence of panic. Not the scene of someone crashing into their death."

"He was an old man," she countered. "His reflexes were shot."

The policewoman filled a paper cup with water and passed it to Katie, then pulled out a manila envelope filled with papers. "According to medical reports, Dr. Olmstead's illness was terminal."

"He was dying," Katie said. "He made no secret of it."

"He was also clinically depressed," she said, fingering through a bright yellow document. "In 1992, he was diagnosed with bipolar disorder. He also prescribed himself a questionable amount of Vicodin this past year. Xanax too."

"Half of America is on those drugs, Captain," Katie said.

"Did you know he spent almost half of 1998 at McLean Hospital?"

She hadn't, but wasn't surprised that Walter had kept this from her. No one she knew blabbed about their dark days. When Katie was away at college, her mother was hospitalized twice following back-to-back nervous breakdowns. She didn't find out about it until three years ago when, after a glass of Scotch, Caroline revealed how their mother went "full-blown cuckoo's nest once us kids were out of the house." She said their father had told her about it just before he died, but he didn't want "Kaitlin" to know as she herself seemed "a bit inconsistent."

"Dr. Olmstead returned to McLean for a checkup in 2000," the captain continued.

"So what?" Katie said. "Just because you've spent time in a psych ward doesn't make you suicidal."

"One of my guys told me it looked like he was smiling when they found him."

Katie finished her water. Since the morning of Walter's death, she hadn't been able to get the cotton out of her mouth. Watching this woman read over his life papers, Katie wished she could articulate the difference between suicide and swan song, but she didn't think the captain had the kind of mind that could discern such a distinction.

"You didn't know him," Katie said, crumpling up her cup. "If Walter was being held up, he'd grin at the gunman."

"Either way, I'm very sorry, Ms. Olmstead."

Katie empties Walter's leftover pills into the toilet and flushes them—Vicodin and Xanax included. At the last second, she drops five of his ten government joints into the dwindling water of the bowl. Feeling both pride and regret, Katie contemplates all that relief swirling down the drain. Before leaving the room, she turns on the green banker's lamp by his desk and lets it burn.

"All done?" C.J. asks, eating from a can of tuna fish.

"Please use a plate," she says, handing him a roll of paper towels. "That fish oil stinks up the marble."

He opens the dishwasher and pulls out a dish. "Did you find the manual?"

"It's on the back of his toilet."

"Cool."

"I thought you had homework?" she asks.

"I can't concentrate if I'm hungry. Besides, I have all Sunday to get it done."

"I wish I only had to study," she says.

"You shouldn't have to work when someone's died."

"It's for the best," she says. "I'll just keep cleaning his room over and over if I stay here."

"Can you drop me at Todd's house on your way in?" he asks.

"Are you staying there tonight?"

"Yeah. His parents will give me a ride back here tomorrow."

She opens the dryer and sticks her head inside the heat. There's enough lint on the filter tray to weave a blanket. "Why don't any of your friends ever come here to sleep over?" she asks, searching for her black pants and apron.

"I don't know," he says.

She folds his shirts over the dryer top. A few of them she doesn't recognize. "Are you ashamed of me, C.J.?" she asks.

"Mommm," he moans.

"Well, what is it then? I'm curious why your friends never come here."

From his seat, C.J. throws his fork into the sink.

"It's just a question," she says.

"What difference does it make?"

"A lot, I think."

"We don't have a flat screen here."

"Then I'll buy a plasma TV first thing tomorrow."

"Yeah, right."

"If our crappy TV is the reason you won't invite your friends over, then I swear I'll get us the biggest one they carry at Best Buy."

"Forget it, Mom."

"What brand do you want me to get?" she continues.

"Cut it out."

"We'll get surround sound too. Heck, you can hook up your Xbox down here so we can all play Halo 3 together."

"Stop it!" he says, slamming his fist on the table.

"What's your problem?"

"I don't want people talking about you, alright?"

"Talking how?"

"Talking, talking," he says emphatically.

"Oh," she says, somewhat flattered.

"Yeah, *oh*."

She begins to blush, then smiles.

"It's not funny," he warns, pointing at her.

"I know, I know," she says. "I'm sorry."

C.J. picks up his tuna can and throws it in the trash. Katie doesn't remind him it's recyclable.

"What about Roxy?" she continues. "Can't I meet your girlfriend at least?"

"I told you she's not my girlfriend. Besides, she's with some senior now."

"Already?"

"She's not my girlfriend," he repeats.

"That's too bad."

"Not really." C.J. opens a can of Rockstar and guzzles. "I'm gonna sign up for a riding course," he announces.

"Great, more motorcycle talk," she says, dragging the lint roller over a sweater, her mind still stuck on his friends.

"I'm just telling you."

"You still haven't seen Dr. Brown," she says. "That's part of this whole deal."

"I'm gonna see him Monday."

"Well, I'm going to establish one other condition," she says.

"What now?"

"No earring. It really looks awful. I'd rather you get a tattoo that no one can see."

"Fine, whatever you want." He removes the stud from his ear. "I'll get a MOM heart tattoo on my shoulder first thing tomorrow."

"That's very sweet," she says.

Katie lays out her work clothes on the butcher block. Inside her apron pocket she finds a crumpled up five dollar bill and a business card from a customer who wanted to take her out for "a steak in Boston."

"No more about this until after Monday, okay?" she pleads. "I'm going to write down a list for you, topics to bring up to the doctor that you and I don't discuss."

"I can handle it myself," he says.

"That remains to be seen." Katie unzips her jeans. "Don't forget to empty Lewis's cat box tonight," she says, wiggling out of her pants. "Your room smells like poo."

"What are you doing?" he says.

"Putting on my work clothes while they're still warm."

"And you wonder why I don't have people over here," he says. "Change in your studio."

"I'm basically in the laundry room."

"Not basically enough," he says, retreating upstairs.

"You used to sit in the bathtub with me," she shouts after him.

"Yeah, when I was three."

"I'm sorry," she calls.

"Whatever," he says. "Just remember to keep your door closed when you get home from work tonight."

"Two Makers and soda, four Patron marg rocks, two no salt," Britney shouts, her waitress tray slick with liquid. "Then a virgin strawberry daiquiri and three Sam Lights. Oh, and no lime wedges anywhere." Britney grabs a clump of cocktail napkins and wipes the sweat from her forehead. Katie repeats the order back to her.

"God, I hate working without a computer system," Britney says.

Katie reaches for the soda gun and makes three Cokes. "When I was your age there were no restaurant computers. We yelled ourselves hoarse every shift. We actually had to remember the orders."

"Did you walk to school in the snow too?" she asks.

"Only when my horse was sick."

"Ha," Britney says. "I wish you worked all my shifts, Katie. Don't tell her I said this, but Paula's a total schizo bitch sometimes. And Jeremy's skeevy. He's hot and all, but a married guy in his forties shouldn't be looking at girls my age."

"Men can't help it," Katie tells her.

The new busser drops a fistful of forks on her way to the dining room. Some of the bar patrons clap. "Assholes," Katie whispers, sprinkling nutmeg over a Brandy Alexander.

"I already forgot table five's food order," Britney continues. "God, I totally have ADHD. Like I test well, but I just can't focus."

"Do you have to take Ritalin?" Katie asks.

"Oh, no," she says, chewing on a cocktail straw. "That's kiddy crack."

Katie returns the Maker's Mark to the shelf, the thick bottle a nuisance for her small hands. She shakes the cramp from her bad palm. "You're all set," she says. "Back you go into the wild."

Katie fills a glass with seltzer and chugs it down. Watching Paula juggle the bar crowd, she's grateful her only responsibility tonight is to the waitstaff. Because Paula likes to be on stage, Katie can just sling drinks and keep her head down. Across the room at the podium, Megan, Harper, and Kayla are overrun with customers. Kayla wears a short black skirt, her gymnast's legs making the hour table wait bearable for the men in line. A group of boat mechanics at the far end of the bar cheer following another Red Sox strikeout, Megan's investment in a plasma TV drawing a more local crowd. Outside, men and women smoke cigarettes and drink complimentary Beaujolais from Styrofoam cups, their teeth blood red by the time they're seated for dinner.

"I'm in the fucking weeds," Paula says, frantically digging a tumbler into the ice bin. Katie cringes, wishing Paula would use the ice scoop instead of risking shattered glass in customer cocktails.

"These pigs on the end are driving me bananas," Paula continues. "They keep asking for more bread. Look at them," she says, elbowing Katie in the ribs. "The fat fucks don't need any more carbs."

"It'll be over soon," Katie says, reaching for a bottle of Patron. She chugs a beer glass full of water. "I'm too old for this shit."

Katie wipes off strawberry sludge from a daiquiri glass and sends Jodie away, the young girl clumsily holding the drink tray above her head.

Britney rushes the bar. "You forgot a Sam Adams," she says, dropping the empty tray on the service counter. "My table is so rude. This job makes me hate people."

Katie hands her the cold beer bottle. "Sorry about that."

"Fuck them," she says, storming off.

Working with so many kids, it's easy for Katie to forget she has almost two decades on some of these girls. At twenty she was just like them. Watching Britney set the beer down in front of the men at her table, Katie suddenly feels sorry for them all, worried they'll get stuck here too. She often wonders if they talk about her when they all go out and party, vowing they'll never end up like her and Paula. When the girls ask about her life outside the bar, Katie won't even tell them she paints, sparing them the sad image of the old starving artist.

A crash sounds from the kitchen; Megan rushes toward the bar. Loud, frantic Spanish voices spill through the kitchen doors.

"Do you guys need help?" Megan asks.

"I'm good," Katie says, refilling her bin with lemon twists, the citrus stinging the nicks on her fingers.

"I'm swamped," Paula says.

"Take a bathroom break, Paula. I'll fill in."

"Thank you so much, Meg," she says, grabbing a straw from the rack and pushing her way into the kitchen. "You can go next," she tells Katie.

Megan ties Paula's soiled apron around her waist and gets to work, displaying a comfort behind the bar way out of Katie's reach. Bonnie comes to the service counter and asks for a Sprite; Katie hands her the drink. She slurps it down to the ice. Katie grabs the gun and refills her glass.

"Thank you," she says.

"How's your first week going?" Katie asks.

"Good. I'm starting to get the hang of it, I think."

"Bussing is hard work," Katie says.

"Yeah."

"Are you from Essex?"

"No," Bonnie says. "Newquay."

"Me too."

"Yeah, your son goes to my school."

"Really," Katie says, hoping she hasn't heard about her drunk walk.

"I don't know him or anything. He's in my little sister's class."

"Two Cosmos," Jodie shouts over them. Bonnie gets out of the way. "Use Grey Goose. And three Mojitos." Jodie dashes back to the dining room, her panty line unflatteringly apparent through her pants.

"He's a good artist," Bonnie continues. "He drew the Viking on our gymnasium wall. Other people filled it in with paint, but Principal Hamilton asked him to do the outline."

"I haven't seen it," Katie says, pulling three frosty martini glasses from the freezer. "He never tells me anything."

"I wish I could draw," she says, "but I'm more numbers oriented." Bonnie grabs a cherry from the garnish bin and plunks it into her mouth.

"Do you know Roxy?" Katie asks.

"Roxy who?"

"I'm not sure of her last name."

"I don't think I know any Roxys," Bonnie says.

A lit birthday cake wheels past the bar, the dessert cart en route to the room reserved for private parties. "Well, I guess I better get back in there," Bonnie says, frowning in the direction of the tables.

Katie prepares a round of Mojitos, "the asshole's drink" as Paula refers to the cocktail.

"Hey," Paula says, "your wrestling coach just walked in."

Behind the first row of customers, Peter stands with his hands shoved in his khaki pockets, eyeing the baseball game on TV. He's a head shorter than the man next to him.

Katie waves, her fingertips green from crushing mint leaves.

"You can give him one on the house," Megan says.

Katie abandons Jodie's drink order and pours Peter a Shipyard from the tap.

"I really need those Mojitos," Jodie says tensely. "This table's up my ass."

Katie reaches over her customers and passes Peter the pint, her elbow just missing a bowl of lobster bisque.

"Thank you much," he says, grabbing the glass with both hands.

She finishes Jodie's drinks, the poor girl's face flushed with urgency. "This too shall pass," Katie says to her.

"I'm getting sooooo annihilated after work tonight it's not even funny," Jodie states, dunking straws into the glasses.

Paula charges back to the bar, eyes ablaze. She snatches her apron back from Megan. "Hey, isn't that your fella over there?" she asks, rubbing her nose. "The wrestling dude."

"Not really," Katie says.

"I'll take him if you're done."

"Be my guest."

"Nah," Paula says, "I can't date a man who weighs less than me."

When the rush finally slows, Megan cuts two waitresses and lets Paula go home. Peter takes a seat in front of the taps and orders a batch of littlenecks and a codburger, no bun. She brushes the crumbs away from his bar space.

"Why are you all alone on a Saturday night?"

"Jenny's on vacation," he says, peeling away at his beer coaster. Katie hates when customers do this, the mess they make, but she won't let herself nag at him.

"You couldn't go with her?"

"She went to Orlando." He points to his empty glass; she pours him another Shipyard. "She's at Disney World with her husband and two kids."

"No way," she says, handing him a fresh pint and coaster. "She's married?"

"Shhh," he says, pressing his index finger to his lips. "God, I already told you about this. I'm not thrilled about it."

Katie turns away and pretends to enter an order on the broken computer.

"You don't remember me telling you that, do you?" he says. "Man, I should never talk to you after ten P.M."

"I remember, jerk," she lies. Katie wipes down the taps and considers how marvelous a cold beer would taste, but when she imagines Officer Rollins waiting for her down route 133, the urge fades. "Is she going to leave her husband?"

"No," he says. "She just wants a boyfriend."

"Now I really feel sleazy about what happened between us."

"I'm going to end it with her," Peter says. "The kids thing is really getting to me."

Nelson, the line cook, steps next to her and fills a pitcher full of Coke for the kitchen. He smells like garlic. Below the speed rack, Katie pours Old Grand-Dad into the pitcher. She drops a five into the register for the bourbon, then hands Nelson a twenty, her tip for the kitchen staff, a practice Paula doesn't share.

"Do you ever go to her house?" Katie asks.

"I'd rather not have this conversation twice." Peter wipes his mouth, then drops the napkin onto his plate. "Do you remember what you said the other night when you called?"

She doesn't. What Katie does remember from Thursday night/Friday morning is finding an AA flyer outside her bedroom door (DO YOU THINK YOU'RE DIFFERENT?) and another on her toilet seat (AA FOR THE WOMAN), which she read with a throbbing head while peeing fire. She doesn't believe AA is her answer, not yet anyway. Once she shakes, Katie swears she'll attend; once she drinks every day, she'll sign the contract. Until then, she'll consult shrinks here and there, stock up on a week's worth of Valium, just enough to get over the speedbumps. When they ask how many drinks she consumes per week, Katie will cut the number in half, not allowing them to link her self-diagnosis of depression with alcohol abuse. At this point, there's simply no call for drastic measures, no need for the extremity of sobriety.

When C.J. returned from school on Friday afternoon, he didn't harass her as she'd expected, didn't quiz her on the brochures he'd left for her to claim. He didn't bash pots and pans demanding she get help, that she fly off to Betty Ford. All he asked instead was that she keep her door closed when using the phone from now on, that he didn't need to hear her "gory details." C.J. was eerily calm, a different son, and Katie was put off by his restraint. She would have actually preferred a full-fledged intervention rather than ruminate over the mystery of what she said, the vulgarity he'd heard from the mouth of his mother.

"You said you wanted to die," Peter continues.

"I was drunk."

"You said you were going to drive into a tree, that you knew the exact trunk you were going to hit."

"What's your point?"

"I just thought you should know how you can get. It's scary."

"Walter had just died. I was grieving. Can't I get a fucking pardon?"

The young couple in the corner look her way. "Would you like more bread?" she asks them. They shake their heads no. She realizes they never even ordered food.

"I'm at work," she tells him. "I'm not talking about this here."

"Is your son home tonight?"

"He's sleeping over at a friend's house, actually."

He looks at her threateningly, what she imagines he thinks is a brooding, sexy stare. "I want you hard," he says sternly.

She laughs in his face. "You want me hard? What does that mean?"

"You know what I'm saying," he says, reaching for her hand, his fingertips cold from the beer glass. "Let's be together tonight."

"For fuck's sake."

"I'm serious."

Katie lets him hold her hand, but not because she wants him. She simply knows that if she brings Peter home, she can't drink herself to sleep in an empty house.

"So what do you say?"

She yanks her hand away. "You'll have to be gone by sunrise," Katie says, reaching for a bar rag. "Plus, you have to let me borrow your truck."

CHAPTER 16

At the halfway point of her three mile jog on Doyle's Beach, Katie threw up in the ocean, the second time in a week she's been sick before noon. Exercising in the sand had been a mistake. While the other joggers seemed to handle the squishy terrain with grace, Katie felt like she'd been running on top of a wedding cake. The third time she caught her ankle in a crab hole, she cut her losses and walked the rest of the way. When she passed a woman her age with a decent body doing yoga, Katie wondered why she bothered with jogging, why she had to drive ten miles from home this morning to feel slow and clumsy.

With a sweatshirt stuffed between her back and the windshield wiper, Katie lays out on the hood of her car. Still winded, she coughs in the salty air, her pulse so strong she feels it in her fingertips. She can smell the donuts from the backseat, the half-dozen glazed she picked up at Dunkin's for C.J.'s birthday. While her stomach craves something sweet, she doesn't want to risk another public heaving.

Popping open a can of ginger ale, Katie watches the little kids climb over the rocks leading up to the wharf, their young mothers eyeing them closely from the shore. One of them films the children's ascent with her cell phone. The first time she brought C.J. here, Katie remembers her five-year-old son got into a territorial dispute with another boy, the two of them trying to shove each other off the rock in question. When Katie told the other mother that "boys will be boys," the woman looked at her like she smelled something foul.

"Your kid started it," she said, pulling her son away from C.J.

"Your boy is twice his size," Katie replied.

"That's hardly the point. He should apologize."

"You should get a grip," Katie said, picking C.J. up. "They're children."

"Ah, I see where he gets it now."

"Oh, go to hell."

"Go to hell," C.J. repeated.

Back on the beach, far away from the rocks, they collected sea shells. C.J. said he'd make her a necklace from the pretty ones, but any shark teeth they found he wanted for himself. Walking side by side, she saw her feet in his own. They shared the same fingers and toes, but the rest of his body was all Craig.

"What were you and that boy fighting about?" she finally asked, sifting through a handful of shattered clam shells.

"He told me not to pull the mussels from the rock. I told him it wasn't his rock."

Katie wiped the water from the back of his bathing suit. A strand of slick seaweed stuck to his knees. "What did he say?"

"He called me a murderer."

She looked back and saw several boys playing nicely on that same rock. "Why?"

"He didn't like that I was smashing the mussels against the seawall."

"Well, you shouldn't be doing that," she said, "but he shouldn't have called you a murderer."

"I like to see the yellow splatter," he said, mashing his hands together.

"Mussels are alive," she said. "You don't want to smash them." She combed back his grainy hair with her fingers. He needed a haircut and was too old for her to keep cutting it at home. "No more of that, okay?" With a stick, C.J. poked an oozing pink jellyfish. "What did I just say?" she asked, snatching the stick away.

"It's dead," C.J. said. "Besides, they sting."

Katie grabbed his hand. "Come on," she said, pointing toward the dunes. "I think there're shark teeth down there."

Just past the washed-up lobster buoys, a boy about C.J.'s age was trying to bury his father in the sand. C.J. dropped his shells and stared.

"Can I bury you?" he asked.

"I'm not in my swimsuit," Katie said.

"You bury me then."

"We don't have a sand shovel. Besides, it's not safe to be in the sand like that."

"Why not?"

"There're parasites."

"What's that?"

"Tiny worms that crawl under your skin," she said, tickling his ribs.

"Parasites can't catch me," he said, darting toward the snack bar.

Katie chased him until she tripped over a piece of driftwood, falling hard onto the gritty sand, skinning her knee.

C.J. caught up to her. "Should I get that man to help?"

"I'm fine," she said, picking herself up. "It's just a scrape."

"You're bleeding," he said frantically.

"It's okay, sweetie. It doesn't hurt."

"It could get infected from the parasites," he screamed, pointing at the beach grime on her shin.

"You can take care of me," she said.

He pointed to the father and son in the sand. "Maybe that man has Band-Aids."

Katie handed him a T-shirt from the beach bag. "Here," she said. "Blot up the blood with this. If you want, you can cup some saltwater in your hands and wash it over my knee."

With the T-shirt, he rubbed the dirt from her skin. When he splashed saltwater over her knee, it burned, but Katie bit her tongue; she didn't want to upset him further. Though she was touched by the attention, Katie didn't think it was healthy for a five-year-old boy to stress so much over his mother's well-being. In the car, he was the first one to lock the doors, reaching over every time to secure her side first. The month before when the plumber came to their house to fix C.J.'s toilet (he had tried to flush a toothbrush), her son insisted the front door remain open in case they had to "get out fast." He was never an anxious baby, generally an easy one to put to sleep. Happy, playful, a bit boisterous maybe, but no cause for alarm. It wasn't until nursery school when he had nothing to make for Father's Day that Katie began to worry. While other kids drew pictures for their dads, he traced his own hand and colored it in black, *For Mom* written in white across the palm.

"What if you die?" he asked, blowing on her cut.

Katie laughed. "C.J., it's a little scrape and you're a very good doctor."

"What if you broke your neck and died. Then what?"

"I'm not going to die."

"Chris Kelly's mother died last summer."

"Mrs. Kelly had cancer. I'm very healthy, C.J."

"Would I go with my dad if you were gone?"

"No," she said, picking the remaining sand sprinkles from her knee. "You shouldn't worry about things like this."

"Then where would I go?"

"Your Aunt Caroline would take care of you, but nothing's going to happen to me anyway."

"I don't even know her."

"She's just like me."

C.J. picked up the piece of driftwood she tripped over and cracked it over his leg. It was too soggy to break clean so he twisted it until it was in two pieces, heaving the remnants toward the sea. "I don't get why Dad lives alone," he protested, picking the fresh splinters from his palm.

"You'll understand when you're older."

"That's what you always say."

"Some little boys don't even have a mommy or a daddy. You're lucky."

"What if he tries to find us?"

"He's not coming to see us."

"Does he know where we are?"

"Of course," she said.

"Would he try and hurt us?" he asked timidly.

"No," she said, grabbing his forearms. "I've told you a million times, sweetie. He loves you, but he has to be away. Some people are like that."

"We're not like that."

"No," she said. "We're not."

A light rain began to fall over the beach. A woman called to her two beagles who were running madly up and down the causeway.

"I feel bad for him," he said solemnly.

"Me too," she agreed, steering him into his jacket. "Tell you what, maybe we'll stop by Dairy Queen on the way home. Sound good?"

"Okay," he said, pulling his red Keds from the beach bag.

"What are you going to get?"

He frowned at his sneakers. "Can you help me with this?"

Katie bent down and used her long fingernails to unravel the knot in C.J.'s laces. "All free," she said.

"Can I get a Peanut Buster Parfait with no peanuts?"

"Anything you want."

"And milk for my muscles," he said, flexing his biceps.

On the walk back to the parking lot, she held his hand, kept him close and to her right, blocking his view of the father and son playing in the wet sand.

"CAN I eat this?" C.J. asks, reaching for the candle-laden donut.

"No," Katie says, slapping his hand away. "Let me light them all first." In her purse she finds a pack of matches from the Chum Line. "I didn't even hear you come in here." She tries to light all sixteen candles with one match.

"Why are you all sandy?"

"I jogged on Doyle's Beach this morning."

"For real?"

"Yes, for real," she says. "I have the pain and nausea to prove it."

"Can I grab a donut from the box while you're doing that?" he asks.

"I'm almost done," she says. "Let me have this moment, will you?"

He sits down at the table and waits for her to finish with the candles. The dryer buzzer sounds from the other room. "Okay," she says, blowing out the match. "Happy birthday." She leans down and kisses his cheek; he winces. "Can't I kiss you on your sixteenth birthday?"

"I just put on Clearasil."

"Well, have at it," she says. "Make your wish."

He closes his eyes and blows out the candles. She tries to capture the moment with her new camera phone, but all she gets is smoke.

"What did you wish for?"

"Peace on earth."

"I'm sure," she says, mussing his bed head. "I have two presents for you."

"Cool."

"Some of them are still lit," she says, pointing at the donut.

C.J. blows out the last of them. He quickly picks the candles from the donut and shoves it into his mouth. Katie licks the waxy ends before throwing them away in the trash.

"Before you get your presents, I want you to tell me what happened with Dr. Brown."

"My wish was you wouldn't bug me about that on my birthday."

"Come on, you have a nice reward waiting."

C.J. licks the frosting from his upper lip, then grabs another donut from the box. He takes two yellow L-Glutamine pills from the pantry and drinks down an entire glass of milk. "He's a dumbass."

She hands him a napkin. "How was Dr. Brown a dumbass?"

"For an hour he was trying to figure out if I've gone through puberty yet. *Do your pants fit from last year? Are your clothes tighter than they used to be?* I don't know why he just didn't ask me. I think it's kind of obvious anyway."

"I'll find you someone better."

"Can I have my present now?"

"Sure," she says, clearing his plate. "Let's go."

Outside, Katie leads C.J. down the driveway toward her car. The sun is white and warm. She sees the winter sealant has been removed from Mr. Kashgarian's sailboat, the elegant white Catalina now on full display. C.J. stops to kick dead pine branches back into the pachysandra, their tiny greenery in desperate need of landscaping.

Katie opens the hatchback. "It was too heavy for me to bring into the house by myself so I wrapped it out here." C.J. peeks into the car. "Go ahead," she says.

He yanks off the yellow bow and tears through the red wrapping paper. Katie's phone vibrates in her hand. The display says *Caroline Olmstead.* "Looks like your auntie is calling for your birthday," she says, ignoring the call. "I wonder how much money she'll send you this year."

"Nice," he says, lifting the Craftsman toolbox from the car. A deep rectangular imprint remains on the yoga mat. C.J. lays the box on the driveway and sorts through the tools.

"The man at Sears said it's a good starter set," Katie tells him. "There's a lifetime warranty on everything in there."

"This is metric," he says, squinting at the tiny sockets.

"What does that mean?"

"It means I can't use these." He closes the lid. "Harley-Davidson is American. I need standard tools, not metric. Inches, not millimeters."

"Okay," she says. "We'll simply exchange it. Not a big deal."

"You should have asked the guy."

"I did ask him. Christ, don't be so ungrateful."

He stands up and pats her shoulder, like he might a friendly dog. She reaches for his hand, but it's already gone. "Thank you," he says, lifting the box back into the car.

Katie points toward the shed. "There's more."

"No way," he says, running off.

The morning after she brought Peter home with her from the bar, they took his truck to pick up the Road King. With a new credit card issued by a Canadian bank she never heard of, Katie paid the dealership to replace the front wheel, tire, and brake system. She bought a two-hundred-dollar helmet, a padded jacket, protective mesh pants, leather gloves and a chic pair of Harley-Davidson boots. Once the master technician and general manager assured her the bike was "ultra-safe to ride," they loaded the Road King onto the back of Peter's Tacoma. After he once again maneuvered the motorcycle into the shed, Katie readied herself for a quick goodbye embrace, but all Peter did was wave out the truck window as he drove away.

With the shammy cloth and Harley Gloss the dealership gave her for free, Katie had wiped the salt layer from the gas tank. The sparkle the polish brought out in the paint actually managed to somewhat feminize the midnight black color. Katie also cleared away the glass shards from the old headlight, scrubbed the stickiness from the grips, and shined the silver cylinder heads into mirrors. With a twig, she dug out the grime between the tire treads, imagining Craig riding through Arizona when he tracked this strange, red dirt. She was surprised how little damage had been done, how the smallest wreck could end a life. At first she mistook the dark streaks on the exhaust pipes for bloodstains, but the technician explained they were probably just heat blemishes. When she opened the saddlebags, she found Walter's last purchase from Christine's Variety: a Tab energy drink, a Whoopie Pie, and three Red Sox lotto tickets, all losers.

Kicking her leg over the rear fender, she sat on the bike for the first time. The tips of her toes barely touched the ground, and she sensed that without the kickstand in place she'd have toppled right over. Even though the bike was at rest, Katie felt terribly unsteady. She couldn't imagine it actually moving, how exposed she'd be on two wheels in the Atlantic wind. Katie likened the experience to horseback riding, the same apprehension she'd endured as a little girl the few times she went to Brooksby Farms. Back then she had desperately wanted to love horses—she'd adored the equestrian's uniform—but sitting so high up only terrified her. Plus she'd felt bad for the poor animals having to lug people around all the time, their eyes so knowing and sad. "You'll break your neck anyway," her mother warned her. "Besides, horse people are tedious."

Katie grabbed the grips and pressed the buttons, clasped the clutch lever and twisted the throttle until it couldn't turn anymore.

"D ID THE mechanics do a frame inspection?" C.J. asks, crouching by the front wheel, tracing his finger along the tire grooves.

"They did everything."

"Good, I don't even need tools now." C.J. mounts the motorcycle and steers the wheel back and forth. "I can't believe it only has five thousand miles," he says, reading the speedometer. "He sure didn't ride it very much."

"I guess he ran out of time."

"Not me," he says, flicking on the high beams.

"You can have this too," she says, handing him the FedEx envelope.

"What's this?"

"The deputy in Nevada told me it's Craig's instructions for giving us the bike. I don't need it."

"That's okay," he says, pushing it away.

"You don't want it?"

"For what?"

"To have."

"You have it."

She tucks the envelope into the waistband of her running pants. "I just thought I should offer."

"Where are the keys to this hog?"

"Hidden away. This bike won't start until you get your license and take that riding course. And a lot of other rules we'll go over once you reach that point."

"Si señor."

"I'm serious, C.J. And when people ask, I want you to say it's from Craig. I don't need to be seen as the mindless mother who got you a motorcycle for your sweet sixteen."

"Did you get a car on your sixteenth?" he asks, tugging on the spark plug wires.

"No," she says. "I got cash. Five hundred dollars in twenties sealed in a business envelope."

"Money's good."

"Not really," Katie says, remembering the curtained darkness she came home to after school that day. The only light she found came from the fish tank in the living room. "My father was in Istanbul for work. He called saying he'd left me a present in his desk drawer." Katie sits down on a milk crate full of hockey pucks. If it weren't for the long hair, C.J. could pass for Craig from behind.

"Where was your mom?" he asks.

"She was upstairs asleep. She didn't realize it was my birthday until I asked to borrow the car keys a week later."

"That sucks."

What really sucks, Katie doesn't tell him, is how she discovered her mother sitting naked in the living room when she got back from a ballet class later that night. A bottle of wine stood upright between her legs and cigarette butts filled the silver cup of her father's golf trophy from Yale. Katie had never seen her smoke inside, not once in sixteen years; and when she tried to shake her awake, Martha bit down on her daughter's thumb—*CRUNCH.*

"Fucking owwww!" Katie screamed, but she couldn't free the skin and bone from her mother's teeth without making a bloody mess. Cocking her leg back, Katie kicked her mother in the groin. As she keeled over, a deep and horrible moan resounded through the living room, the sound of a sick animal. Too confused to phone her father's hotel in Turkey, Katie called Caroline at Princeton. "Just drop a few Valium in her wine glass," Caroline instructed. "That'll keep her upstairs and away from your fingers."

Downstairs, Katie finished her mother's bottle of wine as she straightened up the living room. The next morning, she found Martha frantically spraying the house with Pledge as if it were Lysol. "It smells like an ashtray in here," she said, wrinkling her nose. "Were you smoking in here last night? . . ."

"Anyway," Katie tells C.J., "my sixteenth wasn't all bad. My boyfriend at the time did buy me a nice locket. I think I still have it somewhere. He brought over a six-pack of Ballantine Ale at midnight. We drank it on my bed. I had two, he had four. God, I can't believe I can remember all that."

"You can stop there," C.J. says.

"Don't worry. That's how it ends anyway."

He leans over and picks up his new helmet. "Why did you get me a yellow one?" he asks.

"So people can see you."

"They sure will," he says, maneuvering the helmet over his head.

"Remember, it's not a hockey helmet. No outbursts, please."

He adjusts the chin strap and snaps it closed. The face mask is black and tinted. She'd meant to buy him a clear visor. "Can you see my eyes?"

Katie searches for his face, a blink of an eye or a smile, but only catches her own dubious reflection in the shield. "I can't tell it's you at all, Calvin James."

CHAPTER 17

Calvin James. She hated that name, could never get used to it. Katie had simply wanted *James* after her father, something traditional and distinguished, but Craig was set on Calvin. He told her if she didn't like it she should call him Cal, "like Cal Ripken of the Orioles," as if associating her child's name with a professional baseball player would make it more palatable.

"*Calvin* makes me think of Calvin Klein," Katie had explained, her arms drained from holding their one-month-old baby for so long. "You know, it's still early enough to make a change."

"Get over it," Craig said. "I won the coin toss."

She adjusted her grip on the baby and sat down at the kitchen table, setting a throw pillow between her lower spine and the back of the chair, her lumbar region a constant source of ache since Calvin's birth. With her fingernail, Katie scraped the spit-up milk stains from her sweatshirt. The washing machine and dishwasher had run non-stop since Calvin was born. Craig never asked how the new mommy was feeling, expressed no concern over her body's postpartum adaptation. And Katie refused to expose her pain, perpetually on guard with her emotions since the final trimester. Even though she was exhausted—strung out on Pepsi and Chips Ahoy!—Katie couldn't put the baby to bed or let him nap away an afternoon without concern. She couldn't rest more than an hour at a time, constantly checking to make sure he was breathing, her hand on his back feeling for the reassuring rise and fall. For months she stewed over SIDS, worried he'd die in his sleep, that each time she set him down in the crib was akin to placing him in a grave. Craig had no idea about her unease, how dead and lonely she felt without her son against her skin.

"Calvin," Katie sang, bouncing the baby. "Calvin, Calvin, Calvin. Do you like your name, Calvin? Do you, Cal? I don't think you do."

"He doesn't really look like either of us, does he?" Craig said, fishing a beer out of the Igloo cooler. He took a healthy sip from the can, keeping a safe distance as he inspected his son, squinting over his face as if struggling to read tiny print. "Bits and pieces, maybe, but not on the whole. Not altogether."

Katie scowled at him. "Why do you have to observe him like he's a science exhibit?"

"Because he is."

"And you wonder why he cries around you all the time," she said, kissing the baby's soft spot. "You totally freak him out."

"He's the one freaking me out. It's so weird to see my eyes on another person. It's like I'm staring myself down."

"Christ, are you stoned?"

"I don't think Calvin cares. Right, Calvin?" he said, smiling at his son.

"I care."

As he kicked his chair back from the table, she felt the floor vibrate beneath the soles of her feet. Craig shot up and elbowed open the screen door. Katie could smell the pines as wind blew leaves into the kitchen.

"Where you going?"

"I'm following house rules," Craig said, pulling a crumpled joint from his pocket. "I'll be outside. Just me and God."

Katie locked the door behind him. He'd be gone at least an hour. He usually just hiked to the reservoir, but sometimes he went all the way to Jack's Hill, a six-mile round trip. The house she'd rented was simple and secluded, and if it weren't for her father's checks, they'd be living in some shanty. She figured her place in the middle of nowhere Vermont would have been right up his alley, but most nights Craig lodged closer to work at Mount Frost one hundred miles away. Even though two or three ski resorts were hiring between here and there, he chose to be remote. He claimed he was allergic to her walls, that the previous tenants must have had cats because he was always itchy inside her house. He said that walking in the woods cleared his lungs and soothed his eyes, but when he returned he still looked like a man who'd been crying. What struck Katie was how the isolation of her home only bothered her when he was there, when it was three instead of two.

When Craig was out of sight, Katie microwaved a cold batch of breast milk from the refrigerator, giving her ailing boobs a much needed vacation. Often she found it more comfortable to pump the milk from her body than endure the greed of the baby's mouth. What she did appreciate about breastfeeding was the connection, the way he held her eyes with his own, brushed her hair with his miniscule hand. Those moments mattered.

Six months into her pregnancy, after winning a silver dollar coin toss, Craig declared he was going to name their boy Calvin after his younger brother who was born premature and died nine months into his life. He explained that while his father finished up his spring trucking routes, Craig and his mother virtually moved into the pediatric wing of the hospital. With their foreheads pressed against the glass partition, they watched the infant in the incubator.

While his baby brother's head was enormous, like those starving Ethiopian children Craig saw on TV, his body was soft and flimsy, "watery" the doctor called it. Sometimes Craig saw his toes move, but his mother said his eyes were playing tricks on him, that "when you stare you see things." Craig wondered how his father could stay away, how he could drive a rig with no radio all over western North America while his newborn was stuck in a box. He couldn't imagine being that cut off from his own blood, but he was glad to be alone with his mother. All he had to do was bring her coffee, sugar donuts, and Camels from the cafeteria and she didn't care how much school he was missing. Sometimes he'd pretend he was the father, that it was their wounded baby behind that glass.

Most nights she went to a bar across the street called the Blue Lamp, telling him to sit tight and watch his brother while she "took a break." Twice he stole her lipstick from her purse thinking she wouldn't leave without dressing her face, but she'd just find a nurse and borrow hers. From the hospital's ninth floor, Craig watched his mother far below, losing sight of her once she pushed through the black barroom door, the fake blue torch shining through her frosty hair. That's when he prayed hardest for Calvin to wake up, hoping to teach his mother a lesson for abandoning them. She'd come back ugly, hugging him hard, her neck and hair stinking of smoke, her sloppy fat boobs pressed against his face. He wanted to push her away, but—he explained—"I didn't have the guts to be by myself yet."

Calvin died as Craig was reading a Homer Price book in the handicapped toilet stall. By the time he got back to his brother's floor, Calvin was clean. No more wires and tubes. No bottles of blood and saline. Craig had never seen anyone so naked. His mother's face was smeared black with mascara when she handed him a wad of oily dollar bills, telling him to take a cab home, that she was going to "mourn across the street." After she left, Craig snuck in to be with his brother on the other side of the glass. Before the nurses took him away, Craig kissed his little brother's cold forehead, brushed the soft belly with the palm of his hand, relieved his brother would be spared.

EMOTIONS ONCE concealed bled from Craig when their own son was born. He began to confide in Katie, mulling over a life's worth of regret with a woman too occupied to feign sympathy.

Over and over she heard how jealous he was of his brother Calvin's "clean getaway," but she no longer had the luxury of time to mull over Craig's childhood demons and philosophical ramblings when their own son demanded her full attention. What might have intrigued her months ago about this man was now extraneous. What she wanted, what he wanted, was irrelevant, long gone. As far as she was concerned, if Craig wasn't talking about their son, he was talking bullshit. Most of his laments were voiced through phone lines, Craig far away making snow and digging out banks on Mount Frost, Katie grateful her son wasn't exposed to his father's collapse. On the night of Calvin's six month birthday—"the final chapter" as she refers to it now—Craig called her from a bar.

"Calvin hates me," he stated.

"You're a disgrace," Katie told him, setting her son down on his blankets. Crawling toward his toys, she watched as he picked up a stuffed penguin and bit its tail. Not one item within his reach ever went untested by his tongue.

"He can't even walk or talk and he's already spooked by me."

"What do you expect?" she shouted. "You're a ghost. You're too scared to even hold him." Katie turned on the burner to make macaroni, the smell of propane rushing her nostrils. "You treat him like a time bomb."

"You don't understand."

"I know I don't. You said you wanted this, but it's a fucking disaster."

"I thought it'd be okay."

Katie wheeled one of their four kerosene space heaters closer to Calvin's blankets. She was cold in this house, even when it was warm outside. Light could never seem to find its way inside. She was sick of it, sick to death of the crappy washing machine, the termite-infested wood, the stink of skunks on humid evenings. The romance of country living had run its course. Now that she was a mother, Katie was fed up with the Green Mountain State, through with earthy people like her "husband." What

Katie longed for was a good school district, beaches where her son could swim and build castles, an actual neighborhood with newspaper boys and block parties. A childhood like her own, wholly divergent from Craig's.

"My father used to lock me out of the house," Craig went on.

"So what?" Katie said, dropping handfuls of elbow macaroni into the boiling pot of water. "This drunk talk isn't worth the phone bill." She stepped back from the stove and wiped the steam from her forehead.

"When the dryer was running," Craig continued, "warm exhaust gushed out the vent on the side of the house and I'd huddle there. Outside smelled like fabric softener. Inside, my father drank Early Times and smoked cigarettes while I froze my ass off. His friends would come over and play cards."

"Do you realize that everything you're saying will be forgotten?" she asked. "Lost forever in your blackout."

"Look, this is important, so listen."

"Well, hurry up," she said, eyeing Calvin as he rested his head on the penguin, his toes opening and closing around the blanket end. "I have to put my son to bed soon."

Away from the phone, she listened as Craig called for "another shot of Jack," his voice dark and nasty. She heard country music and shrill voices. She imagined wooden bar stools, sticky tables, and red faces. Seasonal men in Carhartt jeans and work boots. Women on the lam. Before the entrapment of parenthood, she loved these places.

"A different crew seemed to show up for poker each time," Craig explained. "None of them said hello to me on their way in the house. Now and then my mom would peek her head out the bedroom window and smile, but not a real smile. One of those nervous smiles trying to show everything's okay when it totally wasn't. She'd run the dryer as long as she could, until my Dad caught on to her. With all those men inside," he said, his breath seemingly close, "I think things happened."

She turned off the burner. "What things?"

"I'd be left out there all night sometimes. When my father opened the front door the next morning, he'd be shocked to find me there. 'What the hell you doin' out here?' he'd say."

"What things are you talking about?"

He gasped into the phone, the sound that follows a downed whiskey shot. "Tell me what to do, Katie."

"Don't drive tonight. Take a cab wherever you're going. No one where you are can give you a safe ride."

"No, I mean tell me what the fuck to do."

"Not when you're like this."

"You get like this too."

"Not in a year I haven't," she said proudly.

Stirring the noodles, Katie was reluctant to admit she was jealous, that she wanted badly to get drunk and lost. If only for one night, to plunge into that lovely space where she didn't give a shit, where tomorrow didn't matter. She actually missed all the danger, all the desperation.

"Tell me the truth, just for tonight," Craig continued.

The truth: Calvin was hers and she didn't want to share. The second he was born her stomach turned hollow and hungry, and when the doctor cut the cord Katie swore she could feel the blade. Unlike most women, she missed the extra weight and shared responsibility, the annex of another. Even as she held her blanketed newborn, Katie sensed the rupture. Right then as the infant screamed bloody murder, she wanted him back inside.

"Katie, you there or what?"

Kneeling down, she touched her son's stomach with the back of her hand, the rhythm of his sleeping breath heavy in his tummy. She loved the feel of his skin, was absolutely hooked on its delicacy.

"Hello?" Craig shouted.

Katie put the phone to her other ear, away from her baby. Only when he was drunk did he ask for the truth, only then was he ever really honest. And she knew she was no different, knew it because only after half the bottle of raspberry wine was gone did she finally say, "I think you should go."

CHAPTER 18

Katie lights a second cigarette from the burning tip of her first. Her throat tastes like gravel, but the sooner this pack is empty, the sooner she can blanket her body with nicotine patches. A few feet away, sea gulls peck over shiny strips of salmon skin stuck to the base of the restaurant's Dumpster, while the smaller birds beak through an old tomato can full of cigarette butts. A busser she doesn't recognize walks by and dumps a trash bag of liquor bottles into the recycling bin at the end of the loading ramp. Katie can see Paula through the captain's window, hurriedly setting up a row of tequila shots for the college kids who work at the yacht club down the street. Except for the blonde hair, the good-looking one with Mark Wahlberg arms could be C.J. in five years.

Her phone vibrates against her leg. "I can barely hear you, C.J," she says, plugging her free ear with a finger. "Your voice is going in and out."

"I said I fell off Farmingdale's waiting list," C.J. shouts.

She stomps out the cigarette. "Ah, shit."

"I guess I should have applied to more schools, like you said."

"There's always next year."

"Fuck it."

"Katie?" a timid voice calls from behind the plastic kitchen flaps. She guesses it's the new hostess, Alana. "They say they need you back inside."

"Okay, give me a second," Katie says, cupping the phone away from her mouth.

"I bet if we didn't have to apply for financial aid I would have gotten in. Nick Fletcher got into Taft and he's a dumbass, but his father's a rich stockbroker."

"Don't let this set you back. You don't need Farmingdale to play hockey."

"Screw hockey."

Katie spits into a Kleenex. "God, I warned you not to get your hopes up."

"My SSAT scores were higher than Nick Fletcher's," C.J. continues. "Plus he's like five feet five with his skates on. He should have been the one to get fucked over."

"God," she shouts, frustrated that this moment is taking place by phone, "when did boarding school become the be-all end-all?"

"Maybe when my whole class found out you're a drunk."

"Don't pin this on me. You've been fixated on going away since last summer."

"Well, I'm stuck here now."

"It's not about where you are. Look, your Aunt Caroline went to public school and she's a millionaire. A multimillionaire. We'll try again next year. We'll be more prepared."

"Next year I'll be a junior. It's too late."

"I'm telling you, you're overreacting."

"You tell me a lot of bullshit."

"Oh, really, like what?"

"Caroline said you told Craig to leave."

Katie scurries down the ramp, toward the recycling bins, away from the restaurant. "When did you talk to Caroline?"

"She said it was your idea," he continues. "She said you kicked him out."

Britney sticks a hand through the plastic kitchen flaps, careful to keep her frosty hair away from the surrounding filth. "Paula's really losing her shit at the bar, Katie," she calls. "Just hurry."

"C.J., I really have to go."

"Did you tell him to leave?"

Katie pulls on her hair, wishing he'd just hang up on her. "It was both our idea," she finally says.

"Then you're a liar, because you told me he had to live alone. Since I was a kid you said it was his choice to go."

"I'm not a liar," she says. "What difference does it make now anyway?"

"Lots." Katie hears a cabinet slam, the one above the fridge where she keeps the Grand Marnier. "Why did you tell him to go?" he screams.

"Jesus, C.J.," Katie says, kicking the recycling bin. "I can't do this from here."

"You're a fucking liar."

"Stop yelling at me."

"Stop lying!"

"Why are you listening to Caroline anyway?"

"I don't trust either one of you right now."

"C.J., this isn't fair. I'm trapped at work."

"And I'm trapped at home."

"You're just upset about Farmingdale and I understand that, I really do. But this is one of those times to work on your temper. Process before you react, like Walter told you."

"Too late."

"Look, we'll talk about this when I get home," she tells him. "I'm going to get in trouble if I don't get back inside."

"I found your banana-flavored condoms."

"What? Why are you going through my stuff?"

"You like sucking dick?"

"Shut your mouth," she shouts. "They were a gag gift from Lisa for my birthday last year."

"Who's Lisa?"

"She used to work here."

"If they're a joke, why are some missing then?"

On the other end of the line Katie hears a pop-top open. She listens to him chug. "Are you drunk, C.J.?"

"Wonder where I got that from."

"Jesus, C.J., just wait until I get home, okay?"

"Wait for what?"

He hangs up. When she calls him back the ring goes right to voice mail.

"I gotta go," she tells Britney, once she's back inside.

"But the rush is coming."

"Sorry."

"Megan will fire you if you take off."

Katie unties her apron and shoves it into her pocket. "Tell her it's an emergency."

"Is it?"

"We'll see."

As Katie speeds past Officer Rollins on route 133, she dials Caroline's work number. In the rearview mirror, Katie sees him merge onto the road from his hiding place by Woodman's, but he doesn't switch on the police lights. He's three cars behind her. Katie puts on her seat belt.

"Put that cunt on the phone," she tells Caroline's secretary.

"Who may I say is calling?"

"Katie Olmstead. Her sister."

"I'll put you through, Ms. Olmstead."

Wagner's *Ride of the Valkyries* plays as she's transferred. "This is Caroline Olmstead."

"What's your problem?" Katie says, accelerating past a bicyclist.

"Katie?"

"You stupid bitch."

"Well, hello to you too."

"What did you tell him?" The steering wheel vibrates as she drives over the safety grid. Officer Rollins is now only a car behind.

"You sound a bit uneven. Are we drunk?"

"What did you tell my son?"

"I told him happy birthday."

"What else?"

"Uh, we talked about global warming for a bit. Poor kid thinks it's real. Damn that silly movie."

"What did you tell him about Craig?" Before she can turn the wheel, Katie runs over a dead skunk. The smell engulfs the car.

"Nothing, really. I more or less explained that you were a hero to raise him alone."

"God, I hope you didn't fuck me over this time."

"What's wrong?"

"None of your business."

Katie resented her weakness around Caroline, how her sister managed to extract the most personal secrets. Since she was a little girl, Katie couldn't help but spill her guts to her. Aside from Katie's mother, no other woman had ever rejected her quite like Caroline, which made confiding in her a rare and heady treat.

"Don't call me anymore," Katie continues.

"You called me."

"Just fuck off for now."

"Very well," Caroline says. "Call me when you land."

Caroline hangs up before Katie, which feels like one more failure. She throws her cell against the passenger window, but it drops right back in her lap. "Call me when you land," Katie repeats, mocking Caroline's flippant tone. The phrase infuriates her, the way it's flavored with her sister's singular condescension. Since Katie's move to Vermont, it's been Caroline's go-to insult, her way of dismissing Katie's emotions as fickle and unsound, a snide reminder that she's seldom grounded. She remembers how their father used to patronize their mother—*Call me when you land, Martha*, which makes the insult all the more irksome. Now whenever an innocent utters this simple slogan before she boards a plane, Katie can't help but hear Caroline scolding her penchant for retreat.

Katie turns into her driveway and brakes just before the wide-open shed doors. Another foot and the car would have smashed through the rotting wood frame. She leaves the car running.

Inside the shed, C.J.'s milk crate is tipped over, dozens of hockey pucks covering the cement floor like polka dots. She hears Officer Rollins's cruiser pull up into the driveway.

"What are you doing, Ms. Olmstead?" he shouts, rushing toward her, his boots freshly polished, his badge glinting in the sunlight. "I could have pulled you over a handful of times during that ride." He grips her arm with his black gloved hands. "Why do you push me?"

She shoves him away. "There used to be a motorcycle in this shed."

"So what?"

"So my sixteen-year-old son took off on it."

He grabs the CB from his shoulder holster. "Does he have his license?"

"He just completed a rider safety course."

"So he has his license?"

"Yes," she lies.

"What kind of bike is it?" he asks. "I'll call it in."

"No, I don't want you to report it."

"Then what do you want me to do?"

"Just walk me inside," she says.

He follows her to the front door, his right hand tight on his taser gun. The cat peers at them from C.J.'s windowsill. All the lights within are ablaze except Walter's. "I'd really feel better if we reported this," he says quietly.

"Tough shit," Katie replies.

In the kitchen, Katie finds Craig's FedEx envelope on the butcher block. Digging her fingers inside, she discovers it's empty. Officer Rollins points out three empty Coors Light cans in the sink. "That's not good," he says.

"Those are my boyfriend's."

"Where's he?"

"Fishing."

"Where's your son's room?" the officer asks. "There might be clues there."

"Just up the stairs, one floor up. The door with the AFFLICTION sticker on it."

"May I?" he asks, reaching for the banister.

"Fine, but don't go rooting through his things. He'll blame me."

In the studio, Katie notices Isabel's been peed on, a wet spot the size of a softball saturating her hair. Ceramic shards from her French lamp are sprinkled like jewels across the tile floor. The hockey stick she uses to knock on his ceiling has been broken into thirds over the back of her father's chair. In her bedroom, all her bureau drawers are open, the closet ransacked. The Ziploc with Walter's leftover joints is laid out neatly on top of her pillow; two are missing. In the bathroom, the banana condoms and her long-retired diaphragm float in the toilet bowl.

"I found a note," Officer Rollins calls from upstairs. "It was on his bed." Katie stuffs the Ziploc under a pillow and darts toward the kitchen. Shutting the studio door behind her, she's suddenly panicked by the idea that she'd invited a cop into her home.

"Here," Officer Rollins says, handing her the purple Post-it.

Gone to Arizona. Be back soon. —CALVIN.

The cuckoo clock shrieks from Walter's room. "He wrote this with my eyeliner pencil," Katie remarks, tracing the ink with her thumb.

"What's in Arizona?" Officer Rollins asks.

"His father," Katie says.

"Can you call him?"

"No," she says. "I can't."

The officer checks his watch. Like a nervous child, he bites the corners of his lips. Katie can see he's rattled by her stillness. "So what do you want me to do?" he asks.

"I want you to go away," she says. "I want you to forget about it."

"But we can have him pulled over, Ms. Olmstead," he offers. "A few calls and he'll be caught."

"I don't want him coming home like that."

"Like what?"

"You drag him home tonight and he'll be gone again before sunrise. Look, if he wants to find his father, I can't stop him anymore."

"So you're going to just let him go?"

"It's a free country."

"Jesus, what kind of mother are you?"

"I'm his mother," she says. Katie opens the front door and steps aside, encouraging his exit. "If you really want to help us, Mike," she says, grabbing his arm, "then let him come home on his own."

LATER THAT evening—after several glasses of Grand Marnier, twenty-five straight calls to C.J.'s voice mail, and hundreds of refresh clicks on her email inbox—Katie reaches deep into her underwear. Once again her fingers come back dry and white. She dials Peter's number, knowing he won't answer her call this late at night. Not anymore.

"I'm three weeks late," she says after the beep. "No red in sight. Not a drop."

SUMMER 2007

CHAPTER 19

Peter sets a mug of green tea on top of yesterday's *Boston Globe*, careful to avoid Katie's postcard. Above the rising steam, she warms her fingers while perusing old headlines. Sporting a pair of faded lacrosse shorts and nothing else, Peter proudly displays his clean-shaven chest as he zooms about the kitchen. Fresh scabs cover the tops of his feet, a sight which makes her queasy, his toes nicked and slimy under a layer of Neosporin. Just like C.J., Peter's skin is swollen with veins, especially the arms, the wild vasculature of her restless men. Next month Peter's in New Jersey for a grappling match against an opponent half his age; this fall he's running his first triathlon. Peter's routine exhausts her, his pace a burden to behold. Mostly, she can't stand how he flaunts his energy in her face. Sometimes Katie suspects he actually depends on her atrophy, that deep inside he feels empowered if she's a waste.

Katie inhales the aroma of her tea, the SeaWorld image of Shamu faded on the mug from years of dishwasher cycles. "I swear this stuff smells like urine."

"What's the postmark date?" Peter asks, ignoring her observation. He reaches for the remote control and turns down ESPN, though the TV's still quite loud. She doesn't understand why sports reporters always have to yell.

Katie holds up the postcard from Sweetwater, Tennessee to his bug-riddled fluorescent lights. When she tilts it toward the stove, she thinks she can make out C.J.'s fingerprints on the glossy side. "A few days ago," she says, reluctantly handing him the card.

Peter puts on his reading glasses, an obnoxious artsy-fartsy pair with thick black frames, but she's in no position to nag him. "The Lost Sea," he announces, squinting at the picture of a steel raft full of people floating over the emerald-colored water.

"It's fitting," Katie says.

He flips the card over. "It's weird, there's no note," he says. "No words. Only your name and address."

"Right now he wants to be weird."

"Mysterious," Peter says, examining the card as if for clues.

She pours a third packet of Splenda into her tea. "Like father, like son."

"Well, this is actually good news," Peter offers. "I mean, he's obviously okay."

"Yesterday when I called his cell, his voice mail box was full. He can't get any more messages."

"Maybe he's just going to see the Grand Canyon and turn around."

"I don't care if he goes all the way to Alaska, as long as he's careful."

"At least he took his helmet with him, right?"

Katie nods, briefly comforted by the gesture, but helmet or no helmet, she has no leash, not when he's so far from upstairs.

"And he took a riding class," Peter continues. "Most people don't bother with that. He'll be safer for it."

Katie didn't want to discuss safety, didn't want to dissect the obvious dangers. "It's my sister," she says, "if she hadn't sent him stock for his birthday, he wouldn't have been able to afford the gas to get past Connecticut." Katie reaches into her purse and pulls out a cigarette.

"Hold on," he says, pointing at the cigarette. "I thought you were trying the patch."

"I was until I got a postcard from goddam Tennessee. Do you know his friend, Shawn, called my cell to ask where C.J. was? I told him he was taking an Outward Bound course all summer."

"You really shouldn't smoke now."

"I haven't had one since Wednesday."

"Still, I'd rather you didn't. My mom smoked while she was pregnant with me. I'm pretty sure that's why I weighed only three pounds when I was born."

"You were a preemie?" she asks, happy to change the conversation.

"Can you please not smoke?"

Katie places the cigarette behind her ear. "Let's slow down, Peter. Right now I'm just late."

"You seemed sure the other night."

"I know, but I don't want to get into this until I see the doctor, until I'm positive."

"You told me you're never late."

"I'm usually not, but that doesn't mean I'm pregnant. Stress can play a part too."

"Well, I want you to know—"

"Please, Peter, not now," she says.

"Fuck," he says, "you're all over the place."

Without rinsing the plates in the sink, he loads the dishwasher, cramming it past capacity. She'd explained this is why his knives come out crusty with peanut butter. His cheap silverware is enough to make her miss home. Since C.J. left, Katie hasn't spent one night in Newquay. Peter had been kind enough to offer up his room, saying he'd sleep on the couch; but Katie brought over an air mattress instead, which she set up by the living room television. Peter gave her a fan to drown out the sound, but Katie didn't mind the noise coming from the tenants above. She brushes her teeth and washes her face in the kitchen sink, his bathroom an overcrowded mess full of muscle pills, grooming clips, and bandages. Plus, he uses a washcloth for a bathmat so the floor's wet and grimy. While she knows she's in no position to complain, Katie can't help but grumble about the green tea. He doesn't own a coffee machine and calls the Starbucks she loves a "controlled substance"—this coming from a man who has a wilted marijuana plant on his windowsill.

The water pipes thump-thump-thump behind the walls as Peter starts the dishwasher. "You shouldn't have told me yet," he says.

"I fucked up."

"I've heard that before," he bemoans, rolling his eyes. "I gotta take a shower."

"Oh, I got you more Irish Spring," Katie says. "And some decent shaving cream, the gel kind. It's all in the Target bag on the dryer."

Peter leaves the bathroom door open as he showers. He told her he does this so the mirror won't fog up while he shaves. Sometimes he'll walk stark naked from bathroom to bedroom, yet if Katie so much as removes her socks she'll get a nasty look.

"The doctor will know for sure today, right?" he shouts over the water's stream. "Katie?"

"Yes," she calls. "For sure today."

If she hadn't been a drunken drama queen, Katie might have found the restraint to conceal this news, stalled until she was certain before informing Peter. As a result of her impulsiveness, the baby decision now *had* to be theirs, and nothing aggravated Katie more than negotiation. Sixteen years ago she thought she had her pregnancy problem resolved, but once she decided to share the news with Craig, the answer turned back into a question. Back then she waited more than two months after conception, two months after their romp at the Mogul Motel before calling Craig. She phoned him from a Shell station, the first time she'd heard his voice since ditching him. She sought a confirmation, a corroboration from the other half of the guilty party. Then she'd be free.

"I'm pregnant," she'd blurted out.

"Fuck me," he'd said. "Definitely mine?"

"Yeah."

"How can you be sure?"

"The guy before you was last summer and he wore a condom."

"You said you wanted me to come inside you."

"Oh, God," she groaned, slapping the phone against her forehead. She wanted to retch. "Look, I'm not calling to revisit my blackout."

"It's not like there were midgets or farm animals or anything."

"Great, fine, I don't want to talk about it, okay?"

"Do your parents know?"

"My mom's dead, and my dad and sister will think I'm a loser if I tell them."

"So what's the deal?"

"There's a place in New Hampshire that doesn't ask questions."

"An abortion place?"

"I don't like that word."

"Is it safe?"

"Oh, yeah. A girl I work with went there."

"Do you need money?"

"Probably," she said.

"You're sure?"

"Well, I don't think I'll ever be sure-sure. I just have to decide, and taking care of it sounds like something I'd do." She could hear him light up in the background.

"Do you want to come up here and talk about it?"

"Seriously?"

"A girl I know had an abortion and it fucked her up royally," he said, exhaling deeply. "Now she can't go to bed without pills."

"What do you want from me?"

"I don't know."

Katie bit on the loose skin by her cuticles; her fingernails looked like a man's. "I remember nothing about that night," she admits, closing her eyes. "Nothing after the bar."

"You've made that clear."

"It's something to consider, that's all. The embryo or whatever's inside me is most likely already retarded."

"I don't think it works that way," he said.

A truck horn blares outside Peter's kitchen window, the morning hostility starting early on his street, an unfortunately popular commuter route to the highway. Katie absorbs the scene, awed by the stress that driving creates. Living right off route one, Peter can't even open his windows because the exhaust will turn his apartment walls black. This is why the air conditioner churns all day and night during the summer months. Without a breeze and the lively smell of the sea, Katie feels stir-crazy and sickly, the sterile scent of the interior too dreary for her to remain. As she dumps her tea down the sink drain, a vehicle backfires, which sets off a crescendo of car alarms. Seldom does she hear these sounds in Newquay.

"I'm gonna go," Katie announces as she rinses out her mug.

Peter appears from the bedroom, his red wrestling sneakers unlaced and dirty. "Before seven A.M.?"

"I have a ton to do at home," she says, wiping the water from her hands. "And besides, you need your privacy back."

He jams a Q-tip in his ear and swipes. "Not really," he says. "Jenny never comes over here anyway."

She picks up an issue of *Men's Fitness* from the stack on the coffee table. The guy on the cover stars on *Lost*. "Where do you two go?" Katie asks, thumbing through pages and pages of advertisements.

"I'm not talking about that with you anymore."

"I just don't want you to get busted."

"You have your own problems to worry about." He fills a Gatorade cooler with the orange slices he cut the night before. She remembers how she used to bring oranges to C.J.'s hockey games, but the kids never actually ate them, preferring instead to suck out the juice.

"Do the kids wrestle all day long at wrestling camp? They must drop dead when they get home."

"Yeah, the parents love it," he says, stretching his triceps. "But today we're going to take the afternoon off and watch *Vision Quest*."

"I bet C.J. would've made a good wrestler," she says.

"When are you working again?" Peter asks.

"He's incredibly strong," Katie continues. "He can do push-ups on his fingertips."

Suddenly, she wants to talk about her son, not just discuss his retreat. Now that C.J.'s gone, she's not so bent on concealing him, but Peter doesn't bite.

"So, when are you working again?" he asks.

Katie drops the magazine on the couch. "Well," she replies, "first I have to go in and kiss Megan's ass. She wants to demote me to lunch shifts. Then I'm probably gonna have to borrow money from my sister to keep up with expenses this summer."

"You could sell a painting," he offers.

"I'd have to paint one first."

"There are worse things you can do."

In the living room, Katie deflates the air mattress and balls up the sheets. She carries her duffel bag and the bedding to the laundry closet. Inside the washer, she finds a lavender pair of women's panties. Katie picks them out with a clothespin and inspects: Elle MacPherson Intimates, Size Small. She has a similar pair, but in medium.

"Do you want some breakfast before you go?" Peter calls from the kitchen.

Katie drops the panties into the dryer and loads the sheets into the washer. She shuts the lid.

"No." She scoops up the cat and rubs his jowls; he purrs. "Do you mind if I leave Lewis here until later?"

"That's fine," he says. "I really think you should eat before you go, though."

"I'm not hungry."

"You haven't had anything since you've been here."

"Well, there's nothing to eat here. Nothing with carbohydrates, anyway."

"How about a South Beach bar?"

"They're drawing blood," she says firmly. "I'm supposed to have an empty stomach."

"But Cabernet was recommended?"

"I only had a few glasses last night." She takes the postcard from the kitchen table and shoves it into her purse.

"He'll come back," Peter says confidently. "He'll break."

Katie knees open the screen door, the toxic smell of emissions rushing her lungs. "Maybe," she says, braving the sunlight.

"Don't forget to call me as soon as you're done."

"I'll see you," she says, stepping into a dank and humid morning.

Heading south toward Boston, Katie lights up a Dunhill. She shifts the seat back so her stomach won't press against the steering wheel. A line of six bikers pass her on the left, all doubled up with the women on the back, their long hair wild in the highway wind. She tries to keep pace, but her car shakes past sixty.

At the doctor's office, Katie settles into an uncomfortable chair and pages through a worn issue of *Redbook*. A Muzak version of "Light My Fire" plays from the ceiling speakers. Across from her, a little boy tugs on his pregnant mother's jeans as she gabs on her cell phone. Katie sees he's wet his pants. Her phone rings: *unknown number*. She has to answer these calls now.

"Where are you?" a woman says—the voice crisp, cutting, and unmistakable.

"What do you want, Caroline?"

"I want to go inside our father's house."

"What are you talking about?"

"I'm in Newquay," she says. "And you really need a landscaper, Katie. Just because your yard's the size of a trampoline doesn't mean you can let it go. You should put C.J. to work out here. So where are you?"

Katie stands up and takes the conversation away from the waiting room, into the hallway by the restrooms. The agitating way Caroline doesn't pause between statements has already winded her. "I'm in Boston."

"Where's C.J.?"

"Where do you think, you stupid bitch?"

"What did I do?"

"Look, I can't get into this now."

"What are you doing in Boston?"

"I'll be back in a few hours," Katie says. "God, what are you doing here, anyway?"

"I just paid your cable bill from my iPhone. Looks like someone ordered a porno on the eighteenth."

"What are you doing in my mail?"

"You also got an alumni letter from Hobart. A postcard from Santa Fe, New Mexico. A few gallery flyers. A letter from Senator Barack Obama. Oh, please don't tell me you're making the trendy vote, Katie."

"Just leave everything alone."

"So should I not pay your bill from the Royal Credit Union of Moose Jaw, Saskatchewan? Jesus, where the fuck do you do your banking? This interest rate is criminal."

"Fine, pay that and fuck off."

"Very well. In the interim, do you have someone I can call about your so-called lawn? There are pests everywhere. I'm going to catch bird flu out here. I think—"

Katie hangs up the phone and exhales, her stomach lumpy with indigestion. Back in the waiting room, the receptionist slides open the glass partition. Katie notices the little boy and his mother are gone. "The doctor will see you now, Ms. Olmstead," the receptionist says.

CHAPTER 20

Draped in a johnny gown with her legs spread wide, Katie breathes in the rubber smell of latex gloves, the impending entry of a stranger's finger. Beneath the spotlight, she clings to the stretcher's side rails. Almost two years have passed since Katie's been examined and she's wary of what the doctor might find. Last go-around there was no doctor's office, no blood test required to figure out why she'd missed two straight periods.

"Try and relax," Dr. Reed says. "Slow down your breathing."

Katie turns her head to the left and focuses on the framed photograph of the jagged Matterhorn, Dr. Reed's family of four circling its base, the youngest child holding his snowboard above his head. She can no longer behold a mountain range without thinking of Craig, especially when skis are involved. She can't help but recall the stink of popcorn and dirty socks in Craig's apartment on Mount Frost, the crummy black and white tile floor, the assortment of dismantled ski bindings. Resort posters from locales like Whistler and Bridger Bowl were sloppily taped over the grey cinder block walls. On his bedside table lay a book called *The Selfish Gene* and a couple of blue Skoal tins.

"You don't look pregnant" had been Craig's greeting when he answered the door.

"Nice to see you too," she'd replied.

Katie was just relieved to recognize him, to know she hadn't exaggerated his brawn. He wore a black fleece and carpenter's pants, a tan pair of Timberland boots. He didn't say hello, didn't look her in the eye, his undivided attention focused on her belly.

"It's still early," she said, placing a hand over her stomach.

Craig nodded, as if he didn't mean to imply she'd been lying. Once inside, he removed the filthy snowshoes from the couch cushions. "You can sit here if you want," he offered.

"Oh, I'd rather stand," she said. "I feel like I've been driving forever."

"Middleton's only two hours away."

"Yeah, but I drive like a grandma so it took me a while."

Katie bent over to touch her toes, but she could only reach the tops of her ankles. She'd felt so out of shape, so inflexible. What she needed was a massage, some barefoot Japanese girl to walk up and down her back.

"Do you wanna take off your coat?"

"No, I'm still cold," she said, hugging her arms together. "The heater in my car sucks."

"I can turn up the thermostat, if you want."

"No, that's okay. I actually can't stay too long. I have to work tonight."

His eyebrows lifted in surprise. "I thought you said you were off."

"There's a tourist bus coming in tonight from Montreal," she explained. "The bar's gonna be packed and I can't pass up the money."

"Do you want a beer?" he asked, opening the mini-fridge.

"God, yes," she exclaimed.

He handed her a can of Milwaukee's Best, then sat down on the edge of his bed, a single-sized mattress slab like one she had in college. His sheets were a dismal shade of yellow, his pillows flat and lifeless.

"You grew a beard," she said, brushing her own cheek. Katie cracked open the beer. After a few sips, her mood changed; in a flash she felt optimistic and open-minded.

"I remember your hair being more blonde."

"Nope," she said, "always brown." She didn't like the way he was studying her, the way he seemed to appraise her physique. Katie picked up the only picture on his desk, a framed eight-by-ten photograph of him standing next to a red helicopter with his skis. "Can I have another beer?" she continued.

"You haven't finished the first one."

"I like to plan ahead."

"Well, I guess you are drinking for two now."

"Cheers," she said.

When Craig tried to steer the conversation toward New Hampshire, toward "termination," she'd change the subject, preferring to ignore the occasion of her visit. Instead, Katie talked about the minutiae of her job, revealing how she despised the restaurant manager and the sous-chef, the way they treated servers like slaves. She told him how almost everyone partied on shift, that once they started seating tables she'd fill her coffee thermos with a frozen margarita. Katie didn't describe the agony of working with a hangover—the oppressive heat of the kitchen, dry heaving by the Dumpster, last night's booze seeping from her pores.

"As long as I'm not slinging drinks ten years from now," she continued, "I'll be happy."

"What do you do with your free time?" Craig asked.

Katie realized she hadn't skied since the weekend they met on Powderkeg, hadn't left her bedroom much unless drinks and dollars were involved. She'd become lazy in Vermont, complacent. "Hang out with friends, mostly," she finally said.

Katie watched as a burly guy in overalls walked by Craig's only window, dragging a keg of beer through the snow. Behind him, she could make out the chairlift rising over the distant treetops. It was pretty here. Quiet and slow.

"I have to be outside," Craig said. "If I were stuck in a bar, I'd go mental."

"I do go mental," she said, "but I don't think it's because I'm inside."

When Katie asked him what he did in the off-season, when the snow had melted, he explained there was round-the-clock work on a mountain. When she wondered what kind of work, he brushed off her question and asked timidly if he could touch her stomach.

"Are you serious?" she said.

"Yeah."

She suspected he'd been sitting on this question since her arrival. Katie felt herself blush as she clasped the base of her shirt.

"There's nothing there yet," she continued.

"Let me just try."

Katie stood up and sucked in, lifting her shirt just above the belly button. "Be my guest."

He reached out and lightly pressed the back of his hand to her navel. The hairs on his knuckles made her shiver. Katie tried not to laugh, but it tickled. She also felt silly having a stranger pay so much attention to her stomach.

"Your hands are cold," she shrieked.

"I think I felt it kick."

"Bullshit," she said. "All you felt was me digesting cheap beer." She tucked her shirt into her jeans.

"You have a nice stomach," he said shyly. He cracked open another beer, drank, then burped. "Do you ever feel it?"

"I just get crampy sometimes. Nauseous too."

Katie was disappointed the conversation so quickly switched back to the matter at hand; she wanted to hear more about her nice stomach and less about what was growing inside. After a fourth beer she kissed him. Even though she'd promised she wouldn't sleep with him again, Katie was buzzed enough to believe they could somehow screw their way to the right answer. It was easier than talking and she just wanted to close her eyes for a while. His questions made her uncomfortable. She had trouble conveying the change inside her body. Even the doctor in Middleton made her uneasy with his queries. To describe the feeling to a man seemed like wasted breath. Only the women at Planned Parenthood looked at her knowingly.

Craig had handled her aggressively. Twice she had to ask him to let up, to go a little easier. He looked as if he was trying to work something out, something personal, and this made for the loneliest sexual experience of her young life. With her eyes set on the snow bank outside the window, Katie wondered how she was different this time, if she resembled at all the woman he had in the Mogul Motel.

"How did that happen?" she asked afterward, tracing the smooth scar above his belly button.

"Dear old dad," Craig said, "crazy fucker stabbed me with a paint can opener."

"Why?"

"I stopped asking why years ago," he said. "I try not to show my father the respect of understanding him."

"Did it hurt?" she asked, pressing a washcloth to her groin.

He pulled up the sheets. "No one ever hit you?" he asked.

"My dad spanked us a few times," Katie said. "But that only made us laugh."

He leaned up on his elbow and propped his head against his fist. "So how come you didn't let me go from behind today?"

"Jesus," Katie said, covering her face with a pillow "You really have a way with segues."

"Just wondering."

"Sometimes I just don't like people behind me, that's all."

He reached for his water bottle. "Me neither."

She flipped over on her side and picked up a book by his bedside. She preferred fiction, short stories especially, authors like Alice Munro and Raymond Carver. Her favorite was Andre Dubus, who actually lived in Haverhill where she grew up. Craig said he never heard of any of those writers, informing her he was only reading *The Selfish Gene* because it blew his mind when he was high. When he passed her a joint, Katie declined, admitting that she already felt guilty for drinking. He took another hit and held it. She could hear his breath wheeze.

"You should have a baby if you want," he stated, fighting to keep the smoke inside.

"Did this come to you before or after you lit that joint?"

"I think you want to," he added, exhaling a cloud over their heads.

"You think so?"

"You're pregnant," he declared.

"And your point?" She sat up Indian-style, the heels of her feet cold against her thighs.

"When you think about it biologically, the decision has been made. Why stop what's already happening?"

"Because I'm the one who has to carry it for nine months!"

"It could be a fix," he explained.

"A fix?"

"Yeah, a remedy. A solution."

"Are you shitting me?" She slapped him across the face with a pillow. "You want to change diapers and sing lullabies? No offense, but you don't strike me as the type."

"I guess I'm just curious."

"You don't have a baby simply because you're curious."

"Really?" he said emphatically. "What for, otherwise?"

Katie pulled the sheets over her eyes. She wanted to cry, but not in front of him. It would only aggravate her if he tried to console her. "You know, when I picture myself driving back from that New Hampshire clinic, I panic. That drive has the potential to really do me in."

"We just need to be thoughtful," he said softly.

Katie shot out of bed before he could touch her, before he could make any more sense. She wrapped herself in the grungy blue towel hanging from the bedpost. Just as she expected, the terry cloth smelled like mildew, but the room was too bright to prance around in naked.

"Can I use your shower?" she asked. "I don't wanna reek of sex when I get to work."

"Sure," he said, picking pensively at his scar.

When she opened his bathroom door, Katie was distraught to see there was no shower curtain. White calcium deposits stained the shower nozzle. How could she sleep with a man who didn't bother with a shower curtain? How could she bear the child of such a slob? Inside the medicine cabinet, she was surprised to find a fresh bar of Irish Spring, a more attractive option than the hair-encrusted sliver of soap smeared atop the drain. There was not one bottle of shampoo, not even an empty. As she waited for the water to warm, Katie crafted a paper nest and sat on the toilet, not letting her bare feet touch the tiles. She was sick she'd tasted this man, disturbed that she'd licked the skin of a body that bathed here.

Craig knocked on the door. "You want company?"

"I'm going to the bathroom," she said. "Please go away."

Sitting on his toilet, Katie imagined how drastically different this story would have unfolded had she contacted her father or sister before Craig. She'd convinced herself they were cold-hearted brutes, that she needed sensitivity before sensibility, a level of humanity beyond their grasp. For certain, they would have driven her to New Hampshire on the spot, trapped her in the trunk if necessary. And not for a second had Katie considered how they might have helped her, spared her the torment of where she found herself now.

CHAPTER 21

The enormous black Lincoln Navigator parked in front of the fire hydrant has Caroline written all over it. With the engine running brazenly, Katie wonders how long Caroline has been polluting their green-conscious neighborhood. Behind those tinted windows, she imagines her sister's already set up a functional home office. Katie opens the mailbox and digs out a coupon circular and a flyer for an upcoming exhibition at the Lovett Gallery on Stony Neck, where once upon a time she showcased her work. Underneath Walter's latest issue of *Poets and Writers*, a subscription she'd sentimentally renewed, Katie locates C.J.'s postcard from Santa Fe—a crowd of turquoise-mad tourists gathered on the adobe plaza for Indian Market, "the world's most prestigious Native American arts show." On the flip side she sees only her name and address written in pencil, the *t* in *Katie* missing its cross.

The rear window rolls down and Katie recognizes her sister's pale hand waving in the air. "Katie," she calls.

"You're parked illegally," Katie shouts.

As she approaches the car, the gallery flyer takes off into the wind. Katie manages to step on it before it lands in the sewer grate, then picks it up and shoves it into her back pocket with C.J.'s postcard. On tiptoes, she pulls the orange parking ticket from beneath the Navigator's windshield wiper. She can now hear Caroline on the phone. "I'll have to call you later, Bilal," she says. "Just email me the proposal, but spare me the animation this time. All I want to see are numbers." The back door opens and Caroline steps cautiously out of the car, quite a distance to the ground for a woman of five feet four, black Liz Claiborne heels notwithstanding.

"Kaitlin!" she says, opening her arms.

Katie hands Caroline the orange ticket. "A half mile of open street parking and you choose the spot in front of the hydrant."

"Is there a hydrant here?" Caroline says, crumpling up the ticket. "I hadn't noticed. I can barely see over the goddam steering wheel."

Katie crosses her arms and glares at the car. "What's with this monstrosity?"

"All they had left at the rental place was this or some Lexus hybrid," she says, wrinkling her nose, "and I don't know how to work a car that runs on corn on the cob."

"Why can't you rent a Taurus like everybody else?"

Katie keeps her arms crossed as Caroline gives her a quick embrace. Had her sister held the moment longer, Katie would have likely surrendered and hugged her back. "I see you're still driving Dad's old Volvo," Caroline continues. "God, does it still smell like furniture polish?"

"More like hockey equipment."

Caroline grabs her purse from the floor of the backseat. A plethora of lights and switches gleam from inside the car. As Caroline bends over, Katie recognizes her own ass beneath the beige dress pants. From inside, Caroline reaches into the front seat and turns off the ignition. "So, shall we go in?" Caroline says, collecting a Marc Jacobs handbag.

"When did you cut your hair?"

"About a year ago," Caroline says, fluffing the back with her hand. As usual, her sister looks smart and professional, no-nonsense pretty. Never has she worn jewelry of any kind, not even earrings. "The bigger the diamond, the lower the girl," she'd once explained, referring to their cousin Jackie's engagement ring. Caroline's makeup is conservative and complimentary, seldom flashy. And while they share a strong resemblance, neither could pull off the other's look. Both women would be lost in each other's clothes.

"You look like Posh Spice," Katie says.

"Who?"

"Never mind."

"So can we go inside or what?" she asks, eyeing her sister teasingly. "Or are you hiding a man in there?"

"In a minute," Katie says. "I like the sun right now."

The skin under Caroline's eyes is suspiciously smooth, Botox stamped all over her glossy white forehead. Katie bets she has ten pounds over her older sister, which makes her feel dumpy in her jeans and sneakers, her Supercuts hairdo. Even though she's three inches taller, Katie feels the need to be slimmer than her sister, to at least top her physically.

"Well, you look healthy," Caroline says, lighting a cigarette.

"What's that supposed to mean?"

"It's a compliment. You were too skinny last I saw you." Caroline passes the pack of Dunhills to her sister.

"No," Katie says, pushing her hand away. "I'm trying to quit."

Caroline exhales a billowy cloud of smoke. "Good for you."

"So what are you doing here, Caroline?"

"What am I doing here? You've been hanging up on me every time I call. First I get a message from my assistant, Renée, telling me Walter died. Then I call C.J. for his birthday to find out just how he died. I didn't even know Walter was living here. To tell you the truth, I thought he was already dead. I hadn't seen the man in twenty years. And then I hear about C.J.'s father. What's his name?"

"Craig," Katie says.

"Yes, Craig. That's a lot of death for you two to deal with all alone."

"I just got a postcard from New Mexico," Katie says, shoving it in her sister's face. "Your nephew is on a motorcycle walkabout because of you."

"Because of me?" she asks, examining the postcard. "What happened?"

"You were the last one he talked to," she says.

"You think I told him to go off and play *Easy Rider*?"

"All I know is my son is riding a Harley-Davidson through the desert with no license and no insurance."

"Christ, where did he learn how to ride a motorcycle?"

Katie grit her teeth. "I let him take a riding class."

"Are you nuts?"

"Getting in his way only gets me knocked over," Katie says. "And stop with the judgmental tone. You don't have kids. You don't have any idea."

"God," Caroline says, touching Katie's cheek, "You are so alone. I can see Mom in your eyes."

A train whistle shrieks in the distance. Caroline flicks her cigarette into the wind. Katie can see traces of her peach-colored lipstick on the filter as it burns into the grass. She turns away and concentrates on the dark stretch of ocean between the red and green harbor buoys. She watches as the new sandbar rises under the sinking tide. Beyond the breakwater, she can see the tips of the Gunnerside drawbridge. A line of cars waits for the group of fishing boats to pass as jet skiers jump over their wake. Fathers and sons fish off Jacoby Pier, the same spot where C.J. spent many summer afternoons with a line of twine tied around his index finger, his body hanging over the side of the dock waiting for his bobber to plunge. Katie would watch him from the widow's walk, her son a lone silhouette against the horizon.

Caroline reaches into her purse and retrieves a pack of mints. She pops a handful into her mouth and chomps. "We're the product of two lonely parents," she says, suddenly refreshed. "We can't help but breed solitude."

"What the hell does that mean?"

Caroline's phone rings. "Shit, I have to take that," she says, rushing toward the car. "Just give me five minutes."

Katie waves her away, her mind stuck on solitude and how she breeds it, according to Caroline. With a Kleenex, she retrieves her sister's cigarette butt from the grass. *We breed solitude* was a cheap shot in disguise, an accusation, her way of implying that Katie drove C.J. off the property. Caroline's words can be loaded, heavy with double entendres, lingering long after they're spoken. She's always been able to get under Katie's skin without leaving a scar.

Three years ago when she came to Newquay it was no different, Caroline softening up her sister with quick jabs, tiny strikes here and there, preludes to the inevitable uppercut. She remembers C.J.'s math homework, when Caroline showed him how to solve word problems in algebra. "I used to do this for your mother too," Caroline had explained, brushing her son's bangs from his eyes. "She was never very good with the practical subjects." The gesture startled Katie, the way Caroline gently caressed her son's hair, his forehead, the dubious delicacy of her touch. When they were children, Caroline did reveal a softer side with their dog, Stanley, the sole recipient of her adoration; but with family, she'd been deliberately aloof.

Caroline had also presented C.J. with an answer key covering the second half of his math textbook—twenty pages of Excel spreadsheets—which made her an instant hero. Katie didn't intervene, leery of debating Caroline in front of C.J., deciding it would be best to wait until her sister was gone to explain why it wasn't right to cheat. Of course, Katie remembers the politics too, Caroline's rants about "limousine liberals" and "left wing loons." Katie loathed the topic, despised the way Caroline made her feel misinformed and stupid. "Don't let them fool you, C.J.," Caroline warned him, pointing at Dan Rather as he reported the evening news. "Most of them have money, yet they hate the rich. In their mind it's a crime to make a buck."

"I don't hate the rich," Katie called from the kitchen, draining a load of al dente elbow noodles into a strainer.

"Then why did you vote for Nader?"

"Because I like what he has to say."

"Really, Katie, you have to stop basing your political views on Michael Moore films."

"We're going to eat soon," she said, biting her tongue as she ran cold water over the pasta. "Go wash up, C.J."

In private, in his room before bed, Katie asked C.J. if he liked his aunt.

"It's nice having someone else here," he answered.

"It is nice," Katie agreed. "It's a big house for just us."

"But she's kind of weird," C.J. continued. "Like sometimes I don't know what she's talking about."

"Me either."

"I don't think she liked the giraffe painting I gave her," he said.

Katie stiffened—she would have sat on hot coals for such a gift. "She said that?"

"No, I could just tell."

"Well, I love your giraffe," Katie said. "It's exquisite and shows a lot of promise. Believe me, Caroline has no clue about good art."

"You guys don't seem like sisters."

"Why not?" Katie asked, curious about a young boy's evaluation.

"You just don't," he said.

"Try and be specific," she encouraged. "What seems different to you?"

"Did you play together when you were little?"

"She's three years older," Katie rationalized, tucking the covers around his body. "That's a major gap when you're growing up."

"So you didn't play with each other?"

"Not really," Katie admitted. "Caroline was a very busy little girl."

"You kind of look alike, but you're prettier."

She kissed his forehead. "Thank you."

He turned over on his left side, bunching the pillow into a ball. She switched off his lamp. "I wish I knew you when you were little," he said.

Sitting in the dark of C.J.'s room, touched by his parting words, Katie realized she'd been hurt by the tenderness Caroline displayed toward her son. She was surprised and disappointed to discover how jealous she was of the attention her sister showered on him. Never had Katie received a fraction's worth of that same affection when she was a child. God, she'd even left the studio door wide open, all but inviting Caroline to pop inside and admire her paintings, but she never entered, hadn't once asked to see the work that consumed her little sister. Instantly, Katie was convinced that Caroline flew all the way to Newquay now just to make her feel small, to kick her while she was down.

That night after C.J. drifted off, Katie had opened the forbidden cabinet above the refrigerator, twisting open the cap of Grand Marnier she'd fought so hard to keep sealed during Caroline's visit. For a week she'd struggled to remain sober, to keep the drinking polite and social, to avoid the exact situation she was about to find herself in.

Katie had kicked open her sister's bedroom door, splintering the wood across the jamb. "Who do you think you are?" she'd roared, tearing the blankets off Caroline.

"What are you doing?" Caroline shrieked, reaching blindly for sheets. "Have you finally lost it?"

Katie pulled the feeble wicker chair towards Caroline's bedside and sat down. The clock said three A.M. A fan was cranking beside the bed. "We're going to get this out in the open, tonight," she said, poking her sister.

Caroline sat up and calmly located her glasses on the nightstand. "You smell like a bar," she said, squinting through the dirty lenses. "I'd rather not have a discussion while you're drunk."

"It's the smell of labor," Katie said. "You're not the only one who works hard."

"Oh, Katie," she said, laughing, "you're so dramatic."

"You will not belittle me in front of my son," Katie continued. "You'll show me respect in my house."

"You mean our father's house."

"I pay the mortgage," Katie snapped.

"You pay the property taxes."

"Which are higher than many people's salaries."

"Yours included," Caroline quipped.

"You know what you are, Caroline?" she whispered. "You're dead. There's no life inside you."

"And you're a child."

"Dead cunt," Katie said, twirling a finger in Caroline's face. "What's it like being in bed with you? I bet it's like being with a corpse."

Caroline's face blanched. "Look, C.J. and I are going to New York tomorrow for the weekend. Then I plan on leaving for California on Tuesday. You and I will hardly see each other until I go, which makes all this moot."

"I won't let you deny my feelings," Katie said. "I won't let you be the dictator."

"Even if we solved all our differences right now, you wouldn't remember anyway. I can see the blackout in your eyes."

"Why do you hate me?"

"Oh, Katie, this talk is so tiresome," she said, rubbing her forehead. "Just call me when you land."

Katie slapped her sister's face, the crisp sound of a clap. As Caroline's glasses fell to the ground, Katie's pink handprint swelled over her sister's cheek. She actually wanted to hit her again, but decided instead to step on Caroline's glasses, crunching them into the ground.

Right away, Katie picked up the spectacles and clumsily tried to repair them. When Caroline finally took them from her sweaty hand, Katie was plagued by remorse. For a fleeting moment, her sister looked frail and Katie felt terribly sober.

"Jesus, I'm sorry," Katie said, defeated. "That wasn't right."

"You poor thing," Caroline said softly. "You're confused is all."

Only her sister, Katie thought, could maintain such poise after being shaken awake, slapped in the face, and deprived of reading the *Wall Street Journal*'s tiny print.

"I'm not confused," Katie replied.

"You really should see someone, Katie. You have far too much anger."

"I have seen someone," she groaned. "They want to put me on Prozac. Mom's medicine cabinet didn't solve anything, and I'm not one of those spoiled brats who cries when the sun's not out."

"A father in the house would help."

"Help how?"

"Help calm you," Caroline said. "You're obviously beaten down. You just assaulted me, for Christ's sake. And C.J. tells me you return home like this after work quite often. A strong man would keep you both in line."

"Craig was a strong man," Katie said.

"Does it take strength to abandon a wife and child?"

"Actually, it does."

With this confession—instead of getting up and slamming the door like she'd planned—Katie crawled into bed with Caroline, resting her head on her bony shoulder. As she spoke about Craig, about Craig and C.J. together, Caroline rubbed her sister's back, encouraging her to talk.

"I'm proud of you," Caroline said afterward. "You were right to say he should leave. But you should have learned of his skeletons before bearing this man's child."

"Look, he knows his father left. I really don't think he cares why anymore."

"Well, I wouldn't let it go."

"Well, you're not me," she said. "Please, please, please don't make me regret confiding in you."

Katie removed her socks and curled into a ball, pulling the covers snug over both of them. Suddenly the promise of sleep seemed possible.

"You really should go downstairs now," Caroline whispered, nudging her sister away.

"Please can I sleep here? If I move right now, I'll die."

"I don't rest well unless I'm alone," Caroline said. "Besides, you'll want to wash up before passing out or else tomorrow morning will be even worse."

"You're brutal," Katie said.

The very next afternoon, Katie woke up with a spike in her brain. The second her eyes opened she wanted to cry. Her mouth tasted like rotten fruit. Katie wasn't sorry she hit her sister, not at all. What she regretted mightily was how she'd let her guard down.

In the kitchen, Caroline had left the phone number for a boutique hotel in Tribeca. She also jotted down the phone number for a Dr. Marvin Monroe in San Francisco: "Marvin lives in my building. Call him, he can help." Katie crumpled up the note and threw it into the sink.

THE GIGANTIC Navigator door slams shut, rousing Katie. "Sorry," Caroline says, "that call was from Korea and had to be dealt with before sunrise." She approaches Katie and fans a hand over her eyes. "What are you staring at, moon girl?"

Katie considers bringing up the chaos of Caroline's last visit—one more opportunity to validate her rampage, to rationalize her late night attack—but she instead points west. "Check out that sandbar," she says. "It wasn't there a year ago."

Caroline visors her eyes. "I can't see anything but waves."

"The hurricane that hit Florida made that," Katie continues. "The sandbar's part of the aftermath."

"So what?"

"So it's a new part of our landscape," she says. "A reverberation from the storm."

"You have better vision than me," Caroline concedes. "All those years zoning out in front of the ocean has made you keen."

"I think it's interesting. We rarely live long enough to witness geological change."

"Look, no offense, but I didn't come all the way out here to fawn over a sandbox."

"Sandbar," Katie corrects.

"Same difference."

Katie picks up the smaller of Caroline's two bags and slings it over her shoulder. "Jesus, what's in here?"

"Work stuff," Caroline says.

"Well, how long do you plan on staying?"

"A few nights. I'm actually lucky to be here at all," she says, "considering the miserable business climate in California right now."

Her sister walks like she owns the sidewalk, sure about where she stands. As Caroline moves ahead, Katie hopes she displays that same level of confidence.

When they reach the house, Katie searches her crowded pockets for the house keys. Once she unlocks the door, Caroline charges past her into the house—it's obviously imperative that she enter first. Katie kicks her bag into the kitchen.

"You can have the third floor bed," Katie says.

"James and Martha's room again?"

"Walter had it last," she said. "You can sleep down here if you want, but the couch is covered in cat hair."

"Oh, no, I'm sure the psych ward will be fine."

"You'll have to make up the bed," Katie says, instantly exhausted. A half-hour with her sister and she's already whipped. "You know where the linens are."

Caroline surveys the house with a sneer. "Is there a fan up there?" she asks. "I can't sleep without white noise."

"No, but there's a cuckoo clock," Katie says, heading toward the sanctuary of her studio. "It makes noise in all colors."

Once inside, she'll drop to her knees and pray, the door locked behind her so Caroline won't catch her in the act. Hands in a steeple, she'll speak out loud, the tone of her voice weak and unfamiliar in the hollow room. Sometimes she'll even cross herself and whisper *amen*. On the floor she'll feel like an idiot and a phony, but what's important is the ceremony, the state of quiet where she can face her fear, knowing that beyond these walls she's a liar, a coward with her fists cocked. And although she doesn't call him God, Katie is asking someone for help, anyone who will listen—Walter, her mother, her father, Craig—whoever and whatever has the power to lure C.J. home.

CHAPTER 22

From the complimentary slippers to the totem pole coatrack, almost everything about their room at the Summit Lodge had been charming and kitschy, the epitome of country cozy; but Katie couldn't forget for a minute that she was one hundred miles away from her son. Even the bright half-moon in the sky seemed closer than home. Since sundown, she'd been grinding her teeth as if she'd been snorting coke, the filial separation increasing her irritability. Katie resented Craig for bringing her here, for convincing her she needed an evening away from Calvin. For starters, she was certain the babysitter would ignore her detailed ointment instructions—the Desitin for diaper rash, the Vaseline for the eczema, the cortisone for his itchy ankles. Then there was the Tylenol for teething, Benadryl for his restlessness. Lately, she'd been distressed by the condition of his face—the patchy, chapped skin around his lips and chin, the way he rubbed his mouth frantically against his mattress. The pediatrician assured her it would all pass in time, that he was just going through a "rough stretch," laughing it off when Katie suggested that her son's compulsion to scratch was likely genetic.

"Elk stay in single sex groups most of the time," Craig read aloud from a glossy hotel catalog. "And their mating season is called a rut."

"I can relate," Katie said.

"Ha, ha."

A stuffed moose head hung on the wood paneled wall above Craig's head, its black marble eyes watching as Craig sprinkled pot onto a rolling paper. Katie reclined on the soft queen-sized bed and tried to relax by counting all the sappy pine needles that were stuck to the ceiling. Even though it was sixty degrees outside, the kiva fireplace in front of her feet roared, the snapping sound of burning logs reminding her of winter. With his thick legs hidden underneath a canoe-shaped coffee table, Craig thumbed through the brochures for elk hunting trips and water rafting excursions. He pulled on the wooly hairs of the faux bearskin rug as he read, the joint packed and ready, tucked behind his ear.

"The first time I saw elk was in Wyoming," Craig said, lighting the joint. "Yellowstone." Katie counted seven pine needles before she heard him exhale. He held out the joint, but she waved off the invitation.

"You look exhausted," she told him.

"We've been setting up mountain bike trails at work," he said, massaging the bags beneath his eyes. "It does a number on you."

The sweet smell of pot reached her nostrils. Good God, she wanted to let loose, but more than a year had passed since Katie took a hit and she didn't want to risk a major unraveling. She picked up the phone to make sure it was still working. "It's weird not having Calvin around me," she said.

"You said that already."

"Well, I can't get used to it."

"Do you wanna go back?"

"It's too late," she said, twisting open a bottle of red wine. "We're already here."

Craig let the joint burn in the ashtray as he lumbered toward the sink and filled an empty beer can with water. He drank it down. "You told me you liked the babysitter, right?"

"She did have a ton of references," Katie conceded. "What's crazy is I keep hearing him cry. Phantom cries." She sipped from her glass. The acidity of the wine aggravated her tongue. "God, I'm totally not used to alcohol."

"That's funny," he said. "You used to polish off a six-pack with ease. A bottle of wine, no problem."

"Yeah, I was quite the elegant lady back then."

"Moderation is good," he said. "I admire it."

"I guess it beats throwing up first thing in the morning."

Craig took the buck knife from his pocket and scraped the hardened candle wax from the tabletop. "You've done it."

"Done what?"

"You've become a mother," he said.

"We'll see."

"No, seriously," he continued. "I don't have to worry about him with you."

"Probably not," Katie said, impatient with the conversation. No way did she want to spend the entire night dwelling on their decision. She'd been set on discussing trivial matters like what was on TV, what flavor of Ben and Jerry's they'd devour in bed. Just for a night she needed to be spared the angst of her misgivings. There was no reason to ruminate over the impending trials of single motherhood, her son growing up without a father, dealing with a broken home, etc. The script had already been written: Craig was heading west—Wyoming or Montana, maybe California. Katie and Calvin were moving one state south to Massachusetts. It was for the best, they'd agreed. Best for Calvin. All that mattered to Katie was action, to hit the highway running, to see Middleton, Vermont and the man across the room shrinking in her rearview mirror.

Craig drank from his Coors can and burped. "I don't want to have sex," he announced.

"Who said we have to?"

"I just want to make it clear."

Katie kicked off her socks and let her feet breathe. She threw the one with a hole in the heel into the fireplace and watched it burn. "This isn't a movie where the parting couple has to screw one last time."

He opened the bag of deer jerky they bought from a pushcart outside the lodge. Katie could smell the hickory seasoning. "It's too salty," he said, frowning.

"Should we go see a movie tonight?"

"I doubt there's a cinema around here."

"We can go out and eat somewhere," she said, opening a very thin phone book. "We can splurge for once."

Craig picked up the joint and inhaled. "I saw you giving him a bath last night."

"There's an Italian place in Kettle," she said. "That's about ten miles from here. Should I call them?"

"Are you listening to me?"

Katie finished her wine and poured a half-glass. Bottle in hand, she paused, considering the consequence of more. Quickly concluding *fuck it*, she filled it to the rim. "I need to know if you want me to call this place or not," she said, frustrated. "They might close early in these parts."

"I'm trying to tell you something important."

"Well, I'm not going to eat deer jerky for dinner."

"Why aren't you listening to me?"

"Because you're stoned."

"So what?"

"So now it's going to get weird," she said. "We promised we weren't going to be all dramatic tonight."

"I know, but what I want to tell you is for Calvin. Not me and you."

"Christ," she said, opening a small bag of Funyuns. "At least put down the joint for both our sakes."

He placed the joint in the ashtray and with a wet finger extinguished the burning tip. "Can I at least have my beer?" he asked, taking a sip.

"You know what you're doing isn't partying."

"I know, I'm self-medicating, as you call it," he said.

"Well, it's true," she said. "You should be careful."

"Wait ten years and see where you are before pointing fingers at me."

Katie tucked her knees up. "So you saw me giving Calvin a bath, so what?"

"So I hadn't been around for that before. Sure, I've done a few feedings and changed some diapers, but never any baths."

"You've done three diapers max," she said. "And why are you surprised? You're always gone at Mount Frost, or somewhere else, anyway."

"Sunday was my bath night when I was little," Craig said. "It was my dad's job."

Katie picked up the hotel copy of *Bowhunter* from the bedside table. She didn't like the way hunters sat on top of their kill and pulled on the dead animal's antlers. "My mom bathed us," she said, flipping the page.

"That's why he locked the door," Craig said. "He knew it was wrong."

"What do you mean?"

"That final click of a door locking," he said, snapping his fingers.

She dropped *Bowhunter* and reached for the lodge notebook. "I guess we can order room service," she concluded. "All I need are cheese sticks."

Craig shot up, swiped the notebook from her lap and Frisbee'd it into the fireplace. Towering above her, his body blocked all the light. "I really need you to listen, Katie," he said, squeezing her hand.

She could hear the pages of the notebook catching fire. "I am listening."

"This is important."

"Okay," she said. "Calm down."

She tried to twist her hand free, but her wrist was clamped between his grubby fingers. "Cut it out," she shrieked. "You're hurting me."

"When Calvin grows up and wonders what kind of father leaves his child, I want you to be able to explain it right."

"I will," she pleaded. "I can."

"Tell me you'll listen."

"I'll listen, I'll listen, I'll listen!"

He released her.

"Jesus," she said, opening and closing her hand. "I didn't know you were a wife beater."

"I didn't hit you."

"Close enough in my book."

"Sorry," he said, "it just didn't seem like you were paying attention."

"Well, I am now."

He went back to the canoe table and picked up the joint. She didn't bother to stop him. "He had greasy trucker knuckles, my father," Craig said, lighting up. "I remember his hands splashing around me in the bathtub water, my blue tugboat tipping over in the wake."

"What was he doing?"

"He wouldn't talk when it was happening," Craig said. "That was the worst. I wish he would have turned on the fan or ran the faucet, something to cover up that awful sound."

Katie gulped down her wine. "That's terrible," she said.

"I would just shut down," Craig said. "I'd disappear."

Katie sat up, nauseous and lightheaded. "God, how old were you?"

"Young," he said

Katie lit a cigarette. "Why didn't you shout for your mother?"

"I remember I didn't want to get him in trouble."

"How many times did this happen?"

"A few."

"How could your mother not know?"

"I think she knew, but found a way to pretend otherwise. Like him, she was a drunk. Like him, she could forget. Anyway, after my bath, I'd take off," Craig said. "It'd be dark, but I knew the woods by our house pretty well. Sometimes I'd stay out until school the next morning."

"Didn't your mother worry about where you were?"

"Look, I don't know what the fuck my mother was doing, Katie," he said. "Believe me, she wasn't spared his attention either."

Katie put the cigarette out. "You weren't scared in the woods all night?" she asked.

"I don't get scared outside," he mused. "I never feel alone in the woods. Out there, I can hear the earth breathing." Craig pried himself from the canoe table, his knees creaking as he rose. "They say you're supposed to feel better when you talk it out, but I feel like shit."

"I told you not to smoke up," she said. "This always happens to you. Why did you wait until now to tell me this? Nine months after our son is born."

"I didn't think it would matter before. I was delusional enough to believe that having this kid, marrying you, living a normal life might absolve the past."

"And yet it hasn't."

Eyes closed, Craig nodded. "It's only made everything more apparent, more present. Right here, right now."

Katie had tried to skirt the next question—it wasn't her intention to shame and embarrass him—but she needed to know. "Do you think you might be like your father?"

"Shit, no!" he yelled, kicking an empty beer can across the room. "Christ almighty."

She held up her arms in surrender. "Okay, sorry," she said. "I guess I just don't understand."

Craig lifted the shade and cranked opened the window. A handful of moths scattered from the sill. Katie could hear the coyotes howling through the hills. "I don't know what will come over me in five or ten years," he said, staring outside. "Maybe nothing, but who knows? If my dad had the option to be normal or the sick fuck he was, he would have picked normal. But people like him can't see a choice, and that's the problem. I'm not asking for your pity or your counseling. I'm not even asking you to understand. I'm telling you this because I don't want Calvin thinking I left because I couldn't love him. He needs to know there was more at stake. And it will be up to you to tell him that."

"That'll be a fun day," she said, topping off her wine glass. Katie looked past him, out the window. "I feel guilty," she admitted.

"Why do you feel guilty?"

"Because right now I'm not thinking about how your dad ruined you. All I can see is Calvin," she continued, "and what could happen to him."

"And that's all I want you to see," he said.

Music began to play from the lounge across the hallway. She could make out a cover of the Grateful Dead's "One More Saturday Night." Katie took the joint from the ashtray and breathed in the smoke until it reached her toes. "Hello, old friend," she said, exhaling, reaching for a beer.

"Now we're partying," Craig said lamely, clicking cans.

"Cheers," she replied.

WHAT A scoundrel, her father would say a few weeks later.

I told you Vermont was flake central, Caroline followed.

Is there another woman? her father asked.

Now you're stuck for at least eighteen years, Caroline added.

Katie longed to explain about Craig, but she knew people like her father and sister wouldn't care to hear that it was the so-called scoundrels who suffered most.

CHAPTER 23

Along with a couple of crushed Alka-Seltzer tablets, Katie finds her ringing cell phone deep inside the pillowcase beneath her head. She uncoils the bedsheets from her body and lets Peter's call fade into voice mail. For once her hair doesn't reek of cigarettes, but her hands smell like the garlic and clam pizza they ordered last night from Sorrento's. Her T-shirt is damp with sweat, sticking to her back as she tears it from her body. Katie had wanted to bring the air conditioner in from the shed, but it was too heavy for a couple of drunken women to carry alone. And while she has no real memory of going to bed last night, Katie does remember a dream where she tumbled off the widow's walk after the railing collapsed. It was nothing new for her to be free falling in her sleep, but this was the first time she didn't wake up before hitting the ground.

In the bathroom, she grabs the dirty bar apron rolled up behind the hamper. As Katie shakes out the pockets, she regrets having called Megan last night begging for work, drunk and desperate for a shift. Old drink order tickets and beer bottle caps drop into the bathtub, bar residue from ten days ago at the restaurant, the afternoon C.J. started west. A week and a half without her child and the world insisted on spinning. In the mirror, Katie confronts her face, the lines across her forehead, the wrinkles that are deepest and especially prominent after a gluttonous evening. Disgusted by her disheveled appearance,

Katie kills the lights and runs the faucet, dunking her face under the cold blast until her cheeks turn numb.

She still can't believe that Caroline matched her glass for glass through three bottles of Barolo until she threw up in the cat box and surrendered. After a few drinks, Caroline had come unglued, turning uncharacteristically approachable, engaging, and—most astonishingly—fun.

"Let's go out!" Caroline shouted, digging her finger into the hardened cheese on the bottom of the pizza box.

"I'm putting you to bed," Katie said, removing a strand of mozzarella from Caroline's mouth. "You're not cut out for this. Plus, there's a cop out there dying to bust me."

Never had Katie witnessed her sister drink to the point of vulnerability, not even at her parents' funerals where there was an open bar. Displaying the effects of intoxication went against Caroline's code of personal conduct, yet last night she consumed with vigor, as if being around Katie gave her permission to be reckless. Forever the recipient of her sister's wrath, Katie feared the price she'd pay for Caroline's indulgence, the blame that would most certainly land at her feet. So as Caroline crumbled, Katie took great care to nurse her sister, doing what she could to soften the inevitable hangover. Regardless of the aftermath, Katie felt the party was worth any potential repercussions—she was grateful for the company, pleased to witness someone else's decline. Most of all, playing caretaker helped her forget that C.J. was not upstairs.

Once Caroline tripped over the cat, the sisters determined it would be safer for her to crawl rather than walk up the stairs. Katie followed behind, spotting her like a gym coach. When Caroline stopped on the first landing for a break, she knocked on C.J.'s door.

"Don't do that," Katie warned, yanking Caroline's hand away.

"Let me just stay in there," she pleaded. "I don't think I can make it another flight."

Katie slapped her sister on the butt. "Just keep crawling."

The succulents on the windowsill in Walter's bathroom were all dying. A collection of yellow leaves were scattered over the bathmat. Katie filled the basin with warm water, and with a washcloth she began to scrub away what was left of Caroline's foundation. She shoved Caroline's head under the faucet and held it there until all the suds washed down the drain. It occurred to Katie she was enjoying her new role, taking great pleasure as she pushed her sister around.

"I don't take pills," Caroline moaned when Katie forced two Advil gelcaps into her mouth.

"Tonight you do. Drink all of this," she instructed. "Then drink another. And one more after that."

She helped Caroline finagle out of her tight Dolce & Gabbana pants. Tomato sauce and cat hair coated the fabric. Caroline brusquely removed her top and chucked it across the room, the shoulder of her blouse catching the ceiling fan.

"Do you want to borrow some pajamas?" Katie asked.

"Nope," Caroline said, unabashedly kicking off her panties. "I sleep à la carte." She fell back onto the bed with a hefty, creaking thud. Katie tossed her great uncle's green army blanket over Caroline's tiny, naked body. Her sister turned over, her back to Katie.

"Is that one of yours?" Caroline asked, pointing to the painting by the mirror.

Katie had all but forgotten about that painting, had somehow stopped seeing it every time she came into Walter's room. It was unsettling for her to look at her work after it was done, disconcerting because time revealed the flaws, the same way photos of herself twenty years ago with feathered hair, blue eye shadow, and off-the-shoulder blouses made her cringe. But this time Katie didn't turn away from the colors she'd chosen, the style she had chased. What she found instead was a piece of art far more striking two years after she signed *KO* on the bottom right corner of the canvas.

"Who are the women?" Caroline continued.

Katie crossed her arms and considered her subjects. "No one you know," she said.

"Is it us?"

"There're three of them and we're not bald."

"Sensually, it feels like us."

"You sound like a critic," Kate responded, surprised by Caroline's language. "Plus, their faces are blank. They resemble no one."

"One could be Mom," Caroline offered. "You, me, and Mom. That would make three."

"Interesting interpretation." Katie unclasped her sister's gigantic watch and placed it on the nightstand. "It's inspired by Canova's sculpture, *The Three Graces*. Look it up on Google."

"Are they all holding each other because they're scared?"

Katie was both put off and enchanted by Caroline's curiosity. In that instant she missed her sister, missed her because this moment would soon end, never to return. "C.J. actually thinks it's because they're happy," Katie said, "but I call it solidarity."

"I like the wrinkled pink gowns, the way you made it appear like there's wind blowing on them."

"Four thousand dollars and it can be yours."

"You know, you should paint me," Caroline said. "I've always reminded myself of a young Rita Hayworth." She yawned and curled into a tiny ball. "I couldn't paint a fucking fence."

Katie switched off the lamp. "I left a trash can by your bedside."

"I'm spinning like a dreidel," Caroline groaned.

Katie tiptoed toward the door, hoping for a clean break. "Hold tight to the headboard."

"God," Caroline said, "I can't believe you're knocked up again."

"Just pass out already!" Katie ordered.

Caroline sneezed. "What if I die in my sleep?"

"Then you'll be spared a wretched hangover."

"Stay here until I fall asleep."

She kissed her sister's forehead; her hair smelled of Dunhills. "You'll be fine, sweetie."

Quickly, before Caroline could utter another word, Katie made her exit and shut the door.

"Katie!" Caroline called. "Katie!"

"Count sheep!" Katie yelled from the stairwell.

She stopped before C.J.'s door and took a breath. Katie turned the knob, but wouldn't allow herself to open the door and go inside. As if C.J. were watching from afar, she was dead set on keeping his room sacred and untouched.

"Katie!" Caroline called again.

Downstairs, Katie poured a fresh glass of Barolo.

CHAPTER 24

The stench of vomit greets her as she enters Walter's room.

"Good morning," Katie whispers. She turns on the lamp. The walls turns golden. "Caroline?"

From underneath the covers, her sister grunts.

"Are you all right?" she says, gently tapping the lump beneath the sheets.

Caroline slowly pushes the pillows from her head, evidently an exhausting activity. Her face is the color of chalk. "I don't remember going to bed," she mumbles, her voice grainy and feeble.

"I tucked you in."

"In fact," Caroline says, raising an index finger to stress the point, "I don't remember before going to bed either."

"Welcome to my world," Katie says. "Do you want something to eat?"

Caroline frowns. "No, no food."

"How about an Emergen-C? That might help."

Carefully, deliberately, Caroline sits herself up, propping the pillows behind her spine, ignoring Katie's offer. She sighs, cradling her head like it's fragile, mourning her condition.

"You should brush your teeth," Katie says. "That can make you feel better."

Caroline surveys the scene. "What is it you're wearing?"

"I'm going to the gym."

"In 1985?" she asks. "Jesus, get a new outfit. Try Under Armour."

"I'm not going there to meet men."

"Apparently," Caroline says, massaging her temples with a thumb.

Unwilling to entertain her insults, Katie informs her grumpy sister that she's on her own. "I have errands to run before going to work," she tells her. "I won't be back until late, probably after midnight." Katie picks up the trash can by Caroline's bed and dumps the chunky contents into the toilet. In the bathtub, she washes it out and replaces the liner, then returns it dutifully to her sister's bedside.

"Thank you, Nurse Ratched," Caroline says, rolling over, reburying her head beneath the pillows.

"Will you be okay alone?"

"Just shut the lamp."

Katie clicks it off. "I think C.J.'s close," she whispers.

Caroline pokes her head out from beneath the pillow pile. "What's close?"

"I feel like C.J. will be home soon," she says. "I feel it in my bones."

"Let's hope."

Katie collects a dirty glass from Caroline's nightstand; orange juice pulp sticks to the sides. "Maybe I'm just still drunk."

"How can you be so energized?" Caroline asks, eyeing her suspiciously.

"I don't know," she says defensively.

"I can hardly move."

"I warned you last night you're not cut out for this."

"But clearly you are."

"So what?"

"So it's worrisome," Caroline says flatly.

Katie shrugs her shoulders, the only response she can muster. "Look, I have to go. Maybe I'll see you later tonight."

"God willing," Caroline says.

ACROSS THE street from Starbucks, Katie finds a parking space in the lot of a pretty white Baptist church. A cluster of well-dressed children with blue bibles under their arms wave to her when she gets out of the car. As she hurries along the crosswalk, she realizes she left her fake Ray-Bans in the car, the sun like fire in her eyes. Already she's nauseous from the punishing fifty minute spin class she just endured. Katie had wanted to strangle the man on the bike in front of her who kept farting when the music got loud.

"I hate this place," Katie says, plopping down into an uncomfortable love seat. "Why not a rendezvous at Dunkin' Donuts?"

"Good morning to you, too," Peter says sarcastically.

"Good morning," Katie concedes.

"I thought you liked the coffee here."

"I do," she says, removing the purse from her shoulder. "But I hate this faux charm. I mean, look at that jerk." She indiscreetly points at a fifty-something bearded man clad in shiny bicycling gear and reading a hardcover copy of *Ulysses*.

"Are you hungover?" Peter asks.

"What do you think?"

"I think you're an hour late."

"I had to wait to stop sweating before taking a shower at the gym. Otherwise, I'd smell like garlic and clam pizza." She reaches for his Odwalla orange juice and takes a sip. "God, what happened to your lip?"

"I took an elbow during a kickboxing class," he says.

"It looks like a collagen injection gone awry."

He ignores her as he dips the tea bag in and out of his cup. A small gush of steam rises toward his face. Katie can see he's come to expect the sassiness that accompanies the opening phase of her hangovers, the manic state certain to be followed by fatigue, confusion, and anxiety. Hours from now she'll beat herself up mercilessly for behaving so obnoxiously.

"How's your sister?" he asks.

"She's struggling," Katie says, blowing on her venti-sized cup of coffee. "She was in rare form last night. Look at me. I drank twice as much as her and I feel nothing. Not good, not bad. Just nothing."

He squirts a stream of honey into his cup. "You should slow down."

"Ha," she says. "I make that promise every morning."

"There's meetings for that, you know."

"You drink," she accuses.

"Not like you. You vanish." He opens his hand like a magician. "Poof."

"Can we forget the intervention for a minute?"

"Fine, let's talk about the abortion instead."

"Oh, is that what we've decided?"

"Do you remember calling me last night?" he says.

"Of course," she lies. "I called everyone last night. What time did I call you?" The roof of her mouth burns as she takes her first sip of coffee.

"Around midnight. From your cell. You said you were going to terminate the pregnancy."

"Right," she says, nodding affirmative.

Katie wishes she could call a time-out and reevaluate, somehow extract last night's phone conversation from the abyss.

"So where are you going to have it done?"

"Boston, I guess," she says, wondering what town she picked last night.

"You seem nervous."

"No, I'm just a little nauseous," she says, pushing her coffee cup toward the center of the little round table. "I guess I should have tried herbal tea this morning instead."

"Do you want to take a nap and try this again later?"

What she wants is to punch his fat lip and shut him the fuck up, knock him off his holier-than-thou pedestal. "This table isn't steady," she says, moving it back and forth with her palms. Bending over, Katie wedges a clump of brown napkins underneath the far leg. "That's better."

"So let's go over this," Peter says impatiently.

"Sounds like we already have."

"Not face to face we haven't."

"Look, I have to get to work, and pronto. If it weren't for Caroline's financial assistance, the collection agencies would be hounding me."

"But you just got here!"

"No way can I be late," she says. "In fact, I have to be early."

He looks at his watch, the silver Tag he's so proud of, a gift from his last senior wrestling class. "You can stay a little longer. It's barely afternoon."

As Katie stands up, the blood drains from her brain. "I have to go to the bathroom," she says.

"Jenny's leaving her husband," Peter blurts out. "We're going to Oregon together."

With a head full of helium, Katie sits back down. One more surprise today and she'll collapse. "God, I am so upside-down right now."

"I'm sorry."

"When did this happen?"

"Recently."

A pack of girl scouts rush inside the store, their shrieking voices drowning out James Blunt from the Starbucks stereo. "What's in Oregon?"

"We're going to start a little organic farm. Live off the land type thing."

Katie resists the urge to roll her eyes. She can only imagine the arsenal of put-downs Caroline would start firing off.

"What about her kids?" Katie asks, crossing her arms, eager to assume the position of morality.

"She's working on that," he says. "She's a good mother."

"Pray tell, what then is a bad mother?"

"Pray tell? What's with you today?" He fakes a yawn and turns toward the counter. "I'm gonna get a scone. Do you want one?"

When he tries to get up from the table, she grabs his wrist and draws him near. "What if I want this child, Peter?"

"You don't," he says.

"But what if I did?"

He doesn't meet her eyes, his attention on the table, her hands, the shredded Splenda packets. "I'd try and talk you out of it."

"And how would you go about doing that?"

"For one, we're not married," he says, lowering his voice. "Two, you drink too much." He extends his fingers to match the count. "Three, the income between us is a joke. Four, I don't think your son would be too happy about this when he comes back."

"I see you've rehearsed this."

"It's called being thoughtful."

"You know, C.J. used to beg me for a little brother or sister. He absolutely ached for a sibling."

"We'd fuck it up, Katie."

"Apparently," she says airily.

He leans toward her as if he's about to let her in on a secret. "We've slept in the same bed together, right?"

"Yeah."

"We've eaten from the same fork, shared a toilet, have literally been in and out of each other."

"You're really not helping my hangover."

"Yet in spite of all that," he continues, "we can't get close. And that's fine for you and me, but not that," he says grimly, pointing at her stomach.

Katie takes a swig of coffee and swallows it down, striving not to wretch. Staring out the large picture window, she imagines crashing through the pane and making a scene, ruining everyone's latte. "You're right," she tells him.

Their eyes lock for an awkward instant, a momentary stretch of silence.

"I don't mean it like you're bad," he continues.

"I get it."

"Look, I wanna pay if you go through with it," he offers. "I want to cover all expenses."

"I'll bill you," she says.

"Are you pissed off?"

She shakes her head no. "Do you think you could drop off Lewis today?"

"If you want," he says, "if I can coax him into the kitty carrier."

"The front door will be open. Just set him inside."

"Do you want me to take a look at the leak in the kitchen faucet while I'm there?"

"No, it's fine. I wrapped duct tape around the lever."

"That's not a fix."

"It'll do for now," she says, touching his shoulder. "I'll see you."

"We'll talk later," he shouts.

She waves her hand in the air.

"Be good," he calls.

Back in the car, Katie checks the outgoing call log on her phone to see who else she may have drunkenly dialed last night. Scrolling through the list, she sees she made sixteen dead-end calls to C.J.'s cell yesterday. The only other number dialed was Megan Connelly's at eleven thirty-three P.M. She finds no record of Peter's call.

"Be good," she says mockingly, peeling out of the church parking lot. "Son of a bitch."

CHAPTER 25

Under the glow of his track lights, Katie can make out the top half of C.J.'s Godsmack poster from the end of the driveway. With both feet on the brake, she puts the car into park and shuts off the engine. Fireflies flash yellow and green outside the windshield. Spitting what's left of her nicotine gum into the ashtray, Katie dials C.J.'s number while keeping a steady eye on his room. For the first time in days she hears his recorded voice say *this is C.J., leave a message*, but she hangs up a few seconds after the beep. The new greeting had caught her off guard. There was none of the usual commotion in the background—no music, no blaring TV—just the static sound of his voice. Katie calls back and listens to it again, this time detecting an echo, imagining her son in a cavernous bathroom stall as he speaks. She turns off the phone. When she reaches into the backseat to roll up the rear window, Katie notices Caroline's gigantic car is gone. She grabs her purse and heads toward the house.

Once inside, she's surprised to find her sister in the kitchen, sitting at the round marble table, paging through the *Cape Mary Literary Review* like it's a lazy Sunday morning.

"How was work?" Caroline asks without looking up.

Katie unties her apron and lets it fall to the floor. She can see her son's door is shut. "Did you let C.J. take your car?"

Her eyebrows cross. "C.J.?" she says. "What are you talking about? No, some hillbilly towed it because of the fire hydrant." She closes the journal and returns it to the shelf. "Walter's short story is hysterical. What a nut job."

Katie scans the kitchen for signs of C.J. "What are you doing up then?"

"I have to fly out this morning."

Katie dumps her purse on the butcher block. She digs out a compact and tries to fix her hair.

"Your right eye is all red," Caroline says.

"Lime juice. Occupational hazard. So where's C.J.?"

"Arizona." Caroline closes the front door and locks it. She peers through the peephole. "You really need an alarm system."

"He isn't upstairs?"

"Not as far as I know."

"Then why are the lights on in his room?" Katie says, pointing toward his door.

"I turned them on."

"What'd you do that for?"

"The cat wouldn't stop clawing at his door so I let him in. Your boyfriend dropped him off at about six."

Katie slaps the banister with her palm. "Dammit, Caroline."

"Don't you think I would have called you if C.J. came home? Jesus."

In the kitchen, Katie reaches for the bottle of Trader Joe's Shiraz. What she really wants is a fish bowl full of Grand Marnier, but she doesn't want to drink anything hard in front of Caroline. "I really thought he was here," Katie laments, uncorking the bottle. "I'm getting delusional over this."

"You did get another postcard today. From Arizona." Caroline brings her the card from the pile of mail on the butcher block.

Katie gulps down her wine. "The Superstition Mountains," she says, holding the card to the light. She rubs a fingertip over her name. "I knew he'd make it."

"Most mothers would have called the police on him by now," Caroline says.

"I'm not most mothers." Katie finishes her glass and pours another. She doesn't bother recorking the bottle. "Most mothers wouldn't be rooting for him."

"I'm rooting he makes a U-turn."

"There are plenty of worse things he could have done," Katie says. "Things you can't take back. Things you can't make right." Katie affixes the card to the fridge with a magnet.

"Well, I admire your restraint," Caroline says.

"Just once it'd be nice if he wrote *wish you were here*. Some gesture to show he cares. I swear I'd fly out there on the spot if I saw that."

"Why doesn't he just email you? Why be all weird with the postcards?"

"He left his laptop here," Katie says. "Plus, he doesn't really do email. I've sent him messages and he never replies. He probably gave me a decoy address. Anyway, he barely even texts. So the postcards actually make sense."

Caroline gently tucks her iPhone into the valise. "You should come to California."

"Why's that?"

"Because you'll go bananas if you stay here alone."

"This is temporary."

"I don't see anything temporary here," Caroline says, eyeballing her wine glass.

"Where am I gonna go? Everywhere's a downgrade from Newquay. I could barely afford a shitty apartment in Lynn."

Caroline stands up authoritatively, as if she's about to deliver a presentation. "You know I can set you up. I'm part of a LLC that finances condos in Sausalito. You'd love it. Golden Gate views, good schools, great art scene, tons of moon bats for you to befriend."

"You're serious?"

"East coasters do well out there, Katie. Californians are fascinated by our zeal. I could even get you a job that's not in a bar."

Katie places the bottle behind a vase where Caroline won't see that it's already more than half-empty. "I'm too old for a do-over."

"Well, you need to get out of this rut."

"What rut?"

"This rut," Caroline says, taking the wine glass from Katie's hand. She carries it into the kitchen and pours it down the sink.

"You're lucky that wasn't Barolo."

She runs the faucet and pours Palmolive into the basin. "Was last night normal for you?"

Katie sorts through the mail on the butcher block. A tired Lindsay Lohan is on the cover of *People*. "This poor girl looks forty," she says, holding the picture up for Caroline.

"Katie, you drank almost two more bottles after I went to bed last night."

"I'm not the one who puked," she says, opening the pantry door. She reaches for a bag of salt and vinegar potato chips.

"No," Caroline continues, "you weren't sick at all and that's precisely what's so alarming. You were totally unfazed this morning, going about your day like it was any other."

"You prefer I stay in bed all day and stew?"

"Aren't you tired of being hungover?"

"Only when I am hungover."

"Look, you're on your way again tonight," she says. "Once I leave, you'll finish that bottle of wine. You'll keep going."

"This coming from a woman who crawled up the stairs last night."

"But I haven't been drunk like that in years," she says.

"How can you know anything about me after one night?"

"What I know is that you don't really want to be the sorry widow who drinks alone."

Katie heaves the mail off the butcher's block. Lindsay Lohan lands in the cat box. "Why are you coming down on me now? Where the fuck have you been for thirty-nine years?"

"Where the fuck have I been?" she shouts. "Where the fuck have you been?"

"You're the one who's on the other side of the country."

"No one forced you to stay here and play martyr."

"I was a kid with a kid!"

"That's what you wanted. You didn't even tell Dad and me until it was too late to fix."

"At least I tried to do something right." Katie picks up a sponge and furiously wipes down the butcher block, pushing the crumbs from last night's pizza into her hand.

"So you fancy yourself the family savior by having a baby at twenty-three, by having a shotgun wedding in some town hall to a man no one knows?"

Katie flings the dirty sponge back into the sink, just missing her sister's head. "Why do you think Mom and Dad had us, Caroline?"

"They got married. Married people have babies."

"No, we were their last resort, their last chance to try and be like the neighbors."

"So what?"

"So like me they tried, yet you don't shit on them like you do me."

"Forget them," Caroline shouts. "We're here and they're gone and you have a drinking problem."

Katie bites her lip. She can explain until she's blue in the face how she never begins the day with a drink, that she's never missed a shift because of a hangover, that she doesn't shake and shiver. She can cite a million reasons why she's not like their mother, but Katie can also sense how desperate these protests will sound to someone like Caroline, how they will only prove her point.

"Look," Katie says, collecting the mail from the floor, "I've been planning on taking a break anyway. Once C.J. comes home, once I start painting again, everything will go back to normal. If those goddam lights weren't on in his room tonight, I'd be drinking tea right now."

"Back to normal?" Caroline says, pointing at her stomach. "What about that?"

"I'm flip-flopping."

"You want it?"

"Sometimes, yes. A lot of times, actually."

"Are you out of your fucking mind?"

"Yes, I'm out of my mind," Katie screams. "That's what happens when you're pregnant, Caroline. Your resolve changes."

- 226 -

"But you're pro-choice!"

"You don't know what it's like to have someone depending on you for their life, literally kicking you for it. I wish I could be rational and separate myself, but I can't. It's a responsibility beyond me."

Caroline fills a glass with water and drinks. She checks her watch. "You plan on bearing a child with fetal alcohol syndrome?"

"I didn't drink a drop when I was pregnant with C.J. I can stop again."

"What about after you give birth? What about ten months from now when there's nothing to keep you in check?"

Katie kicks off her sneakers and throws them into the mudroom. She curls and cracks her toes against the floor. "We're getting way ahead of ourselves. I haven't really decided anything yet." She fills her mouth with potato chips. The salt burns her chapped lips.

"Did you know I once dated an alcoholic?" Caroline says.

"I'm not an alcoholic."

"This was when I first arrived in California. Douglas and I went out for about a year," she continues. "I was there for the before, and the after. Anyway, about six months into our relationship he flew off to a treatment center in Minnesota. Hazelden, one of the best. He spent twenty-eight days there."

"I'm not going to Minnesota," she protests. "There's no need to be so extreme."

"What do you call your behavior now?"

"Didn't I just say I'm going to take a break?" Katie says.

"So a few nights before Douglas checked himself in," Caroline continues, "he groped some twenty-year-old intern at his company's holiday party. He called her a cunt in front of everyone when she tried to slap his hand away. The entire office staff was there, a few hundred people. I wasn't, thank God. He was a big time analyst at Oppenheimer until that evening."

"I haven't groped anybody."

"That was his bottom, as he calls it. Sure, terribly embarrassing and shameful and certainly not great for his career, but there's plenty worse that happens to otherwise good people. Drunk driving, for example. If you ask me it's our worst pandemic."

"I've never had a DWI."

"What's crazy is Douglas wasn't a lascivious guy at all. Just the opposite. Very timid, very controlled, but shitfaced he was unrecognizable."

"What's your point, Caroline?"

"The point is I have loads of your saved voice mails I'm sure you'd rather die than listen to. You always sound as if you're calling from the bottom of a well."

"Drunk dialing is not drunk driving."

"Douglas told me that every last patient at Hazelden was there for the same reason. All of them had crossed their *own* lines, all of them regularly doing what they didn't want to do. It got to the point where they couldn't help but fuck themselves over. Like Einstein's definition of insanity: 'doing the same thing over and over and expecting different results.' Douglas said everyone there had their own special methods, but the underlying motive was the same."

"What's that?"

"He told me it was all simply self-loathing gone unchecked. His mission when he drank was to get as far away from himself as possible. The only problem was the next morning he'd end up closer than ever, right smack in his face. And the price only got steeper with age, the hangovers so debilitating they demanded alcohol to treat."

"Sometimes it's just a headache, Caroline. Nothing more."

"You're not there," she says. "Not yet anyway. And thank God for that."

"There's a difference between me and Douglas."

"All I know is I saw a very familiar face when you came into my room this morning."

Katie pokes out a square of nicotine gum from her pack. "Where is Douglas now?"

"Florida. Made a fortune building townhouses along the Everglades." Caroline opens the kitchen window a crack, then lights a Dunhill. "Anyway, you're forty in a month, Katie."

"Two months."

"Still," she says, "it's getting late fast."

Headlights stream through the kitchen window. Caroline covers her eyes as Katie watches the light flash across the walls. "Shit, my taxi's here."

"You're leaving now?" Katie says. "It's like three in the morning."

"My flight takes off at five-thirty. I have a dinner meeting tonight in Nob Hill I can't miss." She takes one last drag before dropping her cigarette into the sink.

"What about the Navigator?"

"I paid the rental place off to deal with it." Caroline takes a thin silver pen from her pocket and writes down a bunch of numbers on the back of a business card. "This is my Amex," she says. "Use it up to 10K for whatever you need the next month or two, just until C.J. comes home. Just mail Renée the receipts. And I don't want to see one dime of it spent at Seabreeze Liquors."

"You don't need to help me."

"Here's an AA meeting list I printed out. The whole week is there," she says, pulling a packet of papers from a manila folder. "I highlighted the ones in Newquay in pink, the ones in Gunnerside in yellow. I'm going to have Douglas call you too."

Katie thumbs through the pages. "*Ladies Sane and Sober* tomorrow morning at nine sounds fun." She reads down the list: *Circle of Light, What's Good About Today, You Get What You Give, First Things First.* "I'll talk to Douglas, but AA isn't happening until I rape the cat or drive over a mother and her baby carriage."

"Just humor me and go, okay?"

Katie drops the papers on the table. "Do you want to take the rest of the potato chips?"

"Sorry I said you're like mom," Caroline says, taking her hand. "You're not."

"I know that."

"We all just let her go."

Katie keeps her eyes on her sister's grip, the fingers a mold of her own. "She wouldn't have listened anyway."

"Either way, we didn't help," Caroline says.

"The last month of her life I was her bartender," Katie recalls. "I'd sneak her gin fizzes when Dad was at work. One time I even drank a beer up there with her. I remember she called me the daughter she never had."

"What the fuck does that mean?" Caroline asks.

"Oh, I didn't press it."

"Still," Caroline says, "it was shitty of us not to give her the chance."

She lets go of Katie's hand and brushes the lint from her cashmere sweater-vest. Standing in front of the hallway mirror, she switches on her business face. "Well, thank you for another lovely visit," she says. "Sorry about the cat box once again."

"Our family's all about quick fixes," Katie says. "Getting in and getting out fast. You breeze into town, then fly right out. We all take off. None of us ever stay."

"We're getting better," Caroline replies.

"I hope so."

"Bye," she says, with a fleeting embrace.

Katie closes the door. She can hear her sister's high heels go *clack-clack-clack* over the brick walkway. With her ear pressed against the paneling, Katie can also make out the crickets in the grass, the wind against Mr. Kashgarian's flagpole. Then she hears the taxi trunk slam shut and in a flash she finds herself barefoot outside, waving towards the car.

"Call me when you land," Katie shouts.

"You too," Caroline says, ducking into the backseat. Katie waits until the taxi disappears, until her street goes dark again.

Back inside, she empties the rest of the wine bottle into a glass. The front door is still open, the sound of the crickets so close she wonders if they've come inside.

"Last call," she says.

FALL 2007

CHAPTER 26

Epilogue

Her hair is turning red. Katie hadn't really noticed the change before now, the light being so different this close to dawn. Usually the sun is well past the horizon when she comes into the studio to paint, but this morning she woke up in the dark. From the beginning, she never wanted Isabel's hair to be any other color than brown, any other direction than straight, but as she touches up the wavy strands circling her subject's ears, Katie can now see that Isabel had always been meant for curls. Tonight she'll give her eyes.

C.J. knocks open the door. "What do I need to wear to this thing?"

Katie drops a paintbrush into her water cup and watches the liquid turn smoky. "There's no dress code," she says, turning her stool around to face him. He's an inch taller than last fall. Ten pounds heavier too. All the weight looks like it's gone into his neck and shoulders.

"Can I wear a hat?"

"Whatever you want," she says. "It's not church." She reaches for her cup of chamomile wishing it was Starbucks Colombian. "You don't have to go, you know."

"Whatever," he says, squinting at his iPhone screen, "I have nothing going on until practice at noon." He presses some buttons before shoving it back into his jeans pocket. Caroline had sent him her used iPhone.

"I can't get over how much better your hair looks short," Katie says. "It makes you look older too."

"I hate it," he says, rubbing a hand over his buzzed head. "I look like a jarhead, but long hair under a helmet in desert heat wasn't an option."

"I guess you can grow it back," she says, removing her smock. "It'll never get that hot here."

"Maybe I'll bleach it."

She sticks her tongue out. "Yuck."

C.J. tilts his face toward the window. In the sunlight, she can see the red mark on his forehead has shrunk down to the size of a quarter. He told her how he got the burn from the motorcycle's exhaust pipe as he was checking the rear tire pressure somewhere in Texas.

"Are they gonna have food there?"

"Not your kind. Basically, it's donuts or cookies. Anything with sugar it seems."

"Then I'm gonna make a power shake before we go. You want one?"

"Yeah," she says. "Make me that peanut butter-banana-chocolate one again." Katie stands up and grabs the easel.

"I'll move it for you," he says. Reaching in front of her, C.J. lifts the painting and carries it into the corner of the studio. "What are these holes in her face?" he asks, pointing at Isabel.

"They're going to be eyes, once I fill them in."

C.J. puts his hands on his hips. "What's she gonna look like?"

"I don't know yet," Katie says, engaging her subject's vacant eyes. "Hopefully human."

In the shower, she uses the green cactus shampoo C.J. brought her back from Arizona. She likes the way the little white "star crystals" make her scalp tingle. He told her he bought it in Cave Creek from Craig's mother who "sits outside her trailer all day drinking beer and selling crap nobody wants.

She's older than Yoda," he said, telling Katie how he found her in the white pages. "I felt bad for her, so I also bought a George Strait cassette and some nasty wool socks." He didn't tell Mrs. Hunter who he was as he browsed through her milk crates full of junk, thinking she looked too old to hear that kind of news. Since he was a "Harley guy," she gave him a beer before he hit the road, handing him the half-empty red Tecate can she was drinking from.

"You live alone out here?" C.J. had said, downing the warm beer in one gulp.

"There's cats here too," she mumbled. "Somewhere."

When he asked her if she had any kids or grandkids, she again said she had cats.

"No one comes to see you?"

"My boy used to come around," she said. "But he checked out. Shot his veins up with brown."

C.J. could tell by the easy way she began to talk that she'd told this story many times before, but he wondered if he was the first person to hear it, if her only other audience had been felines up to now. She told him how the Nevada police said her boy paid off the maid to clear the scene at the motel, to make it look like "he went to bed and woke up dead." The maid informed the cops he gave her an extra hundred dollars to hold his hand until he fell asleep. And she did, wearing green latex gloves and smoking cigarettes with her free hand, reciting the Lord's Prayer in Spanish as "the man on the bed waited."

"What did he do that for?" C.J. asked.

"I don't know," she said. "Can't ask him now."

"What was his name?"

"Craig," she said, cracking open another beer.

"Where's he buried?"

"Everywhere," she said. "He was burned up like Gandhi."

C.J. put on his helmet.

"You going to the Grand Canyon?"

"Yeah," he said, mounting the bike. "Thanks for the beer."

"Be careful."

"Of what?"

"It's a hole, man."

C.J. dragged his boots along the gravel as he rode first gear out of the trailer park, pebbles and sand rattling against the fenders. He saw the green signs pointing to the Grand Canyon, but at the last second C.J. found himself turning onto 40 east toward Gallup, New Mexico, towards home.

He pulled into the driveway a week after she got the postcard from the Superstition Mountains. Katie didn't scream and yell when she heard the engine, didn't run outside and grab him. Instead, she calmly dropped to the ground and thanked God, fighting the urge to tear his hair out and scold him. In the studio, she waited for him to find her first.

"What are you doing in there?" he'd finally asked, standing in the doorway.

"Painting," she said. "How was your trip?"

"Good."

"Good," she said.

"Can I come in?"

"Sure," she called, "the door's open."

That night he told her how he was addicted to the smell of gasoline on his hands.

She told him things were going to be different.

He said riding in the desert was like having a blow-dryer in your face on high.

She said they both had to try for change.

He asked her what was with all the supplements in the kitchen. The folic acid, the iron, the zinc and calcium.

The supplements were to help, she said, and added that she was going to need his help too.

She asked him what he learned being away.

What he learned, he said, was how great it was to wake up somewhere different every morning, forgetting where you were when you first opened your eyes.

"I'm trying not to drink," she told him.

"I'm trying to believe you're pregnant," he said.

Katie didn't convey how hard it was not to drink, didn't describe to her son the awful eternity of twenty-four hours. She didn't tell him how the headaches were even worse, how she was terminally hungry, constantly craving sweets, especially after dinner. She didn't mention the high blood pressure and hot flashes. She refused to admit how she woke up furious every single morning, as if she'd been wronged in her sleep. Yet he seemed to know, at times assuming a countenance that recognized her strife, his sudden sensitivity to her private struggle.

THE AA crowd asks her to slow down. "First things first," they remind her. "This too shall pass," they encourage. Most of the time she wishes they'd get a life. Douglas says to just hold on, that there's a world out there she cannot yet discern. Katie wants to believe him—she has to—so she thinks about what he asked her the first time he called.

If someone was coming at you with a knife, would you stop them?

"Sure," she said. "Of course."

When?

This morning they're going to give her a plastic medallion for thirty days of sobriety. She hopes they won't be able to see the lie, these AA folks with their X-ray vision. One glass of red wine ten days ago shouldn't have to cost her now. She had promised C.J. she'd have her thirty-day medallion before her fortieth birthday. He's earned her chip. And that is no lie.

He drives them to the meeting. Thick steam rises from the wet concrete as they pass over the causeway, the mist so dense that Katie can't even make out the twin lighthouses on Hatcher's Island.

"It's just thirty days," she tells him.

"That's a lot," he says, lowering the radio volume.

"I'm not promising I'll keep going to these things."

"You'd be crazy not to," he says, rolling down the window.

"You're probably right."

"Ya think?" he says facetiously. C.J. clicks on the high beams. "Man, it's mad foggy today."

"Turn those off," Katie says. "High beams reflect more light, making it harder to see in fog. Also, keep your foot closer to the brake."

Every few seconds they lose themselves in the grey of the brume, like an airplane inside a cloud.

"Pull over to the side," Katie says.

"It's okay, I can see enough."

"Just pull over for a second," she says. "There's a tsunami in my stomach."

C.J. steers the car toward the Back Beach seawall. He puts it into park. "Are you all right?" he asks.

"I'm good."

Katie takes his palm and places it on her stomach. Against her belly button, C.J.'s fingers are cold and coarse. His hand moves up and down with his mother's breath. He looks at her, startled.

"What is it?" she asks.

"Shhh," he whispers, "I can feel her kicking."